A MOST UNSUITABLE BRIDE

Gail Whitiker

MILLS & BOON®

First published in Great Britain 2004
Large Print edition 2004
Harlequin Mills & Boon Limited,
Eton House, 18-24 Paradise Road, Richmond, Surrey TW9 1SR

© Gail Whitiker 2004

ISBN 0 263 18194 4

Set in Times Roman 16 on 17¼ pt.
42-0804-70181

Printed and bound in Great Britain
by Antony Rowe Ltd, Chippenham, Wiltshire

A MOST UNSUITABLE BRIDE

Gail Whitiker

Chapter One

'Oh, Diana, are you not thrilled at the prospect of being back in London?' asked Miss Phoebe Lowden, her green eyes bright with excitement as she gazed at the bustling streets visible through the carriage window. 'I spent only two months at Narbeth Hall, but they were the longest two months of my life! However do you manage to live there and find any degree of contentment at all?'

Miss Diana Hepworth, the lady to whom the question was put, and aware of the fervour with which it was asked, tried not to smile as she likewise studied the passing scenery. 'Which would you have me answer first, Phoebe? How I feel about returning to a city where social interaction is considered second only to breathing? Or how I have managed to survive in a place where good company must surely provide the *only* relief in an existence otherwise too boring to speak of?'

The younger girl had the grace to look embarrassed. 'Forgive me, Diana, I did not mean to suggest that life in Whitley was totally without amusement. But neither does it offer the variety of entertainments, nor the type of people and conversation, *you* enjoy so much.'

'What? You did not find Squire Hapston's musings on thirteenth-century farming methods enlightening? Or Mrs Dawson's views on the perils of educating females too much for fear of hindering their abilities to be dutiful wives and mothers illuminating? You surprise me, Phoebe. I have spent many a dull winter evening being entertained by such lively discourse,' Diana said, trying not to smile.

'Now you are teasing me, and it is not deserved, for we both know that you are far too intelligent to be amused by such insipid dialogue,' Phoebe retorted. 'You have never been one for dull talk or stupid companions, admit it!'

A slow smile lifted the corners of Diana's mouth. 'True, but not *all* of the residents of Whitley are dull or stupid, Phoebe. And, in case you've forgotten, Narbeth Hall *is* my home.'

'Yes, but even Aunt Isabel says you should be spending part of the year in London,' Phoebe said, refusing to be put off. 'After all, you have already had the advantage of one London Season, yet you choose to remain buried in the depths of the country where you are forced to suffer the attention of gentlemen who would not even approach you in London. Why? Do you truly find life in town so distasteful?'

Comfortably settled against the squabs of the carriage, Diana paused to consider her answer. In truth, she was not terribly pleased about the prospect of returning to London. She had tried to affect an appearance of being so for Phoebe's sake, but as the city drew nearer and the memory of her reasons for having left it returned, Diana was finding it an increasingly difficult charade to maintain.

'I do not find all aspects of life in London distasteful,' she said, deciding to be as tactful, but as honest as possible. 'I enjoy many of the wonderful things it has to offer. Certainly our local productions cannot compare to the performances put on at Drury Lane, and our selection of shops is humble to say the least. But in other ways, I am content with country life. I have never cared for the congestion of town, and as tired as rural discourse may be, it is not always so inferior to what is to be had in London. You will find that out after spending a few tedious evenings in society. However, we are not here to talk about *my* reasons for wishing to remain in the country,' Diana said, abruptly changing the topic of the conversation. 'We are here to watch *you* take London by storm, and hopefully to see you engaged or married by the end of the Season.'

'Oh, I would like that, Diana,' Phoebe cried, clasping her hands together. 'And to the most handsome gentleman in all London! But, in truth, I do not think I shall be taking anything or anyone by storm. There are so many beautiful ladies at court. All so accomplished and witty, and all so very good at flirting. I am sure I should stumble hopelessly over my words if a handsome gentleman were to approach me and try to engage me in conversation.'

'Nonsense. It is no more difficult than talking to me. Besides, I doubt any gentleman will worry about *what* you say when you look at him with those beautiful green eyes. It's probably just as well you did not spend any more time at Narbeth Hall,' Diana said. 'Thomas Stanhope was looking rather smitten with you, and you would certainly have been wasted on him.'

'But so are you, don't you see that? Oh, you must come about with me, Diana!' Phoebe cried in frustration. 'I know you would enjoy yourself, and I would certainly have a much better time if you were with me.'

'And I'm flattered you feel that way, dearest, but that is not what we agreed to when I said I would come to London. I made it quite clear that I was coming in the capacity of a companion.'

'Tosh! Aunt Isabel won't hear of you being used in such a way. If anything, she is more likely to suggest that we *both* go out looking for husbands. Oh, I know you profess a disinterest in such things,' Phoebe said as the familiar expression settled on Diana's face, 'but Aunt Isabel is right. You are far too lovely to sit at home, and you are much more adept at socialising than I. Why should you not go out and enjoy what London has to offer? Did you not say you had friends in town you wished to see again?'

Diana sighed. She did indeed have friends, but how was she to know if any of them wished to see *her*? Worse, how was she to tell Phoebe *why* they did not without getting into a lengthy and somewhat embarrassing explanation as to what had happened four years earlier to make it so?

The arrival of the carriage at their aunt's house on George Street prevented Diana from having to come up with an answer, and in the flurry of activity that followed, the question was mercifully forgotten. Jiggins, their aunt's long-standing butler, greeted them at the door and saw to the removal of their trunks and travelling garments, and moments later, Diana heard the sound of her aunt's voice drifting down the stairs towards them.

'Diana, Phoebe, is that you? Gracious, girls! I thought you would never arrive.''

Diana turned to greet her aunt, and was delighted to see her looking so well. For all her having just celebrated her fifty-third birthday, Mrs Isabel Mitchell was still a remarkably handsome woman. Her hair, once a bright blazing red, had mellowed to a warm shade of auburn, and her eyes, a shade paler green than Phoebe's, still reflected a passion and enthusiasm for life that was so much a part of her personality. Indeed, time seem to have inflicted few of the infirmities so often visited upon women approaching their later years, and though Diana knew that her aunt occasionally suffered with pains in her legs, she nevertheless managed to attend most of the events deemed to be of particular social consequence. A widow for six years, she seldom wore bright colours any more, preferring the dignity of dark blue, lavender and occasionally deep maroon if the occasion warranted it. She referred to it as her cultivated attempt at staidness; something she feared she had been lacking most of her life.

'Well, my dears, did you have a good journey?' Mrs Mitchell asked, drawing them both into an affectionate embrace. 'It is such a pretty drive from Whitley.'

'We had a lovely trip, Aunt,' Phoebe exclaimed. 'But I am ever so glad to be here.'

'Good, and now that you are, we must make ourselves comfortable. Come, there is a nice fire in the parlour. The day has turned unusually chill for April, has it not?'

Diana, who was indeed anxious to warm her hands, fell in beside her aunt while Phoebe trailed a few steps behind. 'How is Chaucer, Aunt Isabel?' she asked. 'Is he here, or did you leave him in the country?'

'Oh, he is definitely here, and well enough, though the wretched creature is never anxious to leave his bed,' Mrs Mitchell said. 'His old bones are no more immune to the cold than mine, But I dare say he will be happy to see you. In fact, I think I hear him scratching at the door. Stop it, Chaucer, or Jiggins will have your coat for a carriage rug!'

Diana bit back a smile. Chaucer was her aunt's dog, and while he was a recognised member of the family above stairs, she doubted he was as warmly welcomed below. The younger maids were afraid of him, and the older ones complained about the amount of hair he shed. Jiggins simply ignored him, which was a considerable feat given that the hound more closely resembled a small pony than he did a diminutive lap dog.

'Down, Chaucer!' Mrs Mitchell scolded as she opened the door and the great beast lunged forward. 'Have you no manners at all? Go and sit in your place and wait to be introduced.'

The chastised animal let go a muffled 'whoof', but wisely did as he was told.

'That's better. Now,' Mrs Mitchell said to her nieces, 'let me have a good look at you. My word, what elegant young ladies you have both become.'

Phoebe rolled her eyes. '*I* am the one who has become elegant, Aunt Isabel. Diana was already that way the last time you saw her.'

'So she was, Phoebe, so she was. And you are, indeed, a good deal taller and prettier than I remember,' Mrs Mitchell said, closing the door to the cosy, if somewhat overfurnished, room. 'Well, let me see what you have learned. Walk the length of the room and back, there's a good girl.'

Phoebe did as she was told, and duly earned her aunt's nod of approval. 'Excellent. I think your time at Mrs Harrison-Whyte's Academy was exactly what you needed. Did you enjoy your studies there?'

'I suppose, though I am very glad to be finished with schooling,'' Phoebe said, sinking with an unladylike flounce into a deep rose armchair. 'Most of the mistresses were exceedingly dour and we were kept to very strict schedules.'

'Of course, dear, that is the nature of school. The question is, did you learn anything, since that *was* the reason for your being sent there in the first place.'

'*Mais, oui. Fait-il toujours aussi froid?*' the girl asked in perfectly accented French. 'That means, is it usually this cold? As well, I am familiar with the teachings of the ancient Greek philosophers, and I can tell you without hesitation the location of Constantinople, the Cape of Good Hope, and many other equally exotic and intriguing places.'

'Good Lord!' Mrs Mitchell looked faintly shocked. 'They've turned you into a bluestocking!'

'Oh, no, never that, Aunt,' Phoebe said, laughing. 'Because I also learned how to paint and arrange flowers, how to manage a household, and how to engage in polite conversation with handsome young gentlemen, one of whom will hopefully wish to marry me.'

'Well, I am relieved to hear that you do not intend to devote your life to bookish occupations,' Mrs Mitchell said, sharing an amused glance with Diana. 'But experiencing one's first Season is always exciting, and you should plan on enjoying it to the fullest, since once you are married there will be all manner of other duties and obligations to which you will be forced to attend.'

'And I shall enjoy every one of them because it means I shall also have a husband, and I am looking forward to that more than anything!'

Settled in her comfortable chair by the fire, Diana smiled, marvelling that only a few short years separated Phoebe's age from hers. At times it seemed a great many more. She, too, had come to London in the hopes of finding the man of her dreams, and with a belief in her heart that life was going to be wonderful. But reality had painted a very different picture, and when Diana had returned to the country only three short months after she'd left it, it was with far more than her childhood dreams shattered.

She looked up to find her aunt's watchful gaze upon her.

'Phoebe, why don't you run along to your room?' Mrs Mitchell said quietly. 'I've had it completely redone for you.'

Phoebe's face brightened. 'You have?'

'Of course. You are a young woman now and must be treated like one. Grimshaw will take you up,' Mrs Mitchell said as the housekeeper appeared at the door.

'Thank you, Aunt Isabel,' Phoebe cried, getting up and impulsively throwing her arms around the older woman's neck. 'Oh, I am *so* pleased to be back in London! I know we're going to have the most marvellous time, in spite of Diana's reluctance to be here!'

With that auspicious pronouncement, Phoebe turned and followed the housekeeper from the room. Mrs Mitchell watched her go, shaking her head as the sound of the girl's chatter echoed all the way up the stairs. 'Dear me, I'd nearly forgotten what it was like to be so young. I vow the child has energy enough for two.'

'Indeed she has, Aunt,' Diana replied in a dry voice. 'She has made me feel quite old and staid these last two months.'

Isabel Mitchell glanced at her favourite niece and her eyes softened. 'There is nothing in the least staid about you, Diana, and at one and twenty, you are hardly old, but you do not look as cheery as I might have wished. Perhaps we can do something to put the sparkle back in your eyes, now that you are here again.'

'Just spending time with you will do that,' Diana said, smiling as she glanced around the room. 'It seems such a long time since I was here.'

'Four years is a long time when you're young,' her aunt agreed. 'At my age, it is a mere blink of the eye. All right, Chaucer, you may go and make your greetings to Diana. But politely, mind.'

The wolfhound, which had been whimpering ever since being told to go to his bed, rose to his feet and slowly headed for Diana. He knew better than to jump on her, but he did rest his great head on her knee, his liquid brown eyes staring up at her with adoration.

Diana wondered how such a huge beast could be so daft.

'Do you still spoil him outrageously?' she said as she buried her fingers in the dog's wiry hair.

'Of course.' Mrs Mitchell reached for the teapot. 'We all deserve to be pampered in our twilight years. Tea?'

'Yes, thank you, that would be lovely.'

Mrs Mitchell poured out two cups of tea and set one on the table before Diana. 'But never mind that great brute, tell me how you really feel about being back in London. Phoebe seems to think you would rather not be here.'

Diana ran her hand thoughtfully over Chaucer's head. 'To tell the truth, I'm not sure how I feel. I had my fair share of doubts about coming, and there were times when I told my-self I would not—'

'But come you did.'

Diana grimaced. 'Yes, due in large part to Phoebe plaguing the life out of me until I agreed.'

Mrs Mitchell laughed. 'Well, if it is of any consolation, there are many in society who are anxious to see you again. I ran into Mrs Townley and her daughter last week, and you should have seen the look of delight on Amanda's face when I told her you were coming to stay with me.'

At the mention of the young lady who had once been her closest friend, Diana's expression brightened. 'Did she look well?'

'Very well. In fact, Amanda has changed considerably since you last saw her. I dare say you'll be surprised when you see her again. But I was pleased to hear her express such enthusiasm at seeing you. Has there been any resumption of your correspondence?'

Diana shook her head as she reached for the china cup. She wasn't surprised that her aunt had asked about it. Everyone knew that she and Amanda had once been the best of friends. Amanda was one of the few who hadn't shunned Diana when news of her rift with Lord Durling had become public. She had even written to Diana for the first few months after her return to the country—until one day the letters had stopped coming and Diana had been forced to conclude that pressures had been brought to bear.

'I read that Amanda is recently engaged,' Diana said, keeping her voice light. 'Has a date been set for the wedding?'

'Yes, and Mrs Townley did tell me what it was, though for the life of me I can't remember. One of the hazards of growing old, I'm afraid. Still, Amanda will be able to tell you herself when you see her.'

Diana looked up. 'I am to see her?'

'Indeed. Mrs Townley is holding a soirée this week, and when she learned that you and Phoebe were arriving today, she told me that I must be sure to bring you both. Speaking of engagements, did I mention that Sarah Harper married over the winter?'

Diana put down her cup. 'Not as I recall.'

Mrs Mitchell tutted. 'Of course not, you have only just arrived. Well, she is now the wife of Mr Anthony Jones-Davis. And Lady Margaret Bellows is to be married in the fall. She has much to recommend her, of course, but I did think her eldest sister would be settled first...'

Diana listened as her aunt told her which of her friends had married and which had not, and tried not to feel envious over the good fortune of the ones who had. After all, she had no reason to be jealous. She too had received a proposal of marriage during her first Season, and would have been a married lady now if all had gone according to plan. One in charge of a large house, and servants, and all the jewels and pretty gowns she could have wished for.

A married lady, Diana reflected sadly. But one blessed with questionable happiness, if any happiness at all…

'Diana? Did you hear what I just said?'

Diana looked up to find her aunt's sharp eyes on her, and felt the colour rise to her cheeks. 'Forgive me, Aunt. I was lost in my thoughts.'

'Yes, and I'm sure I know where those thoughts were taking you,' Mrs Mitchell said kindly. 'But do you still think so much about what happened, my dear? It has been over four years, after all.'

'Yes, and I truly thought I had put it behind me, but now that I'm here…' Diana stopped, and shook her head. 'It's funny, you know. In some ways, I feel as though what happened took place in another lifetime. And yet, in others, it's as though it was yesterday.' She looked at her aunt with troubled eyes. 'Does that make any sense?'

'Indeed. Adversity is a funny thing, Diana. It affects people in various ways, and it always changes them in one way or another.'

'Did it change me?'

'Most definitely. It made you stronger.'

'I wonder.' Diana took a sip of her tea, savouring the hot, fragrant brew. 'Sometimes I think I should have just accepted matters and got on with my life. After all, there is no such thing as a perfect marriage. Perhaps I was naïve to think there was.'

'Do you honestly believe that?'

Diana looked into her aunt's eyes, and knew she couldn't lie. 'No.'

'Good, because I would have been very disappointed if you had said yes. Marriage is about what two people bring to it, Diana,' Mrs Mitchell told her. 'And though no one is perfect, we usually strive to do the best we can. I know that's what you would have done because you had your mother and father's example to follow.'

Diana's smile turned wistful. 'I miss them so much, Aunt Isabel. At times, it feels like a physical pain. And yet, at other times I'm glad they're not here. They would have been so hurt by what happened.'

'Yes, but not for themselves. They would have suffered for you, and for all you were made to go through. But you conducted yourself with dignity and grace, and that is always the mark of a lady.'

Diana sighed. 'Grace and dignity are all very well, Aunt, but what good do they do when one's reputation is so hopelessly tarnished?'

'What good? Why, they are priceless, child! Tarnished silver can always be made to shine again, but grace and dignity, once lost, are not so easily reclaimed.'

The analogy made Diana smile. 'I fear there are many in society who will not expect me to shine again, no matter how thoroughly I am polished.'

'Then we are not interested in them! Life is too short to worry about the feelings of those unwilling to forgive or forget, my dear. I know. I have encountered many such people during my life, and I haven't shed a tear at seeing them on their way. Now, why don't you run along upstairs?' Mrs Mitchell said. 'You've had a long day, and I'm sure you will feel better for a rest.

Dinner is not for another two hours so you've plenty of time to shake off the effects of your journey. I want to see some colour back in your cheeks.'

Diana smiled crookedly. 'I dare say a rest before dinner would be welcome. I love Phoebe dearly, but her chatter can be wearing after a time. All right, Chaucer, it's time to move,' she said, giving him a gentle push.

Lifting his head, the hound gave her a doleful look, then slowly got up and padded back to his place by the fire.

Diana was almost at the door when Mrs Mitchell stopped her with a question. 'Have you told Phoebe what happened four years ago?'

Though half-expecting the question, Diana sighed. 'I didn't have the heart to. She's always been so excited about the idea of falling in love and getting married, I didn't want to sound as though I was warning her away from it. But I have thought about how she would feel if she were to hear anything of a distressing nature.'

'Well, we can't deny that the possibility exists,' Mrs Mitchell said. 'Since you were not willing to tell anyone what really happened between you and Lord Durling, people were left to believe what he told them—that you jilted him. As such, the simple fact of your being in London now may be all that is required to start them talking again. That doesn't mean Phoebe will be exposed to it, of course, and given that one of us will likely be with her when she does go out, we should be able to prevent her hearing anything untoward. But we cannot guarantee that something won't slip through.'

'Are you saying I should say something to her?'

'I'm saying we should probably wait and see. Most people will assume that Phoebe already knows what happened, and since the true pleasure of gossip lies in the telling of it to someone who isn't acquainted with it, they may not waste their breath. However, if it does come up, I have no doubt Phoebe will come to you for the truth. You can make up your mind then as to whether or not you wish to tell her.'

It seemed a logical solution, and Diana accepted it as such. But close on the heels of that came another question. 'Do you think Lord Durling knows I'm back in London?'

'Oh, Diana.' It was her aunt's turn to sigh. 'I think it would be naïve of us to believe that he isn't aware. He's far too well connected for matters like that to escape his notice.'

Diana nodded. Of course Lord Durling would know she was back, it was foolish of her to have thought otherwise. But she'd had to ask. She had to know if the lies Lord Durling had told about her four years ago were still the stories society believed today. She had to know if she was still thought of as the heartless schemer who had jilted her fiancé for the worst of reasons, and on the very day before they were to have been wed!

Chapter Two

In the overall scheme of things, Edward Thurlow, Earl of Garthdale, was not unhappy with his life. Born into a situation most would have envied, he had inherited not only the title upon his father's death, but the extensive lands and wealth that went with it. He enjoyed good health and a wide circle of friends, and a family situation that was, for the most part, agreeable.

He had two sisters, the elder of whom, Barbara, was happily married and soon to bear her second child, and a younger one, Ellen, who had been keeping company with a titled gentleman, who was said to be on the verge of proposing marriage. The only blot on his otherwise happy life, Edward acknowledged, was his mother.

His father, God rest his soul, had died four and a half years ago, and while the rest of the family had come to terms with his passing, his mother quite simply had not. She had stubbornly refused to move on with her life, and had become more fretful and cynical as the months went on. She had taken to complaining bitterly about a variety of physical aches and pains that suddenly seemed to have afflicted her, and as a result, was often to be found in bed, bemoaning the fact that no one truly understood what she suffered.

Edward wasn't surprised that many of her friends had stopped calling. Moreover, he suspected that the ailments from which she suffered were strictly a means of drawing attention her way, since it was clear that her need for her family had increased as dramatically as theirs for her had decreased.

Unfortunately, there was nothing he could do about that. He was hardly in need of a mother's care, nor was Barbara, who had a family of her own to look after. And given that the servants effectively saw to the running of the house, it fell to Ellen to bear the brunt of their mother's persistent attentions. The fact that her younger daughter might soon be engaged did nothing to prevent Lady Garthdale from clucking over her like a mother hen over her chick, which, at times, Edward supposed to be an apt comparison since, at times, Ellen seemed to possess no more sense than one.

Still, she was a sweet-natured child, deserving of happiness and anxious for a home of her own, and Edward was happy to see her courted by a man of wealth and position. Besides, once they were married, his obligation to her came to an end and he would be free to turn his attention to his own future and marital plans.

Not that he had any plans, Edward admitted as he trotted Titan, his large bay hunter, through the early morning quiet of the park. He had managed to reach the age of six and thirty without having been caught in the parson's mousetrap, but he knew it wasn't a situation that could go on forever. It fell to him to ensure the continuation of the line, and until now, he hadn't given that particular obligation much thought. However, with Ellen all but settled, and his mother unlikely to produce another heir, he no longer had a choice. He had to take a wife.

The question was, who? Certainly, there was a long enough list of eligible young ladies from which to choose. His mother frequently rhymed their names off to him, and of late even Barbara had begun introducing the subject of which innocent young miss might be best suited to the role of Countess of Garthdale.

The problem was, Edward didn't want an innocent young miss for a wife. He wanted a woman of character; a woman with whom he had something in common, and with whom he could have stimulating conversations. One who possessed the intelligence and sharpness of mind to have informed thoughts and opinions of her own.

Was that so shocking?

His friends seemed to think so, particularly those who wanted to marry attractive, well-dowered girls who would present them with sons and then leave them to pursue their own interests. But Edward couldn't imagine a more dismal prospect. He could not imagine spending the rest of his life with a woman who did not at least share *some* of his interests, particularly those that related to politics or commerce.

To him, the idea seemed more purgatory than pleasure.

It was true, he would never be called upon to make his living from the land, or to forge his way in business, but as a member of the House of Lords, surely it behoved him to learn all he could about the factors affecting the British economy.

Closer to home, he wanted to be able to talk to someone other than his land steward or secretary about the state of the home farm and the welfare of his tenants. He wanted to be able to discuss such things with his wife. Unfortunately, other than Barbara, Edward had met very few women who showed an interest in anything beyond the latest copy of *La Belle Assemblée*.

His father had understood his desire to marry a woman of sound mind, perhaps because his father had had the misfortune to be married to one who hadn't. Oh, he'd loved her well enough, Edward supposed, but he doubted his parents had shared anything beyond the most basic of interests. He could not imagine his mother stimulating his father in *any* way, and he thought that a sad commentary on two people who had lived under the same roof for nearly forty years.

Perhaps such mismatches were the fault of society, Edward reflected as he eased Titan to a walk. The necessity of marrying well was often more important than marrying for love, and blushing young women were shot out into the social world for a flock of eager young men to look over, with all the objectivity of farmers selecting brood mares. Appearance was everything, followed closely by good bloodlines and careful upbringing. Those ladies fortunate enough to be blessed with all three would be chosen first, and those even more fortunate would make a marriage with a man who loved and respected them. The rest would settle for a pretence of love and make of it what they could.

Edward didn't like settling and he didn't like pretence. He didn't like the idea of choosing a wife based solely on the strength of a few polite and rigidly supervised meetings. After all, what did a man really know about the woman he intended to marry? All ladies appeared poised and polished on first meeting. They all smiled and danced, and sang pretty songs and played the piano, but what did a man *really* know about the inner workings of such a woman? Was she a lady in public and a shrew in private? Did she evidence a sparkling wit, only to fall victim to vapours when no one was around?

And what about sex? Now there was a subject rife with the potential for disaster. What if his wife turned out to be one of those frigid creatures who did her duty in bed but derived no pleasure from it? How did a man go about pleasing a woman who shuddered at the very thought of intimacy?

Edward was so deep in thought that it was a few moments before he realised that someone was approaching on horseback. He looked up, and to his surprise, saw an elegant lady seated atop a fine dapple-grey mare. She was accompanied by a groom, but because it was so early in the day, Edward felt a mild stirring of interest. Most females of his acquaintance didn't even leave their beds before noon, yet this one was dressed and riding in the park at barely half past seven. That in itself gave the suggestion of someone out of the ordinary.

His gaze sharpened as he noticed other things about her: the flattering cut of her mulberry-coloured habit, and the quality of the lace trim. Her bonnet was most dashing, but the unusually heavy veil descending from it made it all but impossible to discern her features, though her figure looked to be that of a young woman—and one who was obviously at ease in the saddle. She held the reins firmly between gloved fingers and gave no impression of being nervous or ill at ease, even though the mare had her ears pricked forward and looked to be skittish.

Edward knew she would have ridden by him had it not been for the cat, a scrawny creature only a few months old that chose that very moment to dart out from the foliage at the base of a tree and run right between the mare's front feet.

Startled, the grey reared.

The lady, not expecting the movement, uttered a soft gasp, and Edward, fearing that she would fall, immediately pushed Titan forward.

The cat, having surely expended one of its nine lives, scampered unharmed into the bushes.

'Are you all right?'' Edward called, wondering if he should make a grab for the mare's reins.

'I am…fine, sir, thank you, but it would seem that…Juliet is not so easy of mind.' The lady's voice was unusually low and husky, but there was no trace of panic in it. 'I hope she did not tread on the poor cat.'

'Rest assured, it escaped with nary a hair flattened. And even had it not, it was more your welfare I was concerned with,' Edward told her.

'It is good of you to be concerned, but as you can see I am fine. I suspect the unexpected arrival of both cat and hunter momentarily proved too much for Juliet,' the lady said, adroitly regaining control of the dancing mare.

'Thankfully, it did not prove too much for you,' Edward observed, backing Titan away. 'Is your mare always so high spirited?'

'I have no idea.' The lady patted the grey's neck with affection. 'This is my first time riding her, but knowing to whom she belongs, I suspect she was merely in need of exercise. I thought a few times around the park would be a good start.'

Edward couldn't remember having heard a voice as husky as hers before, but finding it excessively attractive, decided he wanted to hear more. He also wondered if there was a polite way of asking her to lift her veil. He was suddenly very curious to see her face. 'Do you ride often in the morning? I don't believe I've seen you in the park before.'

'I am newly arrived in London, but ride when I can, and prefer the morning when there are fewer people about.'

'My sentiments exactly. There is nothing more tedious than trying to enjoy the air when one is squeezed cheek to jowl with others intent on doing the same. Perhaps we might ride together and thereby help to relieve the congestion?'

It was a casual remark, lightly offered, perhaps even spoken in jest. Nevertheless, it came as something of a surprise to Edward, who wasn't in the habit of extending invitations to women with whom he was not acquainted. Nor, it seemed, was the lady used to accepting them. 'Thank you, sir, but I do not think that would be wise.'

'Of course.' Edward already regretted having asked. 'I spoke out of turn. You obviously have a husband or brother at home who would object to such an arrangement.'

'On the contrary, I have neither husband nor brother, but my stay in town is of short duration and after that I shall be returning to the country.'

It was not the answer Edward had been expecting. 'Still, that shouldn't preclude us from riding together while you *are* here,' he said, wondering at his need to persist. 'You did say you intended to ride, and, since we both prefer the morning, why should we not ride together?'

'Because it would be difficult to plan such outings when I cannot commit to riding at the same time each day. I prefer the mornings, but go out when my aunt or cousin do not require my services.'

Her *services*? Edward frowned. Was she a companion then? A poor relation dependant upon a rich family member to ease her way?

He glanced at her outfit again and thought it unlikely. A poor relation would not be permitted such elegant clothes, nor be given so fine a horse to ride. 'Forgive me, but in the absence of someone to perform the niceties, may I ask your name?'

'You may ask, sir, but at the risk of sounding rude, I think I shall decline.'

'You would deny me so simple a request?'

'Yes, because you would not have asked had our circumstances been different.'

'What circumstances?'

'Those imposed by an impulsive feline who dashed out and startled my horse, thereby forcing you to offer assistance.'

'I was not forced to offer it,' Edward said, stung that she would think him so cavalier. 'I was happy to do so.'

'And it was very good of you, and I do hope I have expressed my thanks in a way that leaves you in no doubt as to my sincerity. But given the circumstances, I think it would be best if we were to leave it at that. Good morning.'

And with that, she pressed her heels into the mare's side and rode on.

Edward watched her go, aware of having been slighted, albeit politely, by a lady who obviously wished to have nothing to do with him—equally aware that he couldn't remember the last time a lady had done that to him…especially one who claimed to be single. She hadn't offered her name, nor had she enquired after his. In fact, nothing in the way she had behaved had led him to believe that she knew him, or wished to. And as a man used to being the object of intense feminine scrutiny, Edward found it a new and intriguing experience.

True, his impulsive invitation to have her ride with him had come as a surprise, even to him, but in hindsight, Edward realised it had more to do with finding out who she was than anything else. Anonymity always intrigued him, and, as a man who liked to have answers, her continued resistance had sparked more than a passing interest.

Not to mention that she had the most seductive voice he'd heard in a very long time.

The lady's groom tipped his hat to Edward as he rode by, and, not thinking, Edward acknowledged the salute. Regrettably, it wasn't until the servant was too far past that he realised he should have asked the fellow his mistress's name. It might not be the accepted method of gaining an introduction, but when it was the only one available, why should he not make use of it?

Still, if the lady had ridden this morning, chances were good she would ride again. If not today or tomorrow, certainly before the end of the week. And since he rode every day, and more than once if he could, it was only a matter of time before their paths crossed again.

And in matters like this, patience was something Edward had in abundance.

Diana returned to George Street and changed into a round gown of sprigged muslin. After smoothing a few errant curls back into place, she draped a warm shawl over her shoulders and headed downstairs for breakfast.

She was still feeling chilled from the onset of a cold, and though the wretched soreness in her throat had eased somewhat, her voice was still much deeper than usual. But she was glad she had gone ahead with her ride. She had woken to her first morning in London feeling heavy in body and anxious in mind, and because she had put both down to the uncertainty of what lay ahead, she had decided to venture out on horseback. She rode every morning at home, and getting out into the fresh air always seemed to help improve her spirits.

Unfortunately, it wasn't until she had entered Hyde Park that Diana realised the lethargy she had been feeling was more physical than mental, and that while an invigorating ride might help improve her mood, it probably wouldn't do much for her health. Her throat had felt as though it was on fire, so that every time she swallowed, she'd winced in pain. Nor had it made for easy conversation. Diana had hardly recognised the deep, husky voice as her own. She couldn't help but wonder what Lord Garthdale had thought of it.

Oh, yes, she knew who he was. Thanks to her aunt's groom, she knew not only who he was, but where he lived and who his family were. The strange part was, Diana couldn't recall having met the Earl of Garthdale before, nor could she remember her aunt having spoken about him. That in itself was curious, since her aunt had taken great pains to point out every eligible gentleman the last time Diana had been in London, particularly those who were handsome, titled or in possession of a large fortune.

Lord Garthdale was all three. Part of the reason Diana had been paying so little attention to her mare was as a result of admiring the dashing looks of the gentleman riding towards her. Even his voice had been pleasing; neither the affected drawl of the dandy, nor the clipped tones of the aristocrat. It had been a rich, resonant sound that had fallen most pleasantly on her ear.

Yes, all in all, it had been an interesting encounter, Diana reflected as she made her way to the breakfast parlour. If only he hadn't asked for her name, and whether or not she was married—

'Ah, good morning, my dear,' Mrs Mitchell said, looking up as Diana entered. 'I didn't expect to see you back so soon. Did you enjoy your ride?'

'Very much, Aunt,' Diana said, happy to be diverted from her thoughts. 'Juliet suits me very well.'

'I thought she might. I feared her being a bit rambunctious to start, as she's not had much exercise of late, but I knew that wouldn't be a problem for you. You have your mother's skill when it comes to riding. But, my poor girl, whatever has happened to your voice?'

Diana grimaced. 'I wish I knew. I woke up feeling rather muzzy this morning.'

'Yet you still went riding?'

'I thought it might help.'

'Obviously it did not.'

Diana picked up a plate. 'It did clear my head a little, but I fear it has done nothing for my throat.'

'Probably this vile London air,' Mrs Mitchell said as Diana perused the array of dishes set out on the sideboard. 'I always notice it when I return from the country. But I do hope it clears up soon. You have such a lovely clear voice, and it is all but unrecognisable now.'

'I'm sure I shall be fine in a day or two.' Not feeling particularly hungry and wanting something easy on her throat, Diana helped herself to a small portion of eggs. 'So, what have you planned for Phoebe's first day in London?'

'Oh, there are several things we have to do. The child will certainly need clothes, and I suspect you will, too. I doubt you've had anything new made up during the last four years.'

Diana lifted her shoulders. 'I had no need of new gowns. Those I had were sufficient for my purposes.'

'Sufficient for the country, perhaps, but not for going about in London now,' Mrs Mitchell said. 'Fashions change by the month, Diana, never mind by the year, and I won't have you looking like a country mouse when you set foot in society again. You are far too lovely for that. So, we shall call on Madame Claremont and make her a happy woman, then we shall go to the stationers for cards. After that, we shall visit the jewellers. I am having my old pearl necklace reset for Phoebe. She's always admired it, and pearls are eminently suitable for a young girl entering society.'

'Speaking of society, I met an interesting gentleman in the park this morning,' Diana said, having decided, after much thought, to share news of the encounter with her aunt.

'Really? Did he tell you his name?'

'No, but your groom did.'

Mrs Mitchell laughed. 'Of course. Tupper knows everyone, *and* everything about them. Well, who was he?'

'Lord Garthdale.'

'Lord Garthdale!' Mrs Mitchell nearly dropped her fork. 'Good heavens!'

Diana glanced up in amusement. 'Why so surprised, Aunt? Do not most gentlemen ride in Hyde Park in the morning?'

'Well, yes, but Lord Garthdale is hardly like most men! Apart from being one of the most eligible gentlemen in London, he is also one of the most elusive. He rarely attends society events, and, when he does, he seldom offers encouragement to any of the young ladies present. Still, he is a handsome gentleman, is he not?'

'I thought him very handsome indeed, and extremely gallant,' Diana admitted, explaining how the mare had shied and how Lord Garthdale had come to her aid.

'Obviously he didn't realise how little you were in need of it,' Mrs Mitchell said, chuckling. 'But I'm surprised he did not ride off immediately after seeing Juliet settled, for that would certainly have been more his style. Did he enquire after your name?'

'He did, but I did not make it known to him. I feared he might recognise it.'

'And what if he did?' Mrs Mitchell said. 'Your life isn't over because you refused to marry Lord Durling.'

'It would be if Lord Durling had his way.'

'Nonsense. The man went on with his life. Why should you not go on with yours?'

'Because I am the one who jilted him, Aunt Isabel, and I doubt he has forgiven me for it,' Diana said. 'Remember how angry he was at the time? Remember all the hateful things he said? He did everything he could to ruin my reputation and to make me look guilty.'

'Well of course he would try to make you look guilty. The man has an enormous ego, and since *you* were the one who refused to go through with the marriage, he had to make it sound as though your reasons for rejecting him were entirely self-serving. *We* know they were not, of course, but no one else did. And by not saying anything, you allowed society to draw their own conclusions.'

'You know why I refused to say anything,' Diana mumbled.

'Yes, I do, though I still think you were wrong. I'm sure that if you had spoken to someone in authority—'

'Lord Durling is a member of the House of Lords!'

'Be that as it may, he is not above the law.'

'He is beyond reproach in the eyes of society,' Diana said. 'And because we must concern ourselves with Phoebe making a good impression on society, we cannot afford to be careless.'

'But Diana, it has been *four* years.'

'I know. But I do not trust Lord Durling any more now than I did then,' Diana said quietly. 'He is a man who holds a grudge and I would not put it past him to try to make trouble for Phoebe if he thought it might be a way of striking back at me.'

'Which is why I wish you would tell people the truth of the matter,' Mrs Mitchell said in exasperation. 'The man *struck* you, Diana. He raised his hand without thought or provocation, and dealt you a blow hard enough to knock you to the ground. As far as I am concerned, such behaviour is unpardonable. Any man who would treat a lady like that deserves to be exposed for the wicked creature he is!'

'And I don't disagree with you, Aunt, but who would believe me if I were to tell them?' Diana said. 'It would always be my word against his, and society is hardly like to rally behind me. Lord Durling is a respected member of the aristocracy and an extremely charming man.'

On the outside, Diana reminded herself. *On the inside, it was a very different matter.*

'Well, I shall respect your wishes, just as I did four years ago, but that doesn't mean I agree with them,' Mrs Mitchell said tersely. 'Lord knows, I would take issue with the man myself, but, like you, I cannot suppose to trust him, and I should hate to see his vindictiveness turned against Phoebe.'

Diana returned her attention to her breakfast. 'Exactly. Lord Durling effectively destroyed my reputation when I refused to marry him, and I must do everything I can to guard Phoebe's against him. But now we must say no more about it for I hear her coming.'

Nothing more was said over breakfast, and the rest of the meal passed in amiable chatter about new gowns, current fashions and upcoming events. But as the three ladies set off for the shops, Diana couldn't help but wonder if she should have stayed in Whitley and let Phoebe come on her own. After all, she had no reason to be here, other than to keep her aunt and cousin company, and, in truth, both of them had friends enough to do that.

Had her returning to London with Phoebe now been a terrible mistake?

Chapter Three

Diana did not think it folly to ride in the park the next morning. Why would she, when she had absolutely no expectation of seeing Lord Garthdale again? Her aunt had already told her that he wasn't given to encouraging single ladies, so for him to turn up strictly for the purposes of an assignation would have been entirely out of character for him. Diana was also sure that her declaration not to see him again had been firm enough to convince him of her earnestness. As such, it was with little concern that she set off for the leafy lanes of Hyde Park just before half past seven the next morning.

Regrettably, her sore throat hadn't improved. She had gargled with salt water before leaving the house, but it had done nothing to help, and her voice was once again the husky croak it had been yesterday. She also wore the heavy veil in front of her face to conceal her features from those who might recognise her. Though it wasn't her intent to go looking for trouble, Diana knew it was quite possible she might encounter Lord Durling in the park. He used to like riding in the early hours of the day, and the last thing she wanted was to meet him here, with only the company of her groom for protection.

It was just one more of the fears she had harboured about returning to London.

Still, Diana had to admit that her first day in London had been a delightful surprise. Their visit to Madame Claremont had resulted not only in the ordering of new gowns and fripperies for Mrs Mitchell and Phoebe, but of several new ensembles for herself. Diana had been astonished at the wondrous array of fabrics presented to her, and startled by the degree to which fashion had changed. The cut of a sleeve, the fullness of a skirt, even the height of the waistline had rendered her existing wardrobe *démodé*.

Her aunt had been right in saying that she would indeed have looked a poor country cousin had she ventured forth so attired!

After that, they had seen to the ordering of new cards, paid the promised visit to the jewellers, and then returned home to spend a quiet afternoon occupied with individual pursuits. As a result, it wasn't until after Phoebe had gone to bed that Diana had learned anything more about the intriguing Lord Garthdale—and why her aunt had not spoken of him the last time she had been in London.

'Well, yes, dear, of course I would have introduced him to you, but as a result of his father's death, Lord Garthdale was absent from society almost the entire time. In fact, he didn't return to it until early the following year, by which time your relationship with Lord Durling had long since come to an end.'

Her aunt's explanation had certainly helped to explain why there had been no discussion of the Earl of Garthdale that year, Diana reflected now, though she couldn't say with equal certainty that *he* was unaware of what had happened to her. He might well have heard something from his friends upon his return to society. Her aunt had told her there had been much talk of it at the time, and for some months afterwards.

'So, the lady decided to risk another encounter with me after all,' a familiar voice said from the path ahead. 'I am honoured.'

Roused from her thoughts, Diana looked up—and was astonished to see Lord Garthdale riding towards her. Surely he hadn't come specifically to see *her*?

'It is a beautiful morning,' Diana said, determined to remain as cool as the circumstances would allow. 'And I did not think the risk of an encounter was reason enough to stay home. After all, the park is large enough for us both to be here and not see each other, is it not?'

His smile flashed, his teeth appearing very white against the warm brown of his skin. 'I agree that the chances of running into one another were slight, but I also admit I came in the hopes of doing just that.'

Glad for the veil that hid her blushes, Diana said, 'You should be careful, Lord Garthdale. I've been told it is not your habit to offer words of encouragement to single ladies.'

His look of surprise quickly changed to one of amusement. 'So, the lady also took the time to become acquainted with my name? I must profess myself flattered on top of everything else.'

Diana's lips twitched. 'Pray do not be too flattered. Upon returning home yesterday, my groom assured me that he would have come to my aid, had not Lord Garthdale already done so.'

'Ah, so that was the way of it. Well, since you now have the advantage of knowing my name, I think it only fair that you tell me yours.'

Diana had wondered how she would answer this, *if* she saw Lord Garthdale again and he should ask. Not only because she felt it would be rude to continue to deny him, but also because there was a good chance that they would meet in the social world to which they both belonged. But if she told him her name was Diana, it might be enough for him to make the association when she was eventually introduced to him, even though her veil prevented him from seeing her face, and the huskiness of her voice from recognising the sound of her real one. For that reason, she had decided to narrow the risk as much as possible. 'You may call me Jenny,' she told him.

'Jenny?' He looked at her. 'Nothing more?'

'Nothing more. Just Jenny.'

'I assume there is a reason you don't wish me to know your full name?'

'There is, but it is nothing of import.'

'I wonder,' Lord Garthdale said. 'I could think you a famous courtesan looking for a new protector, but I doubt you would trouble yourself with a groom if that were the case.'

Diana's cheeks warmed at the inference, but she didn't look away. 'A logical assumption, my lord, and correct since I am most certainly *not* a courtesan.'

'Perhaps a widow, then, living away from London. One who, upon returning to it, wishes to take a lover and arranges it through discreet meetings with gentlemen in the park.'

Diana felt her colour deepen. 'You seem to think my motives for being in the park are all quite immoral.'

'On the contrary, I am merely trying to ascertain why a young woman would ride in the park so heavily veiled that it makes it all but impossible to see her face, and be unwilling to reveal anything more than her first name.'

'Perhaps I lead such a boring life that keeping gentlemen guessing as to my identity is my only source of entertainment.'

He smiled, but shook his head. 'I don't presume to know you...Jenny, but I doubt you are easily bored. I suspect you are a woman of breeding and intelligence, and one who finds pleasure in whatever she does. But I do think you are hiding something.'

For Diana, the pleasure abruptly went out of the game. 'You may be right, Lord Garthdale. In which case, you will understand why I am reluctant to disclose my identity to you.'

He glanced down at his hands, seemingly in thought. 'If I gave you my word that I would not disclose your secret to anyone, would you answer me differently?'

'No, because I would be a foolish woman indeed to trust a stranger with so important a matter.'

'I do not go back on my promises.'

Strangely enough, Diana believed him, but it made no difference. 'You are able to say that now when you have no knowledge of who I am, but that is not to say that you wouldn't be compelled to do so in order to honour a promise made to another. Now, if you will excuse me—'

'*Jenny!*'

The sound of her name on his lips made her stop. The way he said it made her tremble. 'My lord?'

'I really don't care what you're hiding. As strange as it sounds, I don't even care who you really are. But I would like to see you again, even if it is only in the anonymity of the park like this.'

'But why? As you say, you know nothing of me. And I am sure your time could be better spent.'

'Perhaps, but I have time enough to do the things I must. This I do for myself, and I have already agreed that it makes no sense. Unfortunately, there *is* something about you that intrigues me, and makes me curious to know more.'

Diana gripped the reins a little harder. 'Curiosity is not always a good thing.'

'No, but the lack of it makes for a decidedly boring existence,' he said, nudging the bay closer. 'It is not my intention to make you uncomfortable, Jenny, but if I agree not to press you for details, will you agree to ride with me in the mornings for as long as you are in London?'

Diana hardly knew what to say. She certainly hadn't planned on anything like this happening, hadn't thought she would be called upon to further what had started out as a harmless deceit. And while she had been able to support it for two mornings, to continue it now, when she knew it was a lie, would remove all pretence of innocence. Could she do that?

Did she want to?

'I do not understand what you hope to gain by this, Lord Garthdale,' Diana said, stalling.

'Perhaps your eventual agreement to tell me more about yourself.'

'And if I choose to say nothing?'

His smile was sardonic. 'Though disappointed, I shall no doubt find the strength to go on. If you wish to tell me nothing, I shall have to be content to ride with you and to enjoy whatever conversations we have. There is, however, one request I would make of you.'

Diana caught her breath. *Would he ask her to lift her veil?* 'And that is?'

'That you even the stakes. For all I know, you are a titled lady, and I can hardly be Lord Garthdale to you when you are Jenny to me. My name is Edward.'

It was the strangest conversation Diana had ever had. She gazed up at the man sitting calmly in the saddle beside her, a man who had asked for nothing beyond the pleasure of her company without the slightest knowledge of who she was, and realised that she rather liked the idea. 'It is a peculiar request, Lord Garthdale, and one society would most certainly frown upon.'

'True, but if neither of us is to tell them, how are they to find out?'

Truth be told, it was unlikely anyone would find out, Diana admitted, if neither of them was inclined to mention it. And whatever his true motives for wishing to spend time with her were, they could not be furthered without her complete agreement to the plan, which effectively put her in control of the situation.

Diana looked up at him again, studying the lines and angles of his face, and wondered if any man had ever looked at her so intently. She knew that he was curious to see who she was; curious to discover the details of her physical appearance. What man alive did not wish to see the face of a veiled woman? But she didn't think curiosity accounted for all of his interest. It didn't invoke the kind of yearning she saw in the depths of his eyes.

But what could a man like this possibly yearn for? He had no need of clandestine meetings in the park. If he wished to speak to a lady, he simply went up to her and engaged her in conversation. So what was it about *her* that inspired him to agree to such strange terms? Her aunt had portrayed him as a gentleman of breeding and manners, and certainly his conduct to her yesterday had been proof of that. And yet, he must suspect her of being slightly improper. She had already admitted to having a secret; the kind that would cause a lady to ride heavily veiled, and to resist all attempts at a proper introduction. Why would he not suspect her of being an unhappily married lady looking for a lover?

Did it really matter what he thought?

The question surprised Diana, but the answer surprised her even more. *No, it didn't.* She had come to London to spend time with her aunt, and to see Phoebe presented to society. She had no intention of partaking in the social whirl herself, except where it was necessary to accompany Phoebe, and as soon as the Season was over, she would return to Whitley and resume her life there. For now, Lord Garthdale wished to ride with her and to continue their association on the terms he had put forward.

For once in her life, Diana decided it was reason enough.

They rode for over an hour, staying by mutual consent to the less well-travelled areas of the park, content to let the horses set their own pace. And while they walked, they talked.

Lord, how they talked! Diana couldn't remember ever having spoken so freely to a man before. Certainly, she had never spoken to Lord

Durling like this. She hadn't been at liberty to express her beliefs in such an open and honest way, because Lord Durling hadn't been interested in her opinions.

His opinion, frequently voiced, was that women only had one role to play: that of the subservient, well-mannered wife. It was their duty to raise the children and to tend the house, and if a woman chanced to have opinions of her own, she was free to express them to her female friends and relatives, but not to him.

Lord Durling had expressed absolutely *no* desire to see a more intellectually stimulating side of her.

Fortunately, Edward wasn't like that. He invited her to offer opinions on a variety of subjects, and listened to them all with interest and respect. When he brought up a subject—and he brought up many—he genuinely wanted to know what she thought about it. He even challenged her to think more intensely about a matter if he felt she was missing a certain aspect of it, or if her answers were lacking in depth. And when they exhausted one topic, they went on to another, including those that were of interest to her.

All in all, it was a thoroughly enjoyable experience, and when Diana glanced at the watch pinned to her bodice, she was dismayed to see how quickly time had passed.

'Oh, dear, I really must be returning home. My aunt will be wondering where I am.'

'She won't worry, I hope.' Edward drew the hunter to a halt. 'She knows you ride with a groom?'

'Yes, but she would not expect me to be away so long.'

'Why not? She must already know what an accomplished rider you are.' He slid her a sardonic glance. 'You really didn't need my help yesterday, did you.'

It wasn't phrased as a question, so Diana didn't answer it as one. 'Nevertheless, it did demonstrate what a gallant gentleman you are, and what a helpful nature you possess.'

He gave a short bark of laughter. 'I doubt there are many in society who would credit me with such noble qualities.'

'Why? Do you go out of your way to be discourteous in society?' Diana couldn't resist asking.

'Not as a rule, but no doubt my inclination to remain separate is a constant source of aggravation to mothers who would have me dance attendance upon their lovely daughters.' He smiled, sarcasm vanishing. 'Still, that need not enter into the conversation this morning. It would only serve to spoil what has been a most enjoyable interlude.' He turned to look at her, and his gaze held hers. 'I shall be here again tomorrow morning, Jenny. I hope you will join me.'

Diana felt her pulse beat in her throat. 'It is probably best that I make no promises, Edward, but…I will try.'

'That is all I can ask.' He swept her a dashing bow. 'Until tomorrow, fair lady.' Then he pressed his heels to the bay's sides and set off at a slow canter.

Bemused by it all, Diana turned Juliet's head around, and thought about the meeting that had just taken place. Was she right to say that she was happy? Surely she had nothing to be happy about. She had just agreed to meet with a man she barely knew, and to keep her identity secret from him.

What was there to look forward to in that but the certainty of failure? She knew there was no chance of a relationship developing between them. At least, not the kind of relationship she,

or any other gently bred lady, would entertain.
And yet, on the strength of her two brief meetings with him, Diana was already more aware
of Edward as a man than she had any right to
be. She grew a little breathless every time he
was around, and on several occasions, she had
experienced a curious sense of renewal, as
though her heart was suddenly awakening from
the depths of a long, deep sleep.

Still, there was no point in reading more into
it than was warranted. Once he found out who
she was—the woman who had jilted Lord
Durling—it would surely be over. Edward was
sure to know what had taken place between Diana Hepworth and Lord Durling. Perhaps he
was even a friend of Lord Durling's and had
heard first hand the lies he'd told about her.

Lies, Diana reflected bitterly, told to camou-
flage the depth of his own wickedness.

Unfortunately, Edward wouldn't know that.
He would only know that Diana Hepworth was
a callous, deceitful woman who had pretended
to love a man, only to cast him aside when she
decided to look for someone better. A woman
with no scruples, and who would do whatever
it took to marry the richest man she could—
even if it meant jilting a man who had been

prepared to swear a lifetime of love and devotion to her.

Diana sighed. Those were the stories Edward would have heard, because those were the lies Lord Durling had circulated. They were also the reasons she couldn't tell him the truth. She didn't want to see the expression on his face change, or the softness in his eyes harden into disgust when he looked at her. As foolish as it might be, Diana wanted Edward to think well of her, and for a few days, perhaps even a few weeks, she might be able to do that. They could ride together in the mornings and enjoy their conversations. They would talk to one another as equals, free to voice their respective opinions, and to suffer no consequences as a result, because in that regard Phoebe was right.

There *was* a decided lack of stimulating conversation to be had in Whitley. Try as she might, Diana often found the topics of discussion reverting back to the same old subjects, namely how the rain—or lack thereof—was going to affect the crops, and whether or not old Mrs Fenton would make it through the winter. However, it was where she had grown up, and where circumstances four years ago had compelled her to return. And though Diana was determined to make the best of it, that didn't mean she would willingly give up the opportunity of enjoying intelligent conversation with a man like Lord Garthdale, now that it had been presented to her.

And so, she decided to allow herself these precious moments in time. She knew they would be fleeting, but she would give herself the pleasure of speaking to a man who valued her opinions and to whom she could speak without fear of censure or contempt. Her aunt had said it best. Time did pass quickly. And in the scheme of things, Diana had no doubt that four weeks, like four years, would pass in little more than the blink of an eye!

'Come, Phoebe, we shall be late!' Diana called, stopping by the door of her cousin's room. 'The carriage is waiting.'

'I'm coming, Diana. Just a few more minutes! Marie is finishing my hair!'

Diana silently turned and continued on towards the stairs. They were to attend the Townleys' soirée this evening, and it seemed as though the entire house was at sixes and sevens. Not only because it would mark Phoebe's unofficial entrance into society, but because it was also Diana's first foray into society in over four years.

It was understandable that both ladies were suffering considerable nerves.

It hadn't helped that Mrs Mitchell had forgotten that it was tonight the reception was to be held. Indeed, it was only thanks to her having run into Mrs Townley and Amanda at Layton and Shears that morning that she had discovered her oversight. Then there had been a positive flurry of last-minute preparations as gowns, gloves and other necessities had been pulled out and made ready.

But equally important were Mrs Mitchell's repeated assurances that Amanda was longing to see her dear friend again.

Diana wished she could say the same. That is, she wished she could say that the prospect of attending a society event at which Amanda would be present was not overshadowed by the thought that so many other people would be there as well. Still, it was a special night for Amanda, and Diana had no intention of missing it.

'Ah, there you are, my dear,' Mrs Mitchell said, standing at the foot of the stairs. 'And looking exceptionally lovely, I must say.

Madame Claremont knew what she was talking about when she suggested that gown for you. The simplicity of the design makes it appear very elegant, and I knew the shade would look well on you. You are going to attract a great deal of attention this evening, my dear, and *not* for the reasons you fear.'

Diana smiled, comfortable in the knowledge that she did at least look well for the evening's festivities. The soft apricot gown with demi-train was one of the many Mrs Mitchell had ordered for her. The style was highly flattering to the slender lines of her figure, and the colour was a perfect compliment to the fairness of her skin. Her aunt's petite French maid, Marie, had arranged her dark hair in a cluster of curls atop her head, and had set a dainty gold clip in the back. The rest of her jewellery was simple. Her mother's pearl earrings, and a necklace of gold and pearls that nestled in the shadowy cleft between her breasts.

Phoebe came down not long after, looking radiant in a gown of white satin trimmed with deep rose. Her blonde hair was arranged in a soft tumble of curls to one side of her face, making her appear very young and appealing. Mrs Mitchell, who was herself gowned in deep blue silk, gave her a brief nod of approval, and then led the way out to the waiting carriage.

'Courage, my dears,' she said as they settled in for the short ride to the Townleys' house. 'Keep your chins up, your smiles bright, and, like the inimitable Sarah Siddons, you shall have all of London falling at your feet!'

Diana smiled and sat back against the cushions. Encouraging words, she reflected, though only time would tell how helpful they would be. Nevertheless, she took a deep breath, whispered a silent prayer, and waited for the proverbial curtain to rise.

Chapter Four

It was an evening of surprises for Diana: the first, that Mrs Townley had not invited half of London to her fashionable soirée, and the second, that the Amanda she remembered no longer existed.

Diana could hardly believe that the elegant young lady standing in the receiving line had once truly been her best friend. Where was the awkward girl she remembered? The one who had constantly bemoaned the fact that her hair was frizzy and unmanageable, and that she wasn't as tall or as graceful as her friends. The elegant young woman in the exquisite white gown bore absolutely no resemblance to that painfully shy, stammering girl. No wonder her aunt had said she would be surprised, Diana reflected.

'Diana!' Amanda cried as Diana drew to a halt in front of her. 'Oh, Diana, I am so very pleased to see you again!'

'And I am delighted to see you!' Diana said, returning the girl's enthusiastic greeting. 'But I can scarce believe the change in you. You look beautiful!'

Amanda laughed, and the sound was bell-like and enchanting. 'Yes, is it not astonishing? I stayed with Aunt Hester over the winter and she took my transformation to heart. Mama could not believe how much I had changed by the time I returned home.'

Diana shook her head. 'In truth, I can scarce believe it myself. But I am happy for you, Amanda, and thrilled with your news. You will be the most beautiful of brides.'

'And the happiest, for I am marrying the very kindest of men. Diana, allow me to present to you my fiancé, Lord Eastcliffe,' Amanda said, turning to smile at the handsome gentleman standing next to her.

Diana duly acknowledged the introduction, pleased that Lord Eastcliffe showed no signs of reluctance at meeting her. She knew little about him, other than that he was a pleasant, studious gentleman who enjoyed collecting Greek antiquities. Indeed, some people joked that he was unlikely to notice a woman from his own time when he was so busy studying those of another.

Diana had originally been concerned that he might not give Amanda the attention she deserved, but, when she saw the warmth in his eyes as he smiled at her, she knew her fears were unfounded.

'We have much to talk about,' Amanda whispered as Diana and Phoebe went to move on. 'Promise we shall have some time together this evening.'

'Of course, but if we do not, I shall be sure to come and visit you again.'

Amanda's eyes brightened. 'Oh, yes, I should like that very much!'

The girls exchanged a few more words, and then Diana and Phoebe moved on to join their aunt, who was already talking to a couple neither of the girls knew. They were soon introduced, however, and the first half-hour or so passed in pleasant conversation. Phoebe eventually went off with a cluster of younger girls, and Diana herself made the acquaintance of several amiable people, none of whom looked at her with the censure she had been expecting.

'Oh, look, there is Lady Aldsworth,' Mrs Mitchell said, spying a tall, black-haired woman who had just come in. 'I must have a word with her. Do you mind if I leave you for a moment, Diana?'

'Of course not. I shall be fine on my own.'

As it turned out, however, she wasn't alone long. Only moments after her aunt stepped away, Diana turned to find Amanda at her side. 'Now, we shall have our few minutes alone,' the girl said with evident satisfaction.

Surprised that she had time so early in the evening, Diana said, 'Are you sure you dare? There are many people anxious to wish you well on your betrothal.'

'Yes, but they can hold their good tidings for a few minutes. Right now, I want to spend time with you.' Amanda reached for Diana's hands and held them tightly in her own. 'I truly am so pleased to see you back in town, Diana. When your aunt told me you were coming, I could scarce contain my excitement. But it must seem strange being back after spending so much time away.'

Diana knew what Amanda was referring to, but she only smiled. 'It is better than I expected. This is only my first outing, of course, but I'm feeling more at ease than I'd thought to, and Phoebe is having a wonderful time, which is my main reason for being here.'

Amanda looked at her quizzically. 'What do you mean? Are you not here looking for a husband?'

'Certainly not. I am here to act as Phoebe's companion, and to make sure she has a wonderful time. And, of course, to help her find a husband.'

'But what about *your* future?'

Diana laughed softly. 'I am mistress of Narbeth Hall, and actively engaged in caring for my garden and my flowers, along with my two cats, three rabbits, and a very rambunctious puppy. But never mind my life, tell me all that has been happening in yours!' Diana said, purposely switching the subject. 'I leave behind a fragile duckling, and come back to find a beautiful swan, engaged to marry the Earl of Eastcliffe, no less.'

Amanda giggled, and in doing so, became the ingenuous girl Diana remembered. 'Astonishing, is it not? Especially given the way I used to look.'

'Nonsense. You make it sound as though you were a dowd, and we both know that was never the case.'

'No, but I was not, as Aunt Hester said, ''a lady whom the gentlemen were lining up to meet.'' Fortunately, she taught me how to improve in so many areas, and I will always be grateful to her for that. I don't think Mama ever dreamed I would attract the attention of someone like John.'

'So you are happy about your upcoming marriage?' Diana asked.

'I am more than happy, Diana. I have been fortunate enough to find a man who loves me, and whom I love so very much in return.'

'Then you are truly blessed.'

'Yes, I believe I am,' Amanda said, her happiness shining through. 'John is always bringing me little gifts, or sending me posies. He even wrote a poem to me once, though he made me promise not to show it to anyone.'

'Really.' Diana had difficulty imagining the pedantic Earl of Eastcliffe sitting down to pen romantic prose. 'And have you?'

'I confess, I was tempted to when I heard people constantly remarking on how serious he seems, but I have abided by his wishes and I suppose it is for the best. It was a rather sentimental piece.'

The delicate blush on her friend's cheeks convinced Diana there must be hidden depths to Lord Eastcliffe, and that it was probably best not to delve any further into the content of the letter. 'Well, I am very happy that you have found someone who makes you so happy, Amanda. You deserve the best of husbands. And as the Countess of Eastcliffe, you will certainly have access to all the best houses.'

'Yes, though I confess, the thought of moving in the uppermost levels of society is somewhat daunting.'

'I don't know why. Looking the way you do, you can hold your head up in any crowd.'

'Dearest Diana, you always did say the kindest things,' Amanda said sincerely. 'And that is only one of the reasons I have missed you so much.' Her smile faltered. 'I have missed you. You know that, don't you?'

Diana sighed. 'I wanted to think you did, but I didn't know when your letters stopped coming. I thought perhaps your mother had discouraged you from writing because of what happened.'

'Oh, no, it wasn't like that at all! In fact, I wanted to write because there was something I desperately wanted to tell you. But I didn't know how to say it and, then, as time went by— yes, Parker?' Amanda said as the butler arrived in front of her.

'Pardon the interruption, miss, but Lord and Lady Jenkins have arrived.'

'Oh, yes, of course, and I must go and welcome them.' Amanda smiled an apology at Diana. 'They are relations of John's, come all the way from Yorkshire to meet me. You will forgive me for leaving you?'

'Of course.' Diana gave the girl her most reassuring smile. 'I told you, you shouldn't be neglecting your guests this evening.'

Amanda's face reflected her relief. 'I knew you would understand. But I shall come back, and we will pick up where we left off. There is much I would tell you, Diana!'

She swept away in a rustle of skirts, and, watching her go, Diana felt a momentary pang of disappointment. She was sure that Amanda had been about to tell her something of importance, but she could hardly expect her to ignore her guests so that she might share confidences with an old girlfriend.

Suppressing a sigh, Diana rose and glanced around the room for her aunt. She didn't find her, but she did find—or was found by—Phoebe, who was looking decidedly flushed and not a little breathless.

'Phoebe, whatever is the matter? You look quite disconcerted.'

'That is because I am disconcerted,' Phoebe said, pressing a hand to her heart. 'A gentleman has been smiling at me and I am quite at a loss to know what to do about it.'

'You could smile back at him.'

'Oh, no! I couldn't, because he is truly the most handsome gentleman I have ever seen! And I know that if he comes to speak with me, I shall make a complete fool of myself!'

Suddenly feeling very much older and wiser, Diana said, 'He won't speak to you without an introduction, Phoebe. And if he does speak to you, you shall certainly not make a fool of yourself.' She glanced around the room, looking for the source of Phoebe's agitation. 'To which gentleman do you refer?'

'The tall one in the scarlet uniform,' Phoebe said, not looking at him. 'There, by the wall.'

Diana glanced across the floor and finally located the source of Phoebe's consternation, a handsome young officer, who nevertheless had a most friendly and engaging air. 'I don't know who he is, but I'm sure Aunt Isabel will,' Diana said, looking around for the older woman.

Fortunately, Mrs Mitchell chose that moment to return, seemingly intent on having a tête-à-tête with Diana. 'My dear, I really must have a word with you.'

'Of course, Aunt, but first, who is that nice looking gentleman standing by the *étagère?*'

'Hmm?' Mrs Mitchell turned in that direction. 'Why, bless my soul, it's Nicolas Wetherby. Lord Mowbrey's son. A younger son, I'm afraid, but blessed with the same charm and good looks as his father and older brother. I nearly didn't recognise him now that he's grown into a man.'

'Apparently, he has been smiling at Phoebe,' Diana whispered.

'Has he indeed?' Mrs Mitchell glanced at her still-blushing niece, and raised one eyebrow. 'Perhaps I should see to an introduction. Then I must come back and speak to you.'

'Why? Is something wrong?' Diana said, hearing the concern in her aunt's voice.

'Not exactly wrong, but it's something you won't be pleased about. Come along, Phoebe,' Mrs Mitchell said in a brisk voice. 'Let us make you acquainted with this handsome gentleman and see what comes of it.'

In the wake of their departure, Diana nibbled on her bottom lip. What was her aunt so anxious to tell her? If it wasn't something bad, why would she be disturbed at hearing it?

The sound of new arrivals had Diana glancing towards the door. But when she saw who it was, apprehension welled in her throat, making it difficult for her to breathe.

Edward! He'd entered the room in the company of two ladies—one of whom looked to be around Phoebe's age, while the other looked a few years older than Diana—and a gentleman Diana assumed to be the older lady's husband. As they moved through the receiving line, it was obvious that they were well known. Laughter flowed easily, and both Amanda and her fiancé looked relaxed and at ease in their company.

Diana wished she could say the same.

'Diana, what *are* you doing?' Mrs Mitchell said, suddenly reappearing at her side. 'If I didn't know better, I would swear you were trying to disappear behind that Chinese screen.'

'That is exactly what I am trying to do,' Diana whispered. 'Look there. Lord Garthdale has arrived.'

'He has, indeed?' Mrs Mitchell turned in time to see the family move into the room. 'Well, so he has, and in the company of his family.'

'All of them?'

'Yes, the younger girl is his sister, Lady Ellen. The older one is Barbara, now Lady Black. And that is her husband, Sir Lionel. The Dowager Lady Garthdale is, of course, absent.'

The note of impatience in her aunt's voice caught Diana by surprise. 'You sound as though you do not care for Lady Garthdale, Aunt.'

'In truth, I do not. The woman has become something of a pariah since her husband's death, and has managed to alienate most of her family and nearly all of her friends. But that, my dear, is what I wished to speak to you about.'

Diana's dark brows drew together. 'Lady Garthdale?'

'No, her daughter, Lady Ellen.' Mrs Mitchell stepped around Diana so that she, too, was partially hidden behind the screen. 'Mrs Townley told me there was something you should know. She told me because she thought it would be easier if *I* told you, rather than letting you hear it from someone else.'

'Why? What did she tell you?'

'That it seems news of another engagement is soon to be made public.'

'What? Tonight?'

'I doubt it will be tonight, but it will be soon.'

'But an engagement is good news. Isn't it?'

Mrs Mitchell looked around to make sure that no one was listening, and then leaned in to whisper, 'That depends on the parties involved. It seems that Lady Ellen has just accepted an offer of marriage.'

'How delightful. I'm sure her family must be pleased. But why did Mrs Townley feel that you needed to—' Diana broke off, gasping. 'Oh, *no*, Aunt. *Please* don't tell me what I think you're about to—'

'I'm afraid I must, my dear,' Mrs Mitchell said in the most regretful of tones. 'As lamentable as it is, it seems the gentleman Lady Ellen has agreed to marry is none other than Lord Durling!'

It was the last thing Diana expected—or wanted—to hear. 'Are you sure?'

'I have no reason to doubt it. Mrs Townley has several reliable sources upon which to draw. Apparently, Lord Durling has been courting Lady Ellen for some time.'

Diana glanced with shock and dismay at the girl standing next to Edward, trying to imagine her married to a man like Lord Durling. She was lovely, to be sure, but she was like a china doll, all porcelain skin and flaxen ringlets. And young. So terribly, terribly young.

'She can scarce know what she is about,' Diana murmured. 'Or what he is.'

'If she loves him, she won't care what he's about,' Mrs Mitchell said drily. 'Only that he is handsome, charming, and anxious to marry her!'

'As I was once,' Diana admitted. 'But then, Lord Durling can be a very charming and persuasive man.'

'So could Henry VIII, but look where it got most of his wives,' Mrs Mitchell muttered. Brows furrowed, she watched the family move around the room. 'You don't think it's possible that Lord Durling has changed, do you, Diana? Perhaps he has mended his ways. After all, if he was in any way affected by what happened four years ago—'

'I don't know that a man whose nature tends to violence *can* change, Aunt, no matter how much time he is given,' Diana said. 'But I am curious to know why he hasn't married before now. Surely there was no reason for him to have remained single all this time.'

'I really can't say. He did withdraw from society for some months after you left London,' her aunt said, 'but I am sure that was more as a result of his feeling compelled to do so, rather than out of any deep-rooted feelings of guilt. He *was* the jilted suitor, after all, and it behoved him to show some signs of remorse, whether he felt any or not.'

Diana had no doubt that any remorse Lord Durling had shown was entirely for the benefit of others. 'Has he been seen keeping company with anyone else?'

'There were a few ladies,' Mrs Mitchell said, 'but none with whom he seemed serious. Until now.'

In a decidedly subdued mood, Diana watched Edward and his family move around the room. She couldn't deny that she was deeply troubled by the thought of Lady Ellen Thurlow marrying Lord Durling, but what could be done about it? She certainly couldn't say anything to Edward. She hardly knew him well enough to comment on his family's activities, even in the guise of Jenny. And he wouldn't welcome remarks from Diana Hepworth—a woman who was known to carry a grudge against Lord Durling. On the other hand, how could she just leave the child to her fate, allowing her to be swept into a marriage that could prove not only unhappy, but potentially destructive?

As for herself, she was facing a dilemma of her own. What was she to do about Edward? Diana knew it was quite likely she would be introduced to him. He was obviously a good friend of the Townleys, and Diana had a feeling that Amanda would try to effect an introduction, seeing him as an eligible man, and her as a single lady. Did she want that to happen?

'Aunt Isabel, there is something I must tell you,' Diana whispered, aware that her head was starting to spin. 'Remember I told you that I met Lord Garthdale in the park?'

'Of course, dear. I am not likely to forget something like that.'

'Well, as it happens, I have seen him on…two more occasions since.'

'You have? And you did not tell me? Where? And when?'

'I would rather not go into detail, but it is imperative that he not recognise me as that lady.'

'But you just said the two of you met in the park.'

'Yes, but I was heavily veiled, and my voice was unrecognisable as a result of the cold,' Diana explained quickly. 'Nor did I give him my full name. I told him he could address me as Jenny.'

'Jenny?' Mrs Mitchell's look of surprise changed to one of confusion. 'You gave him your *middle* name? Diana, what on earth is all this about?'

'I promise I shall explain as soon as we are alone, Aunt, but please understand why, if an introduction is made between Lord Garthdale and myself tonight, I must behave as though I am meeting him for the first time!'

Her aunt's eyes narrowed. 'I don't like this, Diana. I've never known you to indulge in subterfuge before.'

'I know, and it's too late to undo what I've already done. I can only say that I did what I did without stopping to fully consider the consequences.'

'So it would appear. I know you too well to doubt your integrity, but I can't help but feel that you have set yourself a very difficult task by pretending to be two people.' Mrs Mitchell cast a furtive glance in the direction of the gentleman. 'Well, do you wish me to effect an introduction for you to Lord Garthdale *as* Diana Hepworth?'

Diana pondered the question for a moment, wondering how best to proceed. She could risk the introduction and get it over with now. Or she could try to elude Edward for the rest of the night in the hopes that when their paths finally did cross, she would be better prepared to deal with it. But would she ever really be prepared?

Hoping to catch a glimpse of Edward, Diana turned her head—and blanched.

He was looking right at her. He was standing very still, watching her across the width of the room. And he wasn't smiling.

Diana felt her heart jump clear into her throat. *He'd recognised her!* He must have! Why else would he be staring at her so intently?

The question was, would he come over and ask to be properly introduced?

Diana went cold as he took a step in her direction. Clearly, that was exactly what he intended!

Then, miraculously, a reprieve. A liveried footman walked up to Edward and handed him a note.

Diana watched, holding her breath as Edward took the letter and broke the seal. He started to read, but within seconds, his face darkened until finally, tucking the letter in his coat, he turned on his heel and left—without sparing her a second glance.

Weak with relief, Diana closed her eyes and let go her breath, scarcely aware that she had been holding it.

'Well, I wonder what all that was about?' Mrs Mitchell said quietly at her side.

Almost having forgotten the presence of her aunt, Diana turned and said, 'I have no idea, Aunt. Whatever news that letter contained obviously didn't make Lord Garthdale happy.'

'No, but at least it spared you the embarrassment of an encounter. Oh, yes, that's precisely what he had in mind,' her aunt said. 'I saw the look on his face. He had every intention of coming over to speak with you, and would have, had the footman not arrived when he did. Are you sure he hasn't seen through your disguise, my dear?'

Diana wasn't sure, and told her aunt as much.

'Well, there is no doubt that he thought he knew you,' Mrs Mitchell said, drawing Diana's arm through hers. 'But whatever the message, it was important enough to make him change his mind and embark on a different course altogether. Perhaps it was just as well, wouldn't you say?'

Chapter Five

Edward jumped down from the hackney cab and mounted the stairs to the elegant four-story town house in two bounds. Rapping his cane against the door, he waited impatiently for it to be opened. It was moments later, and the butler, recognising the late arrival, stood back and nodded. 'She is in the drawing room, my lord.'

'Thank you, Denner.' Edward handed the man his hat and gloves, then made his way up the stairs.

In the formal drawing room, he found his mother much as he'd expected; sitting in the dark, with her chair pulled close to the fireplace, and a handkerchief pressed to her eyes. Knowing that she expected someone else, Edward silently crossed to the sideboard and picked up one of the flickering candles. 'Good evening, Mother.'

Lady Garthdale jumped. 'Edward!' She whirled around, her dark eyes filled with accusation. 'What are you doing here?'

'I came in response to your letter.' Edward went to each of the silver candelabras in the room and lit their candles from the stub of the one in his hand. 'I thought it best not to wait until morning.'

The dowager's eyes narrowed. 'My letter was addressed to Ellen.'

'Yes, but, unfortunately, I intercepted it. Are you feeling all right?'

'No, I am not feeling all right. Not that any of you care,' she muttered. 'Where's Ellen? Why did everyone go out and leave me?'

Edward returned the candle to its holder, and then pulling up a chair, sat down across from his mother. 'Mrs Townley is holding a reception this evening to which we were all invited. Even *you.*'

Lady Garthdale waved her hand in a gesture of dismissal. 'I do not attend parties any more. I stopped socialising the day your father died. I wonder that people fail to remember that.'

'They remember, but they send you invitations in the hopes that you will change your mind and decide to attend.'

The handkerchief stilled. 'I'm not sure I like your tone, Edward. You know how hard this is for me. You know how devastated I was by your father's death. No one seems to care what I've had to suffer! No one seems to think it's right and proper for a woman to grieve for her husband.'

Edward sighed. He had been through this too many times to believe that arguing with his mother would achieve anything, but sometimes it was a struggle to curb his impatience. 'No one is saying that you shouldn't grieve, Mother, but there has to be a limit to it. Everyone knows you still miss Father, but you can't expect the rest of the family to stop living just because you've chosen to.'

'That's not fair!'

'Isn't it? It has been over four and a half years, Mother. And though I am sorry to have to say it, that's long enough for anyone to have recovered from their grief.'

'He was my husband!'

'And he was my father, and I loved him dearly,' Edward was stung into replying. 'But nothing is going to bring him back, and as far as I am concerned, my obligations, like yours, are to the living.'

'I don't have obligations any more.'

'Nonsense! In a few weeks, Ellen will be leaving here forever. You could at least try to make her last weeks at home pleasant.'

His mother turned her face away. 'I have no idea what you're talking about!'

'No?' Edward pulled out the letter and held it up. 'I'm talking about dispatching a letter to her, begging her to come home and keep you company when you know she is engaged at a social function.'

Lady Garthdale's face set in defiant lines. 'I am her mother. I have a right to expect her loyalty.'

'And she gives it to you willingly enough, but it isn't your right to demand it every second of the day. No one owes you that much devotion.'

Suddenly, the woman's face crumpled. 'Why do you attack me, Edward? I have done everything in my power to make you happy. All of you! And yet this is how I am repaid.' She went silent for a moment, twisting the handkerchief between her fingers. 'You should have brought her back. It isn't right that she be left alone and unattended. You know what men are like.'

Wearily, Edward ran his hands through his hair. 'She isn't alone. The last time I saw Ellen, she was having a very good time with Amanda Townley and several of her friends. And Barbara and her husband are there to look after her.'

'Humph! She should be here taking care of me!'

Edward didn't bother arguing. What was the point? 'I'm sorry you feel that way, Mother, because it isn't the case any more. Barbara and I have gone on with our lives, and Ellen is about to go on with hers.' He slowly stood up. 'I suggest you give some thought to what you intend to do with the rest of *yours*, lest it become a very long, boring, and lonely affair.'

He left her then, quietly closing the door behind him even as she railed and cried and swore never to receive him again. It meant nothing, of course, because his mother was the kind of woman who used histrionics to inflict guilt on others. She had done it when her husband had been alive and she still did it now, four and a half years after his death.

Not of a mood to go straight back to the Townleys' party, Edward stopped at his club for a drink. He needed a few minutes to take the edge off his anger. If he went back to the reception now, his patience would be strained and he might end up saying something he'd regret. He would go back eventually, if only to make sure that Ellen got home. Barbara would do it, but it wasn't his way to shirk his responsibilities.

He'd offered to take Ellen to the reception, and he would make sure she got home. That was just what a brother did.

Staring into his brandy, Edward's thoughts turned briefly to the reception, and to how pleased he was at seeing Amanda Townley and Lord Eastcliffe engaged. They were both people he liked, and he knew they would deal well with one another. Though not identical, their personalities were similar enough that they would have no trouble making a life together.

Edward thought for a moment about the young woman he had seen talking to Amanda throughout the evening. He hadn't known who she was, but something about her had seemed familiar to him, causing him to stare at her longer than he might otherwise have done.

Her face had been a constant reflection of her emotions. He had seen warmth and sincerity interposed with concern and amusement as she and Amanda had talked together, no doubt exchanging confidences about Eastcliffe and other gentlemen of the *ton*. And, judging from the way Amanda had held the lady's hands, they were close, yet he could not recall having seen or met her before.

It must be my week for seeing mysterious young women, Edward thought, his mind going back to the lady he had met in the park. To Jenny.

Funny that after three meetings, her name should be the only thing he knew about her. He had no idea where she lived, what her surname was, or who her family were. He didn't know if she had brothers and sisters, if she was a titled lady, or a paid companion in a relative's house.

But even more surprising was the fact that he really didn't care. At least, not enough to jeopardise the relationship by asking her for answers. She likely wouldn't give him any regardless. The lady had a good reason for keeping her identity secret.

The question was, what was it? Edward didn't take her for a courtesan, or for a married woman looking for an affair. Nothing in her speech or conduct had led him to believe that she wished to take their relationship to a more intimate level. She had made no enquiries into his wealth, nor tried to find out who he was protecting, if anyone.

The basis of their meetings was strictly conversation, and he enjoyed them for that reason. Jenny had an agile mind, and was better informed than most women of his acquaintance, and he had certainly tested her in enough areas. Their discussions had touched on politics, foreign trade, the inland economy, and the welfare of the British working class. It was true, she hadn't his in-depth understanding of all the subjects, but she had certainly known enough to be able to hold her own. And what she hadn't known, she had been happy to ask about, demonstrating a willingness to learn more about matters that were unfamiliar to her.

Unfortunately, none of that took away from the fact that she *was* hiding something. No woman with an unblemished past would appear as she did, heavily veiled and mysterious.

Edward wondered if she might be hiding from a man. He assumed she had been out of London for a while. Perhaps upon returning to it now, she was doing all she could to keep her identity hidden.

And yet, how could a young, single woman escape notice entirely? She must be of some consequence, judging by the clothes she wore and the fine horse she rode. She was also attended by a groom, which signified a genteel upbringing. He remembered her brief mention of an aunt and a cousin, which meant she had family living in London. But did she lead the same kind of restricted life at home? Did she never venture into society with those relations? Edward didn't attend all of society's functions, but he went to enough to recognise the faces that kept appearing—and the voices that were always to be heard. And while he might not be able to identify Jenny's face, he certainly wouldn't forget the sound of her voice. The seductive quality of it, deep and smoky, made him think of dark nights in soft arms, and limbs entwined in passion.

Realising that he was starting to spend entirely too much time thinking about Jenny, Edward got up and reluctantly headed for the door. He didn't have time to indulge in such pleasurable thoughts when he had other more immediate concerns to address. Like getting Ellen home and perhaps finding out the identity of the young woman he had intended to speak with just before he had left. To find out why something about her was familiar—and why the thought of his approach had brought such a look of trepidation to her face.

At approximately the same time, Diana, Phoebe and Mrs Mitchell were climbing into their carriage for the short drive back to George Street.

'Oh, what a *marvellous* evening!' Phoebe exclaimed as the carriage door closed behind them. 'Did you not think so, Diana?'

Happy to have quit the evening relatively unscathed, Diana returned her cousin's smile. 'Indeed, Phoebe, it was most pleasant. I was delighted to see Amanda looking so well and happy.'

'She should be happy, she has made an excellent match with Lord Eastcliffe,' Mrs Mitchell commented. 'Mrs Townley is beside herself, and apparently Lady Eastcliffe is pleased with her son's choice of a bride, which bodes well for a happy marriage. So, you enjoyed your first venture into society, did you, Phoebe?'

'Very much, Aunt. Captain Wetherby said he couldn't remember the last time he had attended a livelier reception.'

Mrs Mitchell glanced at her niece sharply. 'I would advise you to be careful in your conduct with Captain Wetherby, Phoebe. You are new to society, and will meet many gentlemen over the next few weeks. Captain Wetherby is a pleasant young man, but he is a second son, and therefore not in line to inherit the title or the estate.'

Phoebe huffed. 'I do not care about such things.'

'You should.'

'I like him for who he is.'

'And there is nothing wrong with that, but it is just as easy to fall in love with a rich man as a poor one, and far more advantageous. Did he tell you he has hopes of being given a living within the church after leaving the militia?'

Phoebe's startled silence told them he hadn't.

'Not that there is anything wrong with the church,' Mrs Mitchell conceded. 'It is a good and honourable profession, and entirely suitable for a younger son. But you must ask yourself if it is the type of life you wish to lead. After all, you could do much better were you to hold out for a title, and preferably one with a fortune attached.'

Phoebe sighed. 'I suppose you're right, but I do wish to marry for love. Is that so wrong?'

'No, and I admit, it is what I would wish for you, but not if it leaves you penniless and living in some far-flung country parsonage. Your parents would not be pleased if I allowed you to make such an alliance. But I am sure we will be able to find a gentleman possessed of the necessary requirements, *and* with whom you can fall in love.'

Phoebe didn't look convinced. 'Lady Ellen Thurlow is marrying for love, and she is delighted about it.'

Shocked to hear Phoebe speak of the lady and of her engagement, Diana said tensely, 'You spoke to Lady Ellen?'

'Yes, when you were talking to Miss Townley. She told me she wasn't really supposed to say anything, but she was so excited about her betrothal to Lord Durling that she could not keep it to herself.'

Diana and her aunt exchanged a glance.

'Did she say anything in particular about her fiancé?' Mrs Mitchell enquired.

'Only that she believes he is the most wonderful man in London. A date hasn't been set for the wedding yet, but she is hopeful one soon will be. Oh, I do hope I see her again. I liked her very much.'

Reasonably assured that nothing had been said about *her* past relationship with Lord Durling, Diana relaxed back against the squabs. She hadn't expected to hear Phoebe mention Lady Ellen's engagement to Lord Durling; not after her aunt had been so careful about telling her. But then, Lady Ellen would have no reason to keep it secret, and if she was as excited as Phoebe said, she would likely want everyone to know. And that was fine, Diana reflected. She doubted that Lord Durling would say anything to Lady Ellen about his past engagement to her, and, obviously, no one else had either.

Diana closed her eyes, glad the day was almost done. She hadn't realised how tense she had been during the evening, but now that it was over and she had come through it without incident, she was feeling decidedly drained. On the other hand, she had drawn no attention to herself, and seen no censure in the eyes of the people she had met, which meant either the scandal had died, or that four years away was long enough to make it fade from people's minds.

There had just been that one moment, when Edward had looked as though he would walk across the room to speak to her, that her knees had started to quake and her heart to pound. But thanks to the timely arrival of a footman, the meeting had been avoided. And once Edward had left, the rest of the evening had passed in a most uneventful manner.

Diana could only hope the duration of her time in London would slip by as peacefully.

It was curiosity and concern that had Diana donning her riding habit earlier than usual the next morning. Curiosity as to whether or not Edward had recognised her, and concern that everything would be different between them this morning. Edward had looked at her so intently last night—had he somehow figured out that she was the same woman he rode with in the mornings? She'd thought her veil heavy enough to disguise her appearance, but his interest in her last night had been unmistakable.

Now, as she rode into the park, Diana went through the various scenarios: the first being that he had recognised her, and that he had been on his way to confront her. The second, that he *thought* he'd known her, and had intended to clarify the issue, and the third, that he hadn't known her but that he'd wished to make her acquaintance for no other reason.

Diana immediately ruled out the third scenario. Why would he have singled her out in a room where there were so many lovelier ladies to choose from?

She wondered about the letter the footman had given him. What kind of message had it contained? Obviously one that had troubled him deeply. She had seen the anger on his face as he'd skimmed over the page, and then, moments later, the purpose in his step when he had left the reception without saying a word to anyone.

Who could have sent such a disturbing letter in the midst of an evening's festivities?

Aware that she was tying herself up in knots again, Diana tried to clear her mind. There was no point in belabouring the issue. She could second-guess herself all day, and still not be any closer to the truth. Her first concern now was to meet Edward and find out if he had recognised her last night.

Her second would be in deciding what to do if he had.

Edward was in his usual place. He looked up as she approached, and in spite of her determination not to let her emotions become engaged, Diana felt the same quiver of excitement she always did when seeing him. The lines of tension that had hardened his features last evening were not in evidence this morning, and he appeared quite relaxed and at ease. And though Diana knew she shouldn't be pleased at the way his eyes brightened when he looked at her, she nevertheless was. It gave her hope that he hadn't recognised her last night, and that nothing need change between them today.

'Good morning, Jenny,' Edward said. 'How are you this morning?'

'I am well, thank you, Edward.' Her sore throat was almost gone and it was becoming more difficult to affect the huskiness in her voice, but Diana had practised it enough to know it was still a credible imitation. 'And you?'

'Well enough.'

She thought she heard a slight hesitation in his voice, and her confidence faltered. 'You sound troubled.'

'It is nothing you need concern yourself with.'

Could she take that to mean it had nothing to do with her personally?

'Sometimes the sharing of one's troubles makes them easier to bear, my lord. If there is something you would like to talk about, I would be happy to listen.'

He looked at her, then at her groom positioned a discreet distance away. 'You say that without knowing the nature of the problem, Jenny, and I can assure you, family problems are not often welcomed with the same enthusiasm as personal ones.'

At hearing him mention family, Diana cautiously inclined her head, 'But we can all identify with family issues, because we all have them. And as much as we feel they should be simple and straightforward, they are often anything but.'

He looked at her as though trying to decide whether she was just being kind, or whether she was indeed, willing to listen. 'Very well, but I would remind you that you were the one who insisted on hearing. It has to do with…my mother.'

His mother! Diana felt a palpable wave of relief at his disclosure. 'I see. And what is the nature of your problem with her?'

'She is not…an easy person with whom to get along,' Edward said slowly. 'She hasn't been since my father died. I thought she would have recovered by now. Indeed, I harboured hopes she might even have remarried, but I realise now there is no chance of that happening. My mother has turned her personal grief into a way of life.'

Remembering not to disclose more than she was supposed to know, Diana said, 'Is it her prolonged grieving that is causing problems for you?'

'Not so much me as it is for my younger sister,' Edward explained. 'Barbara, the elder, is safely married and away, but Ellen is just seventeen and still living at home.'

'But how is your mother being difficult? Other than in struggling to cope with her grief.'

Edward hesitated, as though considering how much he should say. 'One of the biggest problems is that she refuses to be happy. She demands companionship all the time. Not the companionship of friends, of course.'

'She wishes to have her family around her,' Diana said.

'Precisely. For example, last night, we attended a small reception, held in part to celebrate the engagement of a couple well known to my family. We were all invited, Barbara and her husband, Ellen and myself, and, of course, my mother, who steadfastly refused to go. She likes to tell everyone she stopped socialising the day my father died.'

'Not an unusual sentiment for a widow,' Diana said, knowing it to be true.

'No, but the problem was, she ended up sending a letter to Ellen, asking her to come home at once.'

Ah, so *that* was the nature of the mysterious letter. 'Was your mother in need of care?'

'No, she was just lonely and in want of company.'

'I see. And did your sister go home?' Diana asked, remembering that she had to act as though she hadn't been at the Townleys' reception last night.

'No, because I didn't show her the letter,' Edward admitted, though there was little evidence of guilt on his face. 'I suppose it was wrong of me to intercept it, but I recognised the handwriting and had a suspicion as to what it might contain. I also thought, to be fair, that if my mother was unwell and in need of help, I was the best one to go to her. So, I read the letter and decided to go in Ellen's place. Needless to say, my mother and I had words and did not part on good terms.' He looked into the distance. 'It has left me feeling somewhat unsettled ever since.'

Diana looked down at her hands. She thought she understood his sentiment. A family could be close and still suffer from the gaps in their relationships. A family who weren't close would suffer even more. 'How does Lady Ellen feel about her mother's demands on her time?'

'I honestly don't know.' Edward brushed a fly from the hunter's ears. 'She doesn't confide in me. The age difference between us is too great. My sister Barbara and I are closer, which has as much to do with Barbara's spirit and vivacity as with our being of a similar age. Ellen, for all her being a sweet, lovable child, is rather vacuous.'

'I have always felt it important for a woman to have spirit, or perhaps, the ability to stand up for herself,' Diana said. 'There is less chance of society or a husband browbeating her that way.'

Edward's smile was matter of fact. 'I have no cause to worry in that regard. Ellen's future husband is a gentleman, and wealthy enough that I needn't worry that he is marrying her for the wrong reasons. And, once she is his wife, there will be no chance of anyone getting the better of her.'

Diana couldn't speak to Edward's latter statement, but she longed to cry out against the former—until she remembered that she, too, had once believed Lord Durling to be a gentleman.

She was silent for a while, listening to the gentle thud of the horses' hooves as they walked along the path. 'Have you tried talking to your mother?' she said finally. 'Perhaps she has been mired in grief so long she no longer knows how to pull herself out of it.'

Edward sighed. 'I used to talk to her. In the months following Father's death, we spent a great deal of time together, but even then, it was as though she didn't want to hear me. Nothing I said seemed to make any difference, and while I tried to be patient and to mark it up to legitimate grief, as the months passed and she showed no signs of improving, I'm afraid I gave up. Patience is a virtue, and one I had very little of in those days. I loved my father, and his death was very hard. Mother had her family and friends around her, yet she would accept nothing from them. Eventually, they stopped coming. It was as though she wanted to shut everyone out.'

'Grief is not always an easy emotion to understand,' Diana said quietly. 'People have their own ways of dealing with it. Ways that often make no sense to anyone else.'

'Yes, but the problem is, my mother *hasn't* dealt with it. She's still fully immersed in it. Sometimes I think she does it in order to avoid life's other realities,' Edward said, clearly frustrated. 'And the sad part is, she expects everyone to understand. If she was trying to go on with her life and struggling because of it, I could at least feel sorry for her. But when I see what she is doing to her family…to her life…'

Hardly aware of what she was doing, Diana reached out and put her hand on his arm. 'I'm sure she will heal in time, Edward. No one likes to feel the way she does. I honestly believe it is the nature of all people to try to rise above their problems. Perhaps your mother is simply reluctant to show that she *can* go on for fear of what people will say about her. Mayhap this extended display of grief is to show everyone how deeply she loved your father.'

'No one's ever questioned her love for him. More likely, people are wondering about *his* love for her.' Edward sighed, and glanced down at her hand. 'Unfortunately, by behaving the way she is, she is alienating those who still love her. She has turned into someone that none of us recognises. And worse, that none of us likes.' He placed his hand over hers, lightly squeezing her fingers. 'But I think that's enough of my problems. It was good of you to listen, Jenny, but that's not what our time together is about.' He drew back his hand and sat straighter in the saddle. 'I have been enjoying a book by William Roscoe, addressing the life of Lorenzo de Medici. Have you read it?'

Accustomed to his quick change of subjects, Diana replied that she had not, though said she had read one of his other titles and enjoyed it immensely. Thereupon, a lively discussion ensued as to the merits of the author's first book and to Mr Roscoe's skills as a writer. As a result, the time passed swiftly, and when all too soon it was time for Diana to leave, Edward surprised her by reaching for her hand and raising it to his lips. 'Thank you, dear lady, for being willing to listen to my trials. It goes beyond what is expected of such a brief acquaintance.'

For a moment, Diana was at a loss to know what to say. His gratitude for so simple a task was heartbreaking, but the touch of his mouth, even through the fine leather of her gloves, was warm and intoxicating. She found herself imag-

ining how it would feel against her skin…
against her lips—

'It is…only what a friend would do,' she
stammered, drawing back her hand. *Dear heavens, where had that come from?* It was just as
well she wore a veil.

'Is that what we are, Jenny? Friends?'

'I like to think we are, for what would be the
point of our meeting otherwise?'

'People meet for many reasons, some more
noble than others.'

'But is not the need of friendship in and of
itself noble?' Diana said. 'A man can be brave
or creatively gifted, or even a genius when it
comes to matters of science or mathematics, but
what is he if he has no friends? Who can he
celebrate his achievements with?'

Edward smiled. 'You make an excellent
point. Perhaps our meetings in the relative obscurity of this park are nothing more than an
interlude of peace in a world where we are
forced to play our parts, and not always willingly. But, whatever the case, I know how much
I have come to enjoy them, and I hope you will
allow them to continue.'

His words hit too close to the truth, Diana
reflected. Yes, she wanted their rides to con-

tinue, even though she knew they should not. Emotions she had no business feeling, like tenderness, affection, and concern, were already being called into the equation. Emotions that could only cause her heartache in the long run. Because it was safer to say nothing, however, Diana inclined her head, and then slowly turned Juliet around, thankful the nature of her relationship with Edward did not include the necessity of being strictly truthful—or of always giving answers to the questions he asked.

Chapter Six

Amanda Townley paid a visit to George Street that afternoon, with an invitation for Diana and Phoebe to go shopping with her.

Phoebe was delighted, of course, and though Diana's first inclination was to decline, she really couldn't bring herself to do so. Yes, a visit to the shops would put her out into the midst of society, but she was here to act as a companion to her cousin, and there was no denying Phoebe's excitement when it came to perusing the shops. As such, Diana agreed to the outing and the three set off for Berkeley Square, where Amanda was to call at the mantua-maker to check on the progress of her wedding clothes.

It was a lovely day, and Diana made up her mind to enjoy it. She donned one of her new gowns, a stylish pale blue walking dress with a darker blue pelisse, and a rather fetching bonnet tied with ribbands of the same hue. Amanda looked very fashionable in a smart green pelisse over a light green slip, the elegance of it yet another indication of how much she had changed. At one time, Amanda would have been the least noticeable in a crowd of girls. Now, Diana was sure she would be the cynosure of all eyes.

Not surprisingly, talk soon turned to her up-coming wedding, which was, as expected, to be a rather elaborate affair. Amanda was quick to point out, however, that the number of guests owed much to the size of the groom's family, and that it was her future mother-in-law's wish that they all attend.

'Well, I suppose it is only to be expected, given her position in society,' Diana said in re-sponse to the comment. 'But I am happy you get on well with her. That can sometimes be a sticky point in a marriage.'

'I am greatly relieved myself,' Amanda ad-mitted as Phoebe moved away to look at the goods in a shop window. 'Especially since I am well aware that she was hoping John would marry a lady from a titled family.'

Diana frowned. 'Did she tell you as much?'

'No, but I heard it from others who are close to the family. And to be fair, they were comments made before the countess and I met, but I have no reason to believe they were not true. After all, John is marrying beneath him, and given that I am not in possession of a huge dowry, it would seem that he stands to gain little from the alliance.'

'What about love?' Diana asked softly. 'Was that not a consideration in your marriage?'

'It was the only consideration for me,' Amanda said. 'And John says it was the reason he proposed, and I do believe him. He truly is a good man, Diana. I know he seems rather stiff, but at heart he is decent and kind, and after having made the acquaintance of several other so-called gentlemen, I value John's qualities even more.'

Curious about something in the tone of her voice, Diana said, 'Is Lord Eastcliffe the first gentleman you fell in love with?'

Amanda's reaction was startling. Pretending not to have heard the question, she focussed her attention on a collection of china dogs in the shop window they were passing. 'Oh, look, Diana, are they not charming? I must buy a pair for John's sister. She collects them, you know.'

The ploy was so obvious that Diana wondered why Amanda hadn't just said she didn't care to answer the question, because the fact that she had avoided the question raised an even more disturbing one.

Who had Amanda been involved with, and why was she so reluctant to talk about him?

'Are you to attend the Eaglemonts' ball next month?' Amanda enquired after concluding her purchase and resuming their walk.

Diana said she couldn't recall having seen an invitation, but Phoebe piped up that she was quite sure one had arrived just that morning.

Amanda smiled. 'I hope so. Lady Eaglemont has a most glorious ballroom. I attended a soirée there last summer and it was incredibly festive. The flowers were beautiful, and they were all from her gardens. I vow she must employ an army of gardeners.'

Amanda went on to describe everything about the ball, scarcely pausing to catch her breath. Diana listened, but knew there was something odd about her friend's behaviour. It wasn't like Amanda to be evasive.

'Oh, look! There is Lady Ellen,' Phoebe cried, her attention caught by a smart curricle drawing to a halt across the street. 'I wonder who the gentleman with her is. Lady Ellen! Hello!'

The two occupants alighting from the curricle turned at Phoebe's exclamation. Lady Ellen waved back. 'Miss Lowden, hello!' she called. Then, catching the arm of the gentleman with her, she hastily drew him across the street.

Diana felt the hair on the back of her neck stand on end. *Edward!* What was she to do? There was absolutely no chance of avoiding an introduction this time! *Please don't let him recognise me. Not here, not like this!*

'Lord Garthdale, how very nice to see you again,' Amanda said, looking enviably relaxed and at ease.

Edward's smile encompassed them all. 'The pleasure is mine, Miss Townley, at seeing such lovely ladies out on such a beautiful day.'

'You are all kindness to say so.'

Diana stopped breathing as Edward turned to face her. She felt his eyes travel with agonising slowness over her face, resting for a moment on her eyes, lingering a little too long on her hair. She didn't see his expression change, but she wondered if a man like this would ever allow anything of what he was feeling to be reflected on his face.

In the end, he merely inclined his head with a smile. 'I fear I have not made the acquaintance of your friends, Miss Townley.'

'Have you not?' She looked momentarily surprised. 'Forgive me, I thought you had met at Mama's reception. In that case, please allow me to introduce you to my dear friend, Miss Diana Hepworth, and to her cousin, Miss Phoebe Lowden.'

'Miss Hepworth, Miss Lowden.' Edward turned to his sister. 'My younger sister, Lady Ellen Thurlow.'

Lady Ellen smiled at Phoebe, who was already known to her, and surprised Diana by offering her hand. 'Miss Hepworth.'

Diana smiled and took it. 'Lady Ellen.'

So this was the girl who would be Lord Durling's wife. She was lovely, to be sure. Her eyes were a clear, bright blue, and her complexion as smooth as a piece of alabaster. But it wasn't long in listening to her conversation with Phoebe that Diana realised Edward was right. She was a simple creature, pleasant and sweet, but no match for any man who would have authority over her, or who might wish to inflict his will upon her.

'Where do you call home, Miss Hepworth?' Lord Garthdale asked, drawing Diana's attention away from his sister.

For a moment, Diana almost forgot who she was. She had only spoken to him in the guise of Jenny, and she went to do so now, preparing to drop her voice into the low, husky tones she used in the mornings. She caught herself just in time. 'From Whitley, my lord. In Hertfordshire.'

Edward inclined his head. 'I know Hertfordshire well, though not, I confess, that particular town.'

'It is hardly to be wondered at. Whitley is exceedingly small.'

'But charming, I'm sure. Are you staying long in London?'

'We are here for the Season,' Diana told him in a voice that bore absolutely no resemblance to Jenny's. 'Phoebe made her come out this year, and we are staying with our aunt, Mrs Mitchell, in George Street.'

He smiled. 'I know your aunt well. Please extend my regards to her. I regret I did not have a chance to speak with her last night.'

'Edward, would you mind if I stayed and visited with the ladies?' Lady Ellen asked. 'I know we were to have called at the linen draper, but it is not of great importance that we do so today, and I would like to spend some time with my new friends.'

Edward glanced down at his sister, and Diana saw his eyes soften. Despite what he'd said about her, he obviously loved her. 'If that is what you wish, Ellen, and the ladies have no objection…'

'Not at all, Lord Garthdale,' Amanda assured him. 'We would be happy for Lady Ellen's company. In fact, we could stop at Gunter's, now that we are so close.'

'Oh, yes, I should like that,' Lady Ellen said.

'In that case, I shall pay a visit to the tobacconists, and meet you there in—' he pulled out his watch '—an hour?'

His sister was delighted. 'That would be splendid, Edward. Thank you!'

'It was a pleasure meeting you, Miss Hepworth, Miss Lowden,' Edward said, doffing his hat. 'I hope you both enjoy your stay in London.'

It seemed to Diana that his eyes lingered a little too long on her face, but she smiled brightly and bent her knee in a curtsy. 'Thank you, Lord Garthdale, I'm sure we will.'

With a warm smile for Amanda, Edward headed back to the curricle. He tossed a coin to the young lad holding the reins, climbed up into the seat and set the pair of blacks to a smart trot.

Diana watched him go, wondering if she should read anything into that lingering glance.

'Aren't we fortunate that the timing worked out so well?' Lady Ellen said brightly.

Phoebe agreed with alacrity, and Amanda suggested they set off for refreshments. Everyone thought that a wonderful idea, especially Phoebe, who had thus far only heard about the delightful establishment. Diana, who was happy just to have somewhere to sit for a moment, made no demur, for she was all but trembling with relief.

Edward hadn't recognised her. She was sure she would have seen it in his eyes. He was curious, yes, but he'd really had no reason to suspect that the lady who walked freely about London was the same lady who rode with him, veiled and mysterious, in the mornings.

Nevertheless, Diana knew she would have to take greater care from now on. If she forgot herself and slipped into the wrong voice, the consequences could be devastating!

Truly, deceit was a wicked thing, Diana thought as she accompanied the other three into Gunter's. At this point, she almost hoped that

Phoebe *would* fall in love and marry Captain Wetherby, just so that she might safely retire to the country with her fate unchanged, and her secrets undisclosed.

He knew her, he was sure of it—yet he was damned if he could say from where.

Edward stood by the counter at Fribourg and Treyer, waiting for his special mix to be prepared, and tried to remember where he had seen Miss Hepworth before. He'd had the same feeling of recognition last night when he'd stood across the room from her, but by the time he had returned to take Ellen home, Miss Hepworth had already left.

The fact that she appeared to have no recollection of him meant nothing. They obviously hadn't met, but he was sure he had seen her. At court, perhaps? Or out in society? Miss Lowden might just be making her come out, but Miss Hepworth was clearly of an age to have been moving in society for several years. But if that was the case, why couldn't he remember her? He usually had an excellent memory for names, and an even better one for faces, yet on this occasion he could recall nothing.

Was it possible she reminded him of someone else? He was hard pressed to think of another lady with features similar enough to put him in mind of her.

His business concluded, Edward climbed back into the curricle and made two more stops before returning to Berkeley Square. He knew it wouldn't matter if he were late. Having grown up with sisters, he was familiar with the nature of females, and knew they could talk for hours without even being aware of the passage of time. It was one of the things he generally preferred about the company of men.

And yet, that wasn't entirely fair, Edward conceded. Jenny didn't strike him as the type of woman who would be late. She was too conscientious, too mindful of the importance of other people's time to let her negligence infringe upon that.

The realisation that he was thinking about her again set Edward to frowning. It was happening more and more, and he knew it wasn't wise. It would do him absolutely no good to dwell on her. Intrigued as he was by every aspect of her personality, he knew there could be nothing between them. He had a responsibility to his family and she was a lady with a past.

It was just as simple as that.

* * *

As expected, the ladies were still at Gunter's when Edward arrived. They were gathered around a table, laughing and chatting with the familiarity of old friends. The pairings weren't difficult to ascertain. Miss Lowden and Ellen were on their way to becoming close, while Amanda and Miss Hepworth already were.

As when they had been introduced, Edward found his eyes drawn back to Diana Hepworth. He noticed again how lovely she was. Her hair was a rich, glossy brown, drawn back smoothly to reveal the perfection of her features. Her eye-lashes and brows were dark too, and made for a delightful contrast against the peachy warmth of her skin. Nevertheless, he couldn't shake the feeling that he knew her. Something about her was so familiar.

He might have studied her longer, had Miss Lowden not glanced up and caught sight of him. 'Lord Garthdale!'

As one, the ladies turned. Miss Lowden and Miss Townley smiled a welcome at him, while Miss Hepworth glanced at him and then away, barely meeting his eyes. Funny, she hadn't struck him as the shy type.

Ellen's ready smiled faded. 'Oh, dear, is it that time already? How quickly an hour passes.'

'Actually, it has been more than an hour,' Edward said.

'Do you not wish to go home, Lady Ellen?' Miss Lowden asked.

Ellen sighed. 'Yes, of course. It's just that…oh, I suppose I'm just looking forward to being married and having a home of my own.'

'And a husband who loves you,' Miss Lowden said, wistfully.

The other ladies agreed. All except Miss Hepworth, Edward noticed, who suddenly looked rather ill at ease.

'Of course, being a gentleman's wife does carry with it a great deal of responsibility,' Miss Lowden went on, seeming not to notice her cousin's reserve. 'I am anxious to be married, but I hope I will be able to do all that is required of me.'

Edward's lips twitched. 'And what do you think will be required of you, Miss Lowden?'

'Everything to do with the running of her lord and master's home,' Amanda said with a mischievous twinkle in her eyes. 'A wife must be organised enough to manage a household, several if her husband's wealth runs to that, and she must be capable of overseeing the staff that ensure its smooth operation. And, of course, she must be a good mother to his children, and a gracious hostess to his friends.'

'All very necessary skills, to be sure,' Edward murmured.

'What do you see a wife's most important duty as being, Miss Hepworth?' Ellen asked ingenuously.

Curious as to what the lady would say, Edward glanced at her. He wasn't surprised to see her looking a touch uncomfortable at being centred out.

'Oh. Well, I suppose, like Amanda, I would have to agree that…a wife has many duties,' she said, clearing her throat. 'But I think that one of the most important is that she be a source of support and companionship to her husband. A man and his wife should be able to talk about matters beyond the mundane.'

'So you're saying they should be friends,' Amanda said.

'I think so. There has to be a reason for them to wish to spend time together, beyond talking about children, or houses, or problems with servants.'

'*I* think the most important thing between a husband and wife is love!' Miss Lowden cried. 'For surely all things evolve from that?'

'Yes, what about love, Miss Hepworth?' Edward asked in a casual tone. 'Do you place as much importance on that as you do upon friendship and conversation?'

'Of course, for without friendship, there can be no true love.'

'But there can be passion.'

Edward wasn't surprised when all of the ladies blushed, including Miss Hepworth. To her credit, however, she didn't try to avoid his eye. 'I suppose that is…an element to be considered,' she agreed. 'But in reading fiction, it would seem that even the most ardent of passions cool with time, while love only grows richer and more rewarding.'

'I have always thought mutual respect and trust should have a place in marriage,' Amanda spoke up, 'for without trust, what basis is there for a meaningful and lasting commitment? Indeed, I would rather not see the marriage take place than to know there was no respect between the partners.'

'You are absolutely right!' Miss Lowden declared. 'While I would never consider marrying unless I was truly in love with a gentleman, I cannot imagine how I *could* love someone without admiring and respecting him too.'

A lively discussion ensued between Amanda and Miss Lowden, with Ellen offering the occasional, tentative remark. Edward noticed, however, that Miss Hepworth did not take part, a fact he found both interesting and curious.

'Come, Ellen, you can continue this another time,' he interrupted, deciding that he'd had enough feminine chatter for one day. 'Perhaps after you are married.'

'But by then it will be too late!' Diana cried.

Her words fell into a startled silence. The three ladies turned to look at her, but she was looking at him, and Edward had a feeling it was his reaction she was waiting for. 'What would be too late, Miss Hepworth?' he enquired softly.

'It would be…too late to ensure that the man she was marrying was…the kind of man she could trust and respect.'

'Are you questioning the integrity of all men, or only a few specific ones?'

'I am concerned with the integrity of the gentlemen who would marry my friends,' she said. 'I can have no interest in any others.'

Edward watched her in silence. What was she saying? Why did he feel as though she was sending him a message of some kind?

'It is an interesting point, but I'm afraid our discussion will have to wait for another day,' he said, looking directly at her. 'I must take Ellen home.'

Edward waited for her response, but she turned away, hiding the expression in those re-markable blue eyes.

'Thank you for allowing Lady Ellen to visit with us, Lord Garthdale,' Amanda said, getting to her feet. 'And please give my regards to your mother. I was sorry not to have seen her last evening.'

Edward bowed. 'I shall be sure to do so, Miss Townley. Good afternoon, ladies.'

He glanced at them each in turn, Amanda, Miss Lowden, Diana Hepworth. He saw con-tentment on Amanda's face, excitement on Miss Lowden's, but Miss Hepworth kept her face averted. It was only as he went to leave, that she finally turned back to look at him—and it was a look that stayed with Edward for a long time, because it hadn't been a look of anger or hauteur.

It had been a look of supplication.

* * *

Upon returning home, Phoebe immediately went upstairs to rest. They had invitations to a musical evening, and because they hadn't returned from the Townleys' party until nearly half past two, Phoebe was feeling somewhat tired. She hadn't yet become accustomed to town hours.

For her own part, Diana was too upset to rest. She retired to the drawing room where, with Chaucer snoring complacently at her feet, she recounted the details of the afternoon's activities to her aunt.

'How interesting,' Mrs Mitchell said at the conclusion. 'And you are sure neither Lord Garthdale nor his sister have any qualms about the kind of man Lord Durling is?'

'None. I would have seen it, I'm sure,' Diana said, pacing, as she had been doing since entering the room. 'I tried as tactfully as I could to say how vital it is that a woman be familiar with her husband's character before they are married, but I have no idea how successful I was.'

'I wonder if it really matters. It is entirely possible that Lord Durling loves Ellen, but that his unfortunate tendencies toward violence will appear regardless.'

'Then she, or her family, must be made aware of it before the marriage takes place,' Diana said, coming to an abrupt halt. 'And that is the part that troubles me, Aunt. How do you tell a woman that her fiancé is a violent man?'

'To be honest, I think it more important that Lady Garthdale or her son be made aware of the fact. They are the ones who have the power to stop the marriage.' Mrs Mitchell sent her niece a probing look. 'You say you were introduced to Lord Garthdale this afternoon, and that he didn't appear to recognise you?'

'Not as far as I could tell.'

'Have you given any thought to the possibility that Lord Garthdale doesn't know your history, Diana? As we've said, your break up with Lord Durling took place in the months following the old earl's death, when Lord Garthdale and his family were in the country.'

'It is possible that he hasn't heard, but it is also possible that he has and simply hasn't made the connection.'

'Or that he doesn't care to.'

'But how could he not care to?' Diana cried. 'His sister is engaged to marry the man I jilted. If Lord Garthdale is a man of morals, surely he would not be inclined to smile upon a woman who trifled with hearts.'

'Speaking of morality, would you mind telling me what *is* going on between you and Lord Garthdale?' her aunt said. 'The only reason I didn't question you when we returned home last evening was because I was too tired to do so.'

Knowing that she had promised her aunt an explanation, Diana related the events that had taken place between herself and Lord Garthdale in Hyde Park, including his desire to continue riding with her as Jenny.

'My dear girl, I hardly know what to say!' Mrs Mitchell said in astonishment. 'One of the most eligible gentlemen in London has asked you to conduct a series of clandestine assignations—'

'They are hardly clandestine.'

'You are meeting an eligible gentleman with your face hidden and your voice disguised. What is that, if not clandestine?'

Diana blushed. 'It would be far more so if I were to sneak off to meet him at some deserted cottage.'

Her aunt's eyebrows rose expressively. '*That* would be immoral!'

'Exactly. Lord Garthdale and I meet in a very public place, and always with a groom—*your* groom—in attendance.'

'If you knew that Phoebe was engaged in such activities with Captain Wetherby, would you give her your approval to continue?'

Diana fidgeted. 'I would not tell her it was wrong.'

'Well, you should, because it is,' Mrs Mitchell said firmly. 'The outcome of such meetings can only be harmful, Diana, either to your feelings or to your reputation. What do you think Lord Garthdale's opinion of you is? You must know that he considers you a woman with a past.'

'Yes, but he doesn't know who I am! I am simply Jenny, and since he is never going to meet Jenny in a social situation, what does it matter?'

'It might come to matter a great deal. However, turning to a subject where I can have some influence,' Mrs Mitchell said wryly, 'perhaps there is a way we can be of use to Lady Ellen with regard to her forthcoming marriage.'

Hoping her aunt was right, Diana said, 'And what would that be?'

'We could pay a call on Lady Garthdale.'

Diana stared at her, eyes wide. 'You can't mean that we should go to the lady's house and try to dissuade her from allowing the marriage to take place.'

'Of course not. That would hardly be good manners. But if it is clarity we are seeking, we could call on Lady Garthdale, and under the guise of polite conversation conduct a subtle interrogation. Find out if she is at all open to the possibility that her future son-in-law may not be as admirable as she thinks.'

'I fear I am not skilled at subtle interrogation.'

'No, but I am.' Mrs Mitchell winked. 'It is a useful skill for a wife to possess. And don't worry, we shan't call on them this afternoon. You are upset enough as it is, and as we are expected at Lady Aldsworth's house this evening, you hardly need anything else to worry about. So we shall wait a while,' Mrs Mitchell said, seeming content with her decision. 'After all, what harm can there be in waiting a few more days?'

Chapter Seven

Diana always enjoyed musical evenings. Having long held an appreciation for good music, she was often critical of the quality of the entertainments provided at such gatherings, but fortunately, both the singer and the pianist who had been engaged to perform at Lady Aldsworth's house were exceptional. The talented soprano, a dark-haired beauty of Italian origin, performed a selection of pieces that ranged from von Gluck to Mozart, and in doing so, demonstrated a vocal range and control that was truly astonishing.

'Oh, that was splendid!' Diana said as she rose with her aunt and cousin at the end of the first half. 'I haven't heard a voice like that in a very long time.'

'She is certainly talented,' Mrs Mitchell agreed, fanning herself against the heat of the room. 'And judging from the crowd of gentlemen gathered around her, I would venture to say it is not only her voice they find appealing. Well, Phoebe, are you enjoying your first musical evening? I doubt you've heard anything like this in Upper Tewkham.'

Phoebe glanced up, as though roused from a daze. 'Hmm? Oh, no, Aunt Isabel, I haven't. And, yes, I am enjoying it very much.'

'But…?'

Phoebe blushed prettily. 'No, truly, I am. It is just that…I was hoping to see Captain Wetherby tonight.'

'Perhaps he had other plans,' Diana said, trying to lessen the girl's disappointment. 'He may not be partial to musical evenings and has found something more to his liking.'

Phoebe's green eyes held a faint glimmer of hope. 'Do you think so?'

'I wouldn't have said it if I thought it of no merit. But Aunt Isabel is right, you must take care not to wear your heart where all can see it, Phoebe. It is for the gentleman to make known his feelings to you.'

Phoebe sighed. 'But does it have to be that way? I mean, is it not possible to know when you have met the right person?'

Diana hesitated. She was hardly one to offer comment on that. She thought she had met the right man in Lord Durling, and look where that had got her!

'Phoebe, will you make me a promise?' Diana said instead. 'Will you promise that you won't rush into anything? That you will take time to get to know the gentleman you would give your heart to *before* you give it to him.'

'Diana's right, Phoebe, dear,' Mrs Mitchell said. 'It is important to remember that marriage is forever, and it is far better to take a little extra time to get to know someone, rather than give your heart away and find out later that you gave it to the wrong man.'

Prophetic words, Diana thought, thinking again of her own situation. She could only hope that Phoebe would listen and benefit from the mistakes of others.

It was as they were returning to the music room for the second half that Diana saw Edward for the first time. He was standing with Sir Laurence Dinmott, a gentleman whose acquaintance she had made during her first Season. She was not pleased to see him now, however, because at one time, Sir Laurence had been a close friend of Lord Durling's. The fact that he was with Edward now indicated that they all travelled in the same circles.

Hastily averting her gaze, Diana moved into the crowded room and quickly resumed her seat. With any luck, Edward hadn't seen her, and wouldn't for the rest of the night. She wasn't sure why she thought he might come across and speak to her, but it was a feeling she couldn't shake. And she had no desire to talk to him with Sir Laurence hanging on every word.

A few minutes later, the soprano began to sing, and for a while, Diana put aside her concerns and let herself be swept away by the music. The woman's voice was incredibly rich, hitting the notes with effortless grace and unerring clarity, bringing life to her performance through an astonishing depth of emotion. The rest of the audience were similarly entranced, for while there was little sound during the performance itself, at the end of it, there was an enthusiastic round of applause. The lady was then immediately surrounded by admirers, mostly male, all of whom seemed anxious to express their approval, and no doubt, to make plans for a more intimate acquaintance. Sir Laurence Dinmott,

Diana noticed, was one of the latter. But where was Edward?

'Mrs Mitchell, what a pleasure to see you again.'

Stifling a gasp, Diana turned to see him standing directly behind them.

'Lord Garthdale, you are very good to say so,' her aunt replied with the ease of one used to dealing with such situations. 'I am very sorry that we did not have an opportunity to speak the other evening, but one minute you were there, and the next you were gone.'

'Alas, I was unexpectedly called away,' Edward said. 'By the time I returned you and your party had already left. That is why I wanted to make sure I spoke to you this evening.' He turned to Diana and Phoebe, and bowed. 'Miss Hepworth, Miss Lowden.'

'Lord Garthdale,' they replied.

'How is your mother, my lord?' Mrs Mitchell enquired. 'I was surprised she missed the Townleys' reception. I know how close your families are.'

'Alas, she was a trifle indisposed.' Edward smiled as though nothing was amiss. 'It was, in fact, the reason I was compelled to leave.'

'Oh? Nothing serious, I hope?'

Diana watched him carefully. To Edward's credit, his expression betrayed nothing of what she knew he must have been feeling. 'Not at all, but as you know, she has not been well since my father's death, and is often prone to nerves. I am hopeful of an eventual recovery, but lately, she seems to have suffered with more bad days than good.'

'I am sorry to hear it. Is she receiving visitors at all?'

Diana stiffened, knowing where her aunt's questions were leading.

'She has not said otherwise,' Edward said, 'though she receives very few.'

'Then perhaps she would welcome a visit from the three of us,' Mrs Mitchell said brightly. 'I know that when I am feeling low, the pleasure of company more jovial than my own always raises my spirits.'

Diana purposely avoided looking at her aunt, knowing that she disliked nothing *more* than visitors when she was feeling poorly. Edward did reply, though he was obviously being cautious. 'It is sometimes difficult to predict how she will react. But if you are willing to pay a call, I shall not try to discourage you. I know Ellen would enjoy it immensely.'

'Then it is settled,' Mrs Mitchell said. 'We look forward to calling upon your mother and sister in the very near future.'

'I shall not make it known to them, so that it may be more of a surprise.' Edward brought his gaze back to Diana. 'Are you enjoying the performance, Miss Hepworth?'

'Very much,' Diana said. 'The lady is exceptionally talented. She has amazing range and clarity, yet a richness of sound not always to be found in sopranos.'

He smiled. 'True, which is why I generally prefer a mezzo-soprano. I dare say the *signorina* has a promising future ahead of her.'

'If she doesn't give it up for less admirable pursuits,' Mrs Mitchell murmured, glancing at the lady who was still surrounded by admirers.

'What do you mean, Aunt Isabel?' Phoebe asked, brows knitting in confusion. 'If the lady is such a talented performer, why would she give it up to do something less admirable?'

Diana looked at her aunt, who suddenly realised what she had said, and then at Edward, who appeared to be having trouble keeping a straight face.

'Sometimes ladies with talents like Signorina Angelini's find themselves being offered other avenues of employment, Miss Lowden,' he said. 'And you are quite right, in a case like hers it would be a shame to see her give up what is, obviously, a God-given talent. We can only hope that in the advancement of music, she continues to entertain society in just such a way.'

'Yes, that was…precisely what I meant,' Mrs Mitchell said hastily.

Edward inclined his head. 'And now I must be on my way. Enjoy the rest of the evening, ladies.'

'Well, that was…most pleasant,' Diana said after he'd left.

'Indeed.' Mrs Mitchell cleared her throat. 'Phoebe, dear, why don't you run along and secure a table for us in the next room? Lady Aldsworth has been good enough to set out refreshments. I, for one, could use a cup of tea.'

'Yes, of course, Aunt,' Phoebe said, happy to be of use.

In the wake of her departure, Mrs Mitchell shook her head. 'Dear me, I cannot imagine what I was thinking to have made such a tactless remark. Thank heavens Lord Garthdale stepped so smoothly into the breach!'

'Yes, he almost had *me* convinced you meant something other than you did,' Diana said, laughing softly. 'But as regards visiting his mother, I hope you know what you're doing. We now have no choice but to call on Lady Garthdale.'

'I hope so too, Diana,' Mrs Mitchell said, nodding at a passing acquaintance. 'For I share your belief that Lady Garthdale must be made aware of Lord Durling's character *before* Lady Ellen is married to him. But all I have done is told Lord Garthdale of our intention to call. How we are to make known the news once we are there will, I hope, become clear at the time.'

Edward noticed that the crowd of admirers around the dark-eyed soprano was slowly thinning. He also noticed that Sir Laurence Dinmott, who had been one of that crowd, was in much better spirits when he returned to Edward's side than when he'd left it.

'Ah, there you are, Garthdale,' Sir Laurence said, swaggering a little. 'Thought perhaps you'd decided to go on ahead without me.'

'That would have been ill mannered, to say the least. So, did you manage to persuade the lady to meet you?'

'Indeed. I have secured her for an intimate dinner at the Ritz two nights hence.' Sir

Laurence's brow darkened. 'It would have been sooner had that pompous ass Robertson not engaged her for dinner tomorrow evening.'

'Ah, so the lady is not discriminating in her favours. Careful, Dinmott, lest you find yourself cast aside for a man of greater consequence,' Edward warned. 'Robertson is a practised lady's man with a sizeable income.'

'True, but he also has a sister who keeps a very sharp eye on his choice of companions, and everyone knows she is hoping for a match between him and Lady Susan Henshaw.'

'Yes, but who is to say that Robertson isn't hoping for both? An engagement to a lady, and an affair with a ladybird.'

Sir Laurence snorted. 'At least he'll only need energy to deal with one. Lady Susan's a cold fish. I doubt she'll keep his bed warm at night.' He slid Edward a thoughtful glance. 'Speaking of cold fish, wasn't that Diana Hepworth I saw you speaking to?'

Surprised at the implied connection, Edward inclined his head. 'Yes. Why? Do you know her?'

'Of course, though it's been years since I've seen her.'

'It seems Miss Hepworth and her cousin are staying with their aunt for the Season,' Edward informed him. 'Miss Lowden made her come out this year, and I gather that Miss Hepworth is here in the capacity of a companion.'

'Ah, so that's the way of it. I didn't think she would come back looking for a husband after what she did to poor Durling.'

Edward stilled. 'What are you talking about?'

'Don't you remember?'

'I'm not sure I ever knew.'

Sir Laurence's brows drew together. 'I thought Durling would have told you? If not at the time, certainly now that he is engaged to your sister.'

Feeling apprehension take root, Edward said, 'He has told me nothing about Miss Hepworth, now or in the past.'

'Not even that she jilted him the day before they were to have been wed?'

It came as a considerable shock. Diana Hepworth had once been *engaged* to Lord Durling? How the hell had that been kept from him? In a society that put no stock in secrets, why hadn't someone told him about it? He wasn't surprised Ellen hadn't, but there was no excuse for Durling not to have mentioned it. 'How long ago did this happen?' Edward asked.

'I don't know. Three, maybe four years,' Sir Laurence said. 'Some time after your father died. I know you weren't in London at the time.'

Edward thought it through. The year his father had died, he'd cared for nothing beyond his own grief and that of his family. He had completely withdrawn from society, which might explain why he hadn't heard anything.

But to learn now that Diana Hepworth had been engaged to Lord Durling—and that no one had said a word about it...

'She must have had a reason,' he said, trying to be fair.

'Not according to Durling. He said she broke it off to look for a wealthier husband. Shattered the poor bastard, I don't mind telling you,' Sir Laurence confided. 'Didn't show his face in London for months.'

Edward frowned. 'And you say all of this happened the year my father died?'

'As near as I can remember. It is the only reason I can think of for you to have been out of society for that length of time.'

'It must have been quick. Their courtship, and the subsequent ending of it.'

'It was.' Sir Laurence crossed his arms over his chest. 'Your father took ill in…?'

'January,' Edward said in a quiet voice. 'He died the following month.'

'That's right, and you went down to the country straight away. Durling met Miss Hepworth in the April, they were engaged in May, and if memory serves, they were to have been married in the June. Then she pulled her infamous turnaround, told Durling she had no intention of marrying him, and disappeared back to the country. Durling went north to Chipping Park and stayed there. By the time he returned to London the following January, his parting with Miss Hepworth was old news.'

'Still, I'm surprised I heard nothing about it,' Edward said. 'Word like that generally gets around.'

Sir Laurence shrugged. 'To tell the truth, I think Durling wanted it behind him. After all, it doesn't do much for a fellow's ego to have a chit throw him over like that. He was furious at the time, of course, and embarrassed I'm sure, but he didn't say much about it when he returned. And I suppose by the time you reentered society, everyone had forgotten it. But I doubt Durling will be happy to see Miss

Hepworth back in London now. It can't help but dredge up unpleasant memories.'

For him *and* for her, Edward thought, lapsing into silence. But why in the world would a well-bred young woman like Diana Hepworth call off her wedding only a day before it was to have taken place? She didn't seem that flighty. Nor did she strike him as the kind of woman who would do such a cruel and hurtful thing for the sake of money.

Had it had something to do with Durling? Edward wondered. Overall, he wasn't a bad fellow, for all his fastidious ways, and Edward hadn't heard anything about him that would have led him to believe he was anything but honourable.

So why had Miss Hepworth balked with only a few hours to spare?

Sir Laurence's words stayed with Edward long after he left Lady Aldsworth's house. He was still going over them the next morning as he waited for Jenny to arrive in the park. He couldn't get over the fact that Durling hadn't said anything to him about his engagement to Diana Hepworth. Did Durling think he wouldn't care? Surely a brother had a right to know such things about the man who planned to marry his sister.

And what about Diana Hepworth? Why hadn't she made mention of the engagement? She had spoken to him on several occasions, including two when Ellen was present, and given that she knew Lord Durling was now engaged to marry Ellen, why hadn't she made mention of her own relationship with the man? Was it embarrassment that kept her silent? Something to do with the fact that she wanted to start over in society? If that was the case, he supposed he couldn't blame her for not saying anything.

But what if it wasn't? He couldn't recall her having mentioned what her plans were once the Season was over. Would she go back to Hertfordshire, or would she stay here and try to reestablish her life?

Whatever the case, Edward knew he was going to have to get to the bottom of it. Old wounds festered, and if, as Sir Laurence said, Lord Durling wasn't happy about Diana being back in town, things could become awkward for everyone involved, and the last thing he wanted was to see Ellen's wedding day marred by unpleasantness of any kind.

*   *   *

Twenty minutes later, Edward was still waiting in the designated place. Twenty minutes beyond that, and with still no sign of Jenny, he was forced to conclude that she wasn't coming. For whatever reason, she had decided not to ride with him this morning.

It shouldn't have bothered him, but it did. Because even though they had only ridden together three times, Edward was already finding himself looking forward to the next time with greater anticipation than the last. He enjoyed being with her. He enjoyed talking to her, and engaging in interesting and intelligent conversations. He liked challenging her—and, yes, being challenged *by* her, because while he might not always agree with what she said, she always made him think and he valued that.

Edward knew that his growing fascination with Jenny was totally irrational. There was no need for him to play games like this. Lord knew there were more than enough women anxious to show him their face—and whatever else he wanted—to go on entertaining Jenny's particular brand of companionship. He couldn't put it down to a mere physical attraction, because apart from what he could see of her figure, which was alluring to say the least, he had no idea what she looked like under that veil. He couldn't even be sure that Jenny *was* her real name.

But whatever game she was playing, Edward recognised that he was totally involved in it, just as he was thoroughly captivated by her. Her warmth, her spirit, her laughter, all stayed with him long after they parted for the day. He enjoyed the freedom of being able to talk to her the way he wanted, with no need for polite social chitchat or ineffectual posturing. She wasn't trying to impress him, because she felt she had nothing to gain by it. It was as though for those few brief hours, they both existed outside the constraints normally placed on single men and women.

Particularly women, Edward reflected. With him, Jenny had the freedom to say whatever she wanted because he had no idea who she really was.

But where was she this morning? Had something happened to prevent her joining him? He couldn't think what that might be at half past seven in the morning. He hoped he hadn't driven her away by talking about his problems with his mother. Had he made the fatal mistake of bringing family concerns into a situation where they had no business being? Had he cost himself the friendship of a woman he felt more strongly about than any he had ever met, by speaking about matters that by all rights should have remained private?

In her bedroom, Diana sat on her bed and stared at the floor, trying not to think about the fact that even now, Edward was waiting for her in Hyde Park.

What conclusions would he draw from her not being there? Would he assume that she had changed her mind, or that other obligations had kept her from meeting him?

What obligations did a lady of fashion have at half past seven in the morning?

All right, if he couldn't know her reasons for not being there, did he at least miss her? Would he find this morning's ride a little less enjoyable than yesterday's? Might his day not be as bright, perhaps, as the last two? Or was he merely thinking that while she was a pleasant companion to have around, it really didn't matter if she was not there?

Diana found it difficult to come to terms with that—even though she knew it was the answer she should be coming to terms with. It was the only one that made sense. She already cared for him far more than she should, and it was pointless to let it go farther. There could be nothing between them, she had already admitted that. He was an earl; rich, wealthy, and expectant of marrying someone from his own class. What had she to offer? No name, no money, and a reputation as a jilt. Definitely not someone Edward could—or should—consider marrying.

But she had known that all along, yet she had still gone ahead with the meetings. Except for this morning, when the futility of it had finally hit home. What was the point in continuing their rides? If nothing was going to come of it, except the potential for more pain, why not just stop?

Unable to find solace in reading or crafts, Diana wandered aimlessly around the house. She sat down at the pianoforte, thinking to practise her music for an hour or so, but she found it impossible to concentrate on the studies.

It was her aunt who eventually suggested the idea of a drive in the park, and as Phoebe was hopeful of seeing Captain Wetherby again, Diana could hardly refuse. As such, she changed into a dark blue carriage gown, and a bonnet that sported a jaunty blue feather and a wisp of a veil. The netting was nowhere near as heavy as on the bonnet she wore for her morning rides, but it was enough to give her a feeling of protection from curious eyes.

The weather was perfect, and as expected, the park was heavily populated with people enjoying the fineness of the day. Some walked, most rode, others travelled in the comfort of a carriage. But everywhere they went, there was laughter and conversation. Phoebe was fairly bursting with excitement as they moved into the park proper, her eyes vigilant for her gallant captain. Mrs Mitchell waved or nodded to several people, but did not instruct the coachman to stop. Diana suspected that was for her benefit, and though she saw several glances sent her way, there were not as many as she had feared.

Perhaps she *was* old news. Perhaps she was foolish to have held on to the memory of the past for so long, and allowed herself to be weighed down by it. After all, people went on with their lives. Lord Durling was engaged to marry Lady Ellen. What did society care if the woman who had jilted him was back in London?

Diana heard the carriage approaching, but sitting with her back to the horses, she couldn't see the occupants. But Phoebe could, and she raised her hand in greeting. 'Look, there's Lady

Ellen! And she is in the company of a *very* handsome gentleman! I wonder if that's Lord Durling.'

Diana turned panic-stricken eyes toward her aunt, and knew from the look on her face that it was indeed the man she'd tried so desperately to avoid. 'Phoebe, please do not hail—'

But it was too late. Diana heard the sound of horses being pulled to a halt, and steeled herself for the confrontation. Her aunt flashed her a look of extreme sympathy, and then nodded in the direction of the other carriage. 'Good afternoon, Lady Ellen. Lord Durling.'

Chapter Eight

The coolness in her voice was obvious. Diana wondered, if Lady Ellen hadn't been in the carriage, whether her aunt would have given Durling the cut direct.

'Good afternoon, Mrs Mitchell,' came the polished masculine tones. 'It has been a long time.'

'Indeed, it has.' Then, because there was nothing else she could do, she turned to introduce Phoebe. 'Pray allow me to introduce you to my niece, Miss Lowden.'

Lord Durling had moved the smart black curricle far enough forward that he could see all the occupants of the carriage. 'Miss Lowden.' When he looked at Diana, his voice cooled noticeably. 'Miss Hepworth.'

Knowing she had no choice, Diana raised her eyes and saw, for the first time in four years, the man who had struck her. He hadn't changed.

As handsome as ever, he was a man who could steal the breath from a young girl's heart; a practised charmer who wore his clothes with an elegance few men could imitate. Diana had once thought his golden curls beautiful, his blue eyes the most compelling she had ever seen. Now she only found him ugly, knowing all too well what lay beneath the surface. 'Lord Durling,' Diana said.

'I heard you were back in London. I assumed it would only be a matter of time before our paths crossed.' His voice was a thin veneer of polish over ice. 'It's been a long time.'

But not long enough, Diana realised as she struggled to return his greeting. 'Indeed. May I offer my congratulations on your engagement.' The words nearly stuck in her throat, but Diana knew she had to say them, for Lady Ellen's sake, if not for his. To ignore the relationship would have been the height of bad manners.

'Thank you. I look forward to the day Lady Ellen becomes my wife.' Lord Durling glanced at the young woman beside him and smiled in the way of a man utterly entranced. 'She will make a beautiful viscountess, do you not agree?'

Diana had to turn away from the expression of adoration on Lady Ellen's face.

'I am sure any man who marries her would consider himself extremely fortunate,' Mrs Mitchell said drily.

'Miss Lowden also made her come out this year, dearest,' Lady Ellen said, blissfully unaware of the currents swirling around her. 'I told her that if she is as fortunate in love as I have been, she will truly be a happy lady.'

Lord Durling brushed his finger against her cheek. 'Sweet child.'

Diana watched him, feeling an almost overwhelming desire to knock his hand away from her face; to prevent the tainting of something so lovely, by someone so evil.

'Well, we must be on our way,' Mrs Mitchell said briskly, as though feeling the same aversion. 'Good afternoon, Lord Durling, Lady Ellen. Drive on, Johnny.'

A hurried smile was shared between Phoebe and Lady Ellen as the carriages moved on, but Diana was aware of nothing beyond the pounding of the blood in her veins, and a sickening ache in the area of her heart.

She hadn't been ready for that. Hadn't been prepared for the shock of seeing him again. She'd known it would happen, and had told herself she was ready to deal with it. But the reality of seeing him again, and of having to pretend a civility she didn't feel, was far worse than she had imagined.

Thank God her aunt had intervened to bring the meeting to an end. Diana knew she wouldn't have been able to bear much more. The sight of Lord Durling touching that poor child, and then the hostility in his voice when he had spoken to her, had all but made her feel physically ill.

Diana prayed that Phoebe had not detected it. She likely hadn't, given Lord Durling's smiling face and flattering words, but Diana hadn't been fooled. There had been no warmth in his eyes; no sincerity in his tone when he'd spoken to her.

He disliked her as intensely now as he had four years ago.

The only saving grace, Diana realised, was that he hadn't added hypocrisy to his list of sins. He hadn't said how pleased he was at seeing her again, or been foolish enough to offer empty platitudes. He obviously knew enough of her to know that she would see right through him.

'Are you all right, Diana?' her aunt asked quietly.

Diana struggled for a smile. 'Yes, of course. I was just caught a little off guard.'

'I've never heard you speak to anyone like that before,' Phoebe said hesitantly. 'You don't like Lord Durling, do you?'

Diana caught her aunt's eye, saw the concern on her face, but knew this wasn't the time to go into lengthy explanations. 'Not a great deal. But if it is of concern to you, Phoebe, we can talk about it later.'

Phoebe glanced at her aunt, then slowly shook her head. 'Unless you wish to tell me, I have no desire to hear it. I would certainly not wish to spoil our day with talk of anything unpleasant.'

To Diana's surprise, that was all Phoebe said. She didn't seem downcast or upset, and perhaps because she realised what a painful encounter it had been, she purposely set out to distract Diana with light-hearted chatter.

And Diana loved her all the more because of it.

Because of their untimely meeting in the park, Mrs Mitchell did not suggest that they pay a call on Lady Garthdale that afternoon. Diana was grateful for her consideration. It would have been asking too much of her to go and sit in the dowager's rooms now, knowing what they had to do. As such, she spent a quiet afternoon at home, thinking about the events that were going on around her. In particular, about Edward and the question as to whether or not she would ride with him the following morning. After all, missing one day could be easily explained. Missing a second only slightly less so. But if she went three mornings in a row without meeting him, he would know that she didn't intend to continue their liaison. But was that how she wanted to bring matters to an end? By not showing up and allowing him to draw his own conclusions?

Somehow, it didn't seem the honourable way to behave. And certainly not in light of the fact that he had been honest and open with her all along. Did he not deserve to hear from her own lips that she would not be joining him any more?

Unfortunately, Diana wasn't so sure she was ready to say it. She was reluctant to give up the one part of her life that was bringing her happiness. She couldn't deny that she relished the freedom of riding through Hyde Park with a handsome gentleman, and being able to talk about whatever she wished. Diana was sure even her aunt would have understood that!

And, in the long run, what did it really matter if she prolonged their time together? The Season was only a few months long. If Phoebe decided that Captain Wetherby was the gentleman to whom she wished to give her heart, it would be over even sooner. Diana had come to London as Phoebe's companion. Once the child was engaged, her presence would no longer be required. Phoebe's mother would come to London, or Phoebe would return to Derbyshire. And, at the appropriate time, Diana would travel to wherever the wedding was being held.

In the interim, however, there would be no reason for her not to go back to her life in Whitley. Back to paying calls on the local ladies, and to painting pictures in her garden. Back to riding when the fancy took her, and to playing the pianoforte until three in the morning if she wished. And perhaps, in time, she might even find a gentleman who cared enough to offer her marriage, and to settle down with him to a life of comfortable domesticity.

Knowing all that, was it so wrong to allow herself the enjoyment of Edward's company for a few more days?

He had been there nearly an hour before he saw her. Almost an hour during which Edward had told himself that she wasn't coming and that their brief interlude was over. And though he berated himself for counting the minutes and for caring whether or not she came, it didn't change the fact that he did. Because during those sixty minutes he'd felt a sense of desperation entirely new to him, and realised that it did matter—and why.

As a result, when Jenny came around the corner and into view, he closed his eyes and released his breath on a long, grateful sigh. She'd come. She hadn't decided to stop seeing him.

It shouldn't have made him happy, but it did. Because he knew that if she had not come today, there would have been no point in looking for her tomorrow. And be it right or wrong, he wanted to keep riding with her, and to keep on enjoying their conversation and laughter. Was that foolish?

Definitely.

Ill planned?

Of course.

Necessary?

Absolutely.

'Good morning,' Edward said, hoping his voice didn't reflect the extent of his relief. 'I missed you yesterday.'

There, he'd said it. Not with the strength of emotion he was feeling, but hopefully with enough to let her know how sincerely he meant it.

'Forgive me, I was…unable to come.'

Was that regret he heard in her voice? 'It is of no consequence. You are here now.'

'Yes, and is it not a lovely morning?'

It was, and he wanted to say it was *because* she was there, but he had a feeling Jenny would not look for such declarations from him. Besides, it would have been exposing too much of himself.

They drew their horses side by side and began to walk in the direction of the Serpentine. And perhaps for the first time in his life, Edward found himself wondering what to say. Where was his effortless command of the language now? Where were the glib phrases he tossed off so easily when in the company of other young women? Women who didn't care what he said as long as he spent time in their company.

'You're very quiet this morning,' she said in that low wonderful voice.

Strange. It didn't seem as husky as it had been in the past. Had she been suffering with a cold when first they'd met? It seemed silly to ask.

'I suppose I have things on my mind,' he said, using the excuse in place of the truth. 'So, you have been here over a week now, Jenny. What have you been doing to amuse yourself?'

She glanced ahead of them, rather than at him. 'The usual things one does when in London. Visit friends, pay calls, go shopping.'

'Ah yes. Shopping. The panacea of the well-bred lady.'

'You make it sound as though all females are alike,' she objected, though Edward heard the amusement in her voice. 'That would be like my saying that all gentlemen drink, gamble, and fritter away time in pursuit of their own pleasure, simply because I happen to know of one who does.'

'Is it not a fact that most ladies like to shop?'

'Ah, but you did not say *most* ladies,' Jenny pointed out. 'Your statement led me to believe that you were referring to *all* ladies.'

Edward admitted it was a fair point—since that was what he had meant. 'Tell me, who is this reprobate who has given you such a poor opinion of men? For I can assure you, we do not all drink, gamble, and fritter our time away.'

'No?'

'I seldom have time for any of the aforementioned.'

'Not even for one vice?'

'Well, I suppose if I must confess to one, it would be gambling. At least that calls for a man to use his head.'

'I thought cards were nothing more than a game of chance. That Lady Luck rules the fates of those who sit at her table and, with the turn of a card, she can bring delight or despair to their lives.'

'That's true, depending on the nature of the game,' Edward said. 'But I prefer to play games where there is an element of strategy, where it behoves a man to pay attention to the cards already played. For would you not agree that such things stimulate the mind, rather than numb it, as do too much wine or idleness?'

'I begin to think you should have taken up politics, Edward,' she said, laughing at him. 'You have a way with words that leaves one ready to believe anything you say.'

'Ah, but I would never abuse such a power, for I believe there is enough corruption in politics as it is. If I could use my oratory powers to persuade men to do good, I might consider it.' He tilted his head back to gaze at the sky overhead. 'For now I am happy enough where I am, content to enjoy these discussions with you.'

She made no reply and, not expecting one, Edward fell silent too. Unfortunately, it wasn't long before other thoughts began to intrude into his peace. Memories of what Sir Laurence Dinmott had told him a few nights ago about Diana Hepworth. It had bothered him then, and it bothered him now, and Edward didn't particularly like being bothered.

'Jenny, I wonder if I might ask your opinion on something.'

'You may ask, though the answers may not be of merit.'

He smiled. 'I'll take my chances. The fact is, I would like a woman's opinion on a problem I have, but I need an objective one. I believe you're in a position to be entirely objective.'

'Very well, ask your question.'

Edward took both reins in one hand and rested his other on his thigh. 'It recently came to my attention that a gentleman of my acquaintance had encountered a problem with the woman he intended to marry. It seems that on the eve of their wedding, she jilted him.'

Diana froze, aware of a sudden tightness in her chest that made it difficult to breathe. 'Indeed.'

'Now I should say that I don't know the gentleman well, and that I know even less about the lady,' he went on. 'But I am aware of *his* reputation in society and that *she* seems to be very pleasant.'

'Then…what is the nature of your dilemma?'

'The gentleman in question is now engaged to my sister, though neither he, nor the lady who jilted him, made any mention of their previous association to me.'

Diana no longer had to feign the huskiness in her voice. It was all she could do to get the words out. 'Why would you expect the lady to say something?'

He looked at her in surprise. 'Because she is known to my sister, and knows that she is engaged to marry the man she once jilted.'

'Are you saying you would like to know why she refused to marry him?'

'Yes, I suppose I am.'

Diana took a moment for a few deep breaths. What a precarious situation! Especially since it was imperative that she remember she was supposed to be impartial, and that she was hearing this for the first time. Pretend it wasn't *her* Edward was talking about!

'What about the gentleman?' Diana said, deciding to approach it from another direction. 'Would you ask him the same question?'

'Of course, that would only be fair. The gentleman who told me the story obviously had it from the jilted party, and was therefore biased in his direction. But there are always two sides to a story.'

'If you are willing to entertain such thoughts, why would you not question the lady as well?'

'Because if she speaks ill of the gentleman, how am I to know whether it is personal bias or a legitimate concern?'

'Do you think there could be a legitimate concern?'

Edward shrugged. 'As I said, there are always two sides to every story, and while I don't know the lady well, there is that about her which leads me to believe she would not be flighty or selfish. Yet the reasons given for her behaviour would indicate that she is both.'

'But you also said if the person who told you the story is a friend of the man who was jilted, his view would certainly be prejudiced.'

'When a man is jilted by a woman, his ego is naturally bruised,' Edward said. 'In his attempts to rationalise the situation, it's possible he may try to blame the woman for something she didn't do.'

'What reason did your friend give you for the man's having been jilted?'

'Apparently, the lady found out he wasn't rich enough and went in search of someone who was.'

Diana pulled up on the reins, bringing Juliet to a halt. 'And did she find one?'

'I beg your pardon?'

'Has she found a rich husband?'

Edward likewise reined Titan in. 'No, she is still single.'

'Do you know if she is actively seeking a husband?'

'I do not believe so.'

'Is she living in the country?'

'Yes.'

'Then I would be inclined to say she is either extremely fickle or not looking at all. Tell me, Edward, does she strike you as a woman on a desperate quest for a husband?'

Edward frowned. 'Not in the least.'

'Is she in possession of a fortune, which would preclude her from having to marry?'

'Not to my knowledge.'

'Then it seems obvious to me that the lady is not looking for a husband, and that the charge brought against her of leaving one man for a richer one is not credible. A fortune hunter sets her mind to one thing and one thing alone. She does not consider love, but weighs all by financial or social gain. Once she sets her eyes on a man, she does her best to cold-bloodedly ensnare him.'

'You make her sound like a huntress baiting a trap.'

'In a way, that kind of woman is,' Diana said softly. 'She doesn't have to worry about love, because love doesn't enter into it. She is desirous only of bettering herself through him. Is that the kind of woman about whom we are speaking?'

There was an edge to her voice that Diana couldn't control, and she was sure it was the reason Edward was looking at her so quizzically. 'No, though she could have been biding her time,' he said.

'Perhaps, though I doubt if that was her purpose, she would be living anywhere but London.

That's where the wealthy and powerful gather. And she would not rest until she had either one or the other, or both. Which brings me back to my original point. If she is so consumed by money and left one man because he hadn't enough, why does she now seem content to live in the country without any?'

It was an argument he couldn't refute.

'Now, if you will excuse me, my lord, I feel…a return of the megrims I suffered yesterday,' Diana said. 'I think I shall return home.'

He was instantly all concern. 'Jenny, forgive me, you didn't tell me you were indisposed yesterday.'

'I had no reason to. And I did not…expect it to be a factor in our meeting today.' Diana drew a deep breath, and gathered the reins in her hands. 'I hope what I've said will help resolve your dilemma.'

He inclined his head. 'You have given me a great deal to think about. A great deal indeed.'

'You asked me to bring a lady's opinion to the situation, and that's what I've done. And though I may not be right about any of it, I know how easy it is to prejudge a person based on what you hear, rather than on what is truth.'

With that parting remark, Diana rode away, leaving Edward to mull over everything she had said.

Chapter Nine

Her meeting with Edward that morning disturbed Diana more than she cared to admit. As a result, she decided not to accompany Phoebe and her aunt to a series of at-homes that afternoon, but to stay home and read.

The truth was she hadn't expected Edward to bring up the relationship between Diana Hepworth and Lord Durling, nor to put her on the spot by asking for her opinion about it. She supposed she should have been grateful to him for having had the open-mindedness to ask, and she had spoken to him as freely as she dared, but how did she know where to draw the line? If he had asked the question of a woman with no knowledge of the situation, would that woman have answered differently? Was she at risk of exposing herself by the honesty of her reply?

Diana knew that Edward had no idea who Jenny really was, but she had not improved her situation by having talked to him *about* Diana. There could be no exposing her true self now. In the guise of Jenny, she had talked to him about Diana as though she was a distinct and separate person.

That was out-and-out lying, which meant there was very little chance of his forgiving her, if he did eventually find out that she and Diana were the same. She had wilfully misled him. He could even accuse her of manipulating him, and of trying to put herself—Diana—in a better light. In which case, he wouldn't think her only deceitful and untrustworthy, he would accuse her of being a merciless schemer who played with people's hearts and spared no thought or regard for their feelings.

Exactly the kind of woman Lord Durling had accused her of being!

Was it any wonder that with an opinion like that, there could be little hope of salvaging anything out of this relationship?

Inclement weather the next morning prevented Diana from having to decide whether or not to ride with Edward, and for once, she was grateful for it. The rain fell in a steady downpour that started before dawn and continued until late afternoon.

Unfortunately, it didn't prevent another equally disturbing event from taking place. Over breakfast, Mrs Mitchell announced that they would pay their respects to Lady Garthdale that afternoon.

Diana truly wished she had decided not to get out of bed at all!

They were greeted at the door by Lady Garthdale's butler, and, upon presenting her card, Mrs Mitchell and her party were shown to a first-floor drawing room. It was an elegant room, spacious, with high ceilings intricately plastered, and walls heavily ornamented with mouldings and elaborate cornices. The colours were a touch dark for Diana's liking. Striped wallpaper in a deep gold and blue silk covered the wall, and the curtains were dark blue velvet. The furnishings were gold with blue piping, and a beautiful carpet in shades of blue, gold, and cream covered the floor.

Diana was sure the room would have looked more appealing had the heavy curtains been pulled back to allow some light into the place, but it seemed that Lady Garthdale was not inclined to brightness. Diana also noticed that although the furnishings were of excellent quality, and upholstered in the richest of brocades, there was a shabbiness to the place that signified a lack of care. Or of interest.

The Dowager Countess of Garthdale was a woman who could have looked younger, had she taken the time and effort to do so. She was not unattractive, but the unrelieved black she wore did nothing to enliven a sallow complexion, and her hair was drawn back so tightly, Diana was sure it affected her ability to smile. Lady Ellen, wearing a pretty lilac gown trimmed with cream lace, sat quietly at her side.

'Mrs Mitchell,' Lady Garthdale said without particular warmth, 'it is good of you to call.'

Mrs Mitchell inclined her head. 'I thought that on such a dreary day, it might be nice to enliven it with a visit, Lady Garthdale.'

The woman's smile was hard-edged. 'It matters not to me whether the sun shines or the rain falls. All my days are dreary now.'

Determined to persevere, Mrs Mitchell took a chair close to the lady and sat down. 'Well, we must see what we can do to make this day a little less dreary than the others.'

Once their aunt was seated, Diana and Phoebe did the same, taking chairs on either side of the fireplace. Lady Ellen sat quietly, watching her mother's face and those of her guests.

'Are these your daughters?' Lady Garthdale enquired.

'They are my nieces. Diana is my eldest, and Phoebe, my youngest.'

'I take it they are both unmarried?'

'At present.'

The dowager glanced sharply at Diana. 'The eldest looks to be well of an age to be married.'

Diana stiffened a little at being spoken of as though she wasn't in the room, but she saw her aunt shake her head and knew she wasn't expected to reply. She was tempted to nevertheless.

'Diana has of late been in the country, and is only recently come to London. Phoebe has made her come out this year, and is enjoying her first Season very much.'

'This is my youngest daughter, Lady Ellen,' Lady Garthdale said listlessly. 'She is also enjoying her first Season, but has fared better than your nieces. She is soon to be married.'

Diana saw the momentary look of dismay on Phoebe's face, and knew she hadn't missed the cutting remark. Mrs Mitchell heard it too, but carefully concealed her feelings. 'Yes, so we heard. To Lord Durling.'

'A most satisfactory match,' the dowager countess said. 'I was pleased to give it my blessing. Our social standing is, of course, higher than Lord Durling's, but there is considerable wealth in the family and the title is an old one. It is not,' she said archly, 'like the situation between the Earl of Eastcliffe and the young woman *he* is engaged to marry.'

'Miss Amanda Townley,' Mrs Mitchell said.

'Yes. Pretty enough, though totally without connections. Eastcliffe should have done better. I would certainly not have countenanced such a liaison.'

'But Miss Townley is a gentleman's daughter,' Diana said, unable to withhold comment in the face of such blatant condescension.

The woman fixed her with a hard gaze. 'Be that as it may, there are significant differences between them and a man must be mindful of such things.'

Lady Ellen began to look decidedly uncomfortable. 'Mama, I—'

'As for Ellen, the alliance is far more suitable,' Lady Garthdale went on. 'There were several gentlemen courting her, but when my daughter told me she was kindly disposed toward Lord Durling, I did not hesitate to approve the match.'

'Yes, a mother must always keep the best interests of her children at heart,' Mrs Mitchell observed. 'Especially her daughters. I understand your eldest is expecting another child?'

The dowager inclined her head. 'Barbara will bear her second in October. Naturally, she is hoping for a boy.'

Mrs Mitchell smiled. 'I'm sure she will be delighted with whatever it is.'

'She can be delighted *after* the succession is secured,' Lady Garthdale said in a chilly voice. 'Girls are well enough as companions, but it is boys that ensure the future of the line.'

There was a brief silence, as though no one quite knew what to say.

'Do you know Lord Durling well, Lady Garthdale?' Mrs Mitchell enquired.

Diana's hands tightened on the arms of the chair, but the older woman merely shrugged. 'No better or worse than any other. I am aware that he has a fine appearance, and of his standing in society. What more need I know?'

'Good afternoon, Mother. I hope I am not in-terrupting.'

Diana glanced toward the door, feeling her chest constrict as Edward walked into the room. His hair was damp from the rain, but his boots were dry, indicating that he must have taken time to dry them before entering the salon. Diana wondered if that was natural considera-tion, or a result of years of having lived in his mother's house.

What must it have been like for him, she wondered, growing up in this house where love and laughter seemed to have no place? Had Lady Garthdale been different before her hus-band died? Had she been a loving mother, de-voted to her children? Had she lavished care and attention on her first-born son, knowing that he would one day carry on the family name? Or had she been selfish and self-centred as she was now, leaving the raising of her children to nurse-maids and governesses, and giving them only the most cursory of affection.

Looking into Lady Garthdale's eyes, it was hard to imagine her laughing with her children, or holding them in her arms, Diana decided. She couldn't picture her surrounded by three chil-dren, all of them anxious to play, and to earn her approval and admiration. It was hard to picture her doing anything that involved the giving or receiving of love.

'Edward. I did not expect to see you back so soon.'

Lady Garthdale's greeting was decidedly reserved, and though Edward smiled, Diana knew it was an effort. 'I thought to come and relieve the boredom of a rainy day, but I see Mrs Mitchell has beaten me to it.'

'I do not like going about in inclement weather,' Lady Garthdale professed. 'Most sensible people stay indoors and keep themselves warm by the fire, rather than gallivanting all over town.'

Diana heard Phoebe's quickly indrawn breath, then glanced at her aunt, to whom the thoughtless remark had been addressed. Fortunately, she was too well mannered to indicate that she had taken offence. 'I agree, it is very pleasant to sit in front of a fire when the day is grey and chill, but we must not let weather stop us from paying calls, or we should soon find ourselves spending a great deal of time indoors.'

'Is that not what one's house is for?'

Diana risked a quick glance at Lady Ellen, who was looking quite mortified by her mother's unkind words, and wondered how the child had managed to remain so bright and cheerful in the face of such unadulterated bitterness?

'Has my mother offered you refreshments, Mrs Mitchell?' Edward asked quietly.

'No, but there is no need, my lord.' Mrs Mitchell's voice gave no indication of her feelings. 'My intention was merely to call and make my nieces known to her, and for Phoebe to spend some time with Lady Ellen, but perhaps it is best that we take our leave for today. I am sure there will be other opportunities for longer visits.'

'I regret I did not have more time to visit with you, but I'm glad I arrived in time to catch you.' He turned and looked at Diana. 'I was wondering, Miss Hepworth, if you would be good enough to—'

'Miss Hepworth?' Lady Garthdale suddenly snapped out of her lethargy. '*Diana* Hepworth?'

All eyes turned to the dowager countess, and then to Diana, who was already raising her chin in defiance of what she knew was about to happen. 'Yes, Lady Garthdale. My name is Diana Hepworth.'

The woman's face went white. 'No wonder your aunt did not give me your full name,' she hissed. 'I am surprised you would dare show your face in this house!'

Lady Ellen gasped. 'Mama!'

'Silence!' Lady Garthdale snapped, holding up her hand. 'You do not know who this person is.'

Edward stepped forward. 'I know who she is, Mother, and this is neither the time nor the place.'

'On the contrary, it is very much the time, and since it is my house, it is definitely the place.' Lady Garthdale turned haughty eyes on Diana. 'You are not welcome in this house, Miss Hepworth. I do not know what kind of manners you have, but I am not taken with them or with those of your aunt.' She turned a blistering gaze on Mrs Mitchell. 'You should have known better than to bring her here.'

Two spots of angry colour appeared on Mrs Mitchell's face, but she didn't back down. 'We had a reason for coming, Lady Garthdale. A reason it would be in your best interests to hear.'

'There is nothing I wish to hear from you!'

'Nevertheless, it is something your daughter deserves to know. In fact, it was for her sake—'

'Leave this house!' the dowager countess ordered. 'Without another word for my daughter or myself. I will have none of your stories here.'

Diana felt sick, repulsed by Lady Garthdale's vicious condemnation. She glanced at Phoebe, saw that her face was deathly white, and knew it was essential that they leave before anything more was said and any further damage done.

Fortunately, Mrs Mitchell was already on her feet and staring with hard eyes at the countess. 'You do your family a great disservice, Lady Garthdale. I hope you will not have cause to regret it in the future!'

'Get out!'

Mrs Mitchell did not have to be told twice. She headed for the door, head held high, nodding at Edward as she passed. Diana followed, one arm wrapped protectively around Phoebe's shoulders. She could feel the girl trembling, and knew that she was close to tears. Before she left, however, she risked a quick glance at Lady Ellen, and could have wept for the look of shock and horror on the poor girl's face. Obviously, there would be a great deal more said before the end of the day.

Finally, stealing herself to do so, she looked up and met Edward's gaze. She saw anger, mortification, and regret. Whether he fully understood the reason for his mother's behaviour Diana couldn't say. But she knew that he would before the day was out.

Without a word, she swept Phoebe out of the room, bringing to an end one of the most unpleasant confrontations of her life!

To say that Phoebe was shocked would have been understating the situation. The poor girl didn't say a word on the drive home, and when they arrived at George Street, she went straight to her room, tears pooling in her eyes and running down her cheeks.

Feeling considerably shaken herself, Diana accompanied her aunt to the drawing room.

'Ring for Jiggins, please, Diana,' Mrs Mitchell said, jerkily removing her gloves. 'I find I am quite in need of refreshment.'

Diana did, then likewise removed her own gloves and bonnet. Chaucer, having sensed the tension in the room, sat down and waited for someone to pay attention to him.

'I'm sorry, Aunt Isabel, I had no idea that would happen,' Diana said quietly.

'Of course you didn't, child, and you certainly owe me no apologies. That wretched woman's conduct was shocking. Shocking! I can only pity her poor children. No wonder Lady Ellen is so anxious to leave home. I would be too if I was forced to endure such treatment.'

Diana sat down and, taking pity on Chaucer, called him over. He came, adoringly.

'I am more concerned with Phoebe than I am with Lady Ellen right now,' Diana said, her voice filled with regret. 'The poor girl will surely be wondering what that was all about.'

'She will indeed, and I am hard pressed to know what to tell her.' Mrs Mitchell began to pace. 'I fear *you* may have to say something in light of what happened. Phoebe may be young, but she is not completely naïve, and she will know there is something going on between you and Lady Garthdale. Oh, I could shake the woman!' Mrs Mitchell said, raising her fists in the air. 'How dare she say such things to you, as though you had no heart or feelings. How dare she order us from her house, as though we were utterly beneath her contempt!'

Trying to take a more philosophical approach to the situation, Diana lifted her shoulders. 'I cannot claim to like anything she did, Aunt

Isabel, but I suppose she is within her rights. She obviously feels I am a bad influence on Lady Ellen, since I am the one who jilted her future husband, and naturally, she did not wish to hear anything derogatory I might have said about him.'

'But how was she to know that we intended to say anything derogatory?' Mrs Mitchell exclaimed. 'Just because we were hoping to *advise* her to take another look at Lord Durling is certainly no reason to cast us out on our ears before a single word was spoken! There are limits to how one conducts oneself, Diana, and to my mind, Lady Garthdale overstepped them all! I would never embarrass my family or my guests in such a way. Never!'

Mrs Mitchell stopped pacing, realising the futility of it, and abruptly sat down. 'The problem is, it will certainly make things difficult for you and Phoebe now. No doubt Lady Garthdale will forbid Lady Ellen to see Phoebe, and she will certainly not allow you anywhere near her.'

'Of course not. She will tell her daughter that I was previously engaged to Lord Durling, that I broke it off for the very worst of reasons, and that if I do have a conversation with her about him, she is not to believe a word I say.' Diana paused as Jiggins entered with a tea tray. She waited while he set it on the small table beside her, and silently withdrew, before resuming. 'Lady Ellen may or may not believe her, but it won't change Lady Garthdale's opinion of me, and *she* is the one who will force her to go through with the marriage.'

Her aunt tutted. 'It is a convoluted situation, is it not? By trying to do good for the daughter, we have now alienated the mother, who is determined to see her daughter on a tragic course. Which means we cannot look to Lady Garthdale or Lady Ellen to resolve this.'

Pouring out tea, Diana sighed. 'Then there is nothing for it, I suppose, but to accept the fact that the marriage is going to take place.'

'Not necessarily.' Mrs Mitchell glanced up. 'There is still one person to whom we can turn.'

'Who?'

'Lord Garthdale, of course.'

Diana nearly dropped the teapot. 'Why would you expect him to treat the situation any differently than his mother?'

'Because he is not so embittered as she is. Indeed, I've met few people who are. But if he cares for Lady Ellen, as I believe he does, he may be more willing to listen.'

'I doubt he will be willing to listen to anything *I* have to say.'

'No, but what about Jenny? You told me that she...that is, that *you* are able to talk to him about all manner of things, and that he listens to what she...what you, have to say. And since he has no reason to connect Jenny with Diana Hepworth, or to suspect her of underhanded dealings, it is quite possible that you could do some good for Lady Ellen in that guise.'

'I wish I could, Aunt, but I've already mentioned the idea to him, and he said there would be no point. But I would be manipulating him,' Diana said, setting the teapot down. 'Using what I know of the situation to influence him. I would feel as though I were deliberately deceiving him.'

'Come, Diana, now is not the time for false pride,' Mrs Mitchell said. 'Are you not already deceiving him by concealing who you are? Are you not hiding your face, and disguising your voice every time you ride with him?'

Diana flushed. Of course she was deceiving Edward. Hadn't she already admitted that? Wasn't that part of the reason she felt so guilty about everything? So what reason did she have for objecting to introducing one more element into the deception?

'There is one small problem with your plan,' Diana said, resting her cheek on Chaucer's bristly head, smiling as his tail thumped the floor. 'If I am only recently returned to London, and am not mixing with society, how am I to know any of this? How am I to know what effect the past actions of a lady by the name of Diana Hepworth could have on Lord Garthdale's family now?'

'The same way you found out that the gentleman who is engaged to his sister was once jilted by a woman on the eve of their wedding. By gaining Lord Garthdale's confidence and encouraging him to talk about it. You must somehow contrive to bring up the topic of Lord Durling in conversation, and then have Lord Garthdale tell you what you need to know. That will then give you opportunity to address it. You're not a stupid woman, Diana,' Mrs Mitchell said. 'I feel sure there must be a subtle way of having him bring up a subject that is causing him so much distress. He *must* be made to talk about this. And to listen with an open mind to what he has to be made to hear!'

* * *

Diana was not the only one experiencing anxious thoughts. Edward too, was burdened with anger and surprise after the alarming confrontation between his mother and Diana Hepworth. But in trying to find answers, he only seemed to come up with more questions.

What was he to make of the young woman? Was she a heartless jilt or an unfortunate victim of circumstances?

His mother clearly believed her to be the former. Lady Garthdale had held nothing back when telling Edward what she thought of Miss Hepworth. After her visitors had left, she had sent a tearful Ellen to her room and then launched into a blistering tirade, accusing Mrs Mitchell and Miss Hepworth of entering her house under the guise of friendship, and of then trying to poison poor Ellen's mind against the man she had chosen to marry.

The fact that neither of them had said a word about Lord Durling didn't seem to matter. Diana Hepworth was guilty simply as a result of having once been engaged to him, and of having the audacity to call.

The bitterness in his mother's diatribe had left Edward shaking his head, mainly because he hadn't understood it. Ellen was engaged to marry Lord Durling. What was the point in victimising a woman who had decided, for whatever reason, not to marry the man four years earlier? It didn't necessarily reflect on either of them as people, despite what Sir Laurence had said. Perhaps Miss Hepworth had simply decided they didn't suit. Things like that happened, and surely it was better to discover such incompatibilities *before* a marriage rather than after.

It was also likely, Edward reflected, that Miss Hepworth had absolutely no intention of bringing up the topic of her engagement to Lord Durling today. Why would she? Apart from it being an uncomfortable topic of conversation with Ellen in the room, it would surely have been embarrassing, if not painful, to her.

On the other hand, why would Mrs Mitchell have decided to pay a call on his mother now? He couldn't remember the last time the two women had socialised together. He wasn't even sure Mrs Mitchell *liked* his mother, so it had to be viewed as something of a coincidence that she would just happen to pay a call when her niece was back in town.

A niece who *happened* to be the woman originally intended to be Lord Durling's wife?

Chapter Ten

Diana thought a lot about her aunt's words as she dressed for that evening's engagement, a reception being held at the home of one of her distant relations. And while she agreed that a solution could no longer be reached through Lady Garthdale or Lady Ellen, she really wasn't sure that talking to Edward about it—as Jenny—was the way of doing it either. But there had to be some way of making him aware of the potential danger for Lady Ellen.

Phoebe was noticeably quiet as they set off. Diana did everything she could to try to restore her cousin's good spirits, but nothing seemed to bring the sparkle back to her eyes, which only made Diana regret more deeply the fact that her past was having such an adverse effect on Phoebe now. But she supposed it would have been foolish to believe it would not. If they hadn't met Lady Ellen and her family, all might have been well, but the moment a friendship had been established between the two girls, it was only natural that concern for Lady Ellen would become a personal issue. Diana was surprised that Phoebe still hadn't come to her and asked her to explain what had happened, although, after this afternoon's disaster, Diana wasn't so sure that silence would continue.

Fortunately, help in restoring Phoebe's spirits came from an unexpected source. They had been at the reception no more than fifteen minutes when Captain Wetherby came up to Phoebe and asked her to dance.

At once, Phoebe's uncertain smile vanished, and colour surged back into her cheeks. And as she went off with him, Diana prayed that he would be willing to spend enough of the evening in Phoebe's company to keep her smile in place and hopefully banish the memory of what had taken place earlier in the day.

'Miss Hepworth, I wonder if I might have a word.'

Diana's hands closed convulsively on her fan. 'Lord Garthdale!' She turned, aware that her heart was beating unusually fast. 'Yes, of course, though I am surprised you would wish to have conversation with me.'

He was elegantly dressed, handsome in formal attire, and with simple, but elegant jewellery. 'On the contrary, I wish to apologise for my mother's behaviour. I deeply regret the embarrassment it caused you.'

His words brought a reluctant smile to Diana's face. 'It is kind of you to say so, but it is more my cousin for whom I am concerned.' She raised her eyes to his, and decided to speak plainly. 'Phoebe is not aware of what happened in the past, Lord Garthdale. As a result, you can understand why she was so shocked at hearing your mother speak to me the way she did.' Diana paused, glancing past him to where Phoebe danced with Captain Wetherby. 'I'm sure Lady Ellen was equally taken aback.'

Edward locked his hands behind his back. 'Unfortunately, Ellen has seen my mother in a temper a number of times. But I admit, she's usually more restrained in the presence of guests than she was with you.'

'Not all guests come with the kind of history I do.'

He watched her, and slowly nodded. 'I admire your candour, Miss Hepworth. And though I do not claim to know all of the details surrounding your relationship with Lord Durling, I am sure that whatever happened between the two of you has caused you both a great deal of distress. However, because it is my sister's happiness I must now concern myself with, I think it is probably best that you do not see Ellen again.'

It was much as she'd expected, Diana reflected sadly, but she had hoped for better. 'Does that restriction also apply to Phoebe?'

'Why would it not?'

'Because my cousin knows nothing of what happened, and is, therefore, unable to spread tales to your sister. It doesn't seen fair that she should be penalised for something I did.'

'Unfortunately, my mother sees your cousin as an extension of yourself, therefore, she would frown upon her friendship with Ellen as well.'

'And are you also of that opinion, Lord Garthdale?' Diana asked. 'Do you feel that my entire family must be avoided because of something I did?'

Edward shook his head. 'I don't believe in visiting the sins of the father upon the son, if you take my meaning. And I'm sure that if I were in a similar position, I would feel exactly as you do. Your cousin was still in the schoolroom when you were engaged to Lord Durling.

But if there is a chance she has learned of this since coming to London—'

'Phoebe has heard nothing,' Diana told him. 'She would have said something to me if she had. There is nothing deceitful about my cousin, Lord Garthdale. She lives in Derbyshire with her parents, and has been away at school for the past two years. I have maintained a sporadic correspondence with her mother, but had little to do with Phoebe herself until she came to spend two months with me prior to coming here. We did it with a view to getting to know one another better before coming to London.'

'Why did the girl's mother not accompany her?'

'Because she is crippled, and not easily able to travel,' Diana said. 'And apart from the pain, she is deeply embarrassed by her injury and does not participate in society. However, she wanted Phoebe to have a chance at making a good marriage, and wrote to ask if I would act as her companion. I agreed, and Mrs Mitchell, who is aunt to us both, kindly offered to sponsor her, and to provide a place for us to stay.'

'And what of you, Miss Hepworth? Do you not seek a husband while you are here?'

The flush started in her cheeks and spread outward. 'No, my lord, I do not. When Phoebe is settled, I shall return to Whitley. My exposure to society has been painful, and I have no desire to prolong it.'

'With all respect, Miss Hepworth,' Edward said slowly, 'that is a shame.'

Diana blinked hard, and looked away. She had heard the sincerity in his voice, the concern expressed behind the softly spoken words, and because she didn't feel deserving of it from him of all people, she abruptly took her leave. She feared that if she stayed, she would say or do something to embarrass herself.

Skirting the crowd of people helping themselves to an elaborate array of delicacies, Diana slipped out a side door and into the evening air. There were couples scattered along the terrace, some looking toward the ornamental lake, while others moved through the gardens. As she watched them, Diana was aware of feeling terribly alone.

What had Edward meant by that last remark? Was he suggesting it was a shame that circumstances had brought her to the position she found herself in now and that she still felt so unwelcome in society? Or was he suggesting that she wasn't as bad as she believed herself to be, and perhaps that she deserved another chance at finding happiness?

'Good evening, Diana.'

The unwelcome voice stopped her in her tracks. *Lord Durling!* Had he seen her talking to Edward? Was that why he'd followed her out here now?

She turned to face him, drawing on whatever strength remained. She would not let him fluster her. Not now. Not again. 'Lord Durling,' she said in a cold, hard voice.

He smiled, and Diana hated him for it. He knew he had her at a disadvantage, and they both knew he was enjoying her discomfort. 'You needn't sound so hostile, Diana. *I* am the one who should be feeling put out.'

'You?' Visibly surprised, Diana said, 'Why? What have you to be vexed about?'

'The fact that you went to see Lady Garthdale and her daughter.'

Caught off guard that he knew, Diana stammered, 'H-how did you know?'

'It doesn't matter how I know. The question is, why did you go?'

'I really don't think that's any of your business.'

'On the contrary, any contact you have with my future family is most certainly my business. I simply wondered what prompted the call. I can't think it was because Mrs Mitchell is a great friend of Lady Garthdale's.'

'No, but you are surely aware that…Phoebe has become very friendly with Lady Ellen,' Diana said, knowing she had to find an answer that would satisfy him. 'As such, my aunt thought it would be nice for Phoebe to make the acquaintance of her mother. And since Lady Garthdale does not go about in society, it was necessary that we pay a call upon her at her home. Now, if you don't mind—'

Lord Durling put his hand on her arm, stopping her. 'I do mind, Diana, because I'm not finished with you yet.'

She looked down at his hand, the loathing in her heart reflected in her voice. 'Kindly remove your hand. I have no desire for your touch, nor is there anything you can say that I wish to hear.'

'But you *will* hear me,' Durling said, though he did withdraw his hand. 'You've changed, Diana. There was a time when you were only too glad to have me beside you, and when you longed for my touch.'

It was all she could do not to shudder. 'That was before I learned what you are.'

'I can't think what you mean.'

Diana curled her fingers into her palms, itching to slap the smugness from his face. She knew what he was doing. From the moment she had accused him of striking her, he had denied it. Denied ever having touched her, or of having caused her any kind of emotional distress. It seemed that nothing had changed. 'What do you want?'

'Only that you stay away from Ellen and her family. I intend to marry her, and there's nothing you can do to change that.'

'There are things I could say—'

'But not that anyone would believe, so why set yourself up for more ridicule? Wasn't it bad enough the first time?'

It was, but Diana refused to let him see it. 'If there's no truth to what I say, why are you so fearful of my telling anyone?'

The smile stayed on his lips but fell short of his eyes. 'Because I want no unpleasantness surrounding my marriage. Ellen is a sweet, gentle girl. A delicate flower. One I intend to nurture and love.'

'I hope you remember that, my lord, for it would be a shame to destroy something so beautiful.'

His expression didn't change, but Diana saw the darkness that crept into his eyes. 'You should be careful, Diana. No one else holds me in the contempt you do, I cannot think what has caused it.'

'But that's just the point, isn't it, Lord Durling,' she said quietly. 'You're not capable of honesty. I learned that four years ago and nothing in your conduct has led me to believe you've changed. I know what you are.'

'And I would remind you,' he said, forcing her to retreat until she felt the coolness of the stone wall against her back, 'that if you want your cousin to succeed in London, you would be well advised to keep your opinions to yourself!'

Diana recoiled as though he'd struck her. 'Phoebe will succeed because she is beautiful and charming.'

'Yes, but isn't it strange how rumours can start about even the most charming of people?' Durling whispered close to her ear. 'Rumours, that when started by a person whose reputation is beyond reproach...'

Diana shivered. Horrible, horrible man! He was saying exactly what she had been afraid of hearing. He was threatening to ruin Phoebe, just as he'd ruined her.

'You may have spoiled *my* chances of making a good marriage, Lord Durling, but I will not stand by and allow you to spoil Phoebe's. If you do anything to malign that girl's reputation, I will do everything I can to bring the truth to light.'

'And you listen to me, Diana. If you take me on, you *will* lose,' Lord Durling said calmly. 'Because if you think I damaged *your* reputation four years ago, just wait until you see what I do to hers!'

He left her then; standing with her back against the wall, her body quivering with anger. Dear Lord, what was she to do? Durling hadn't changed at all. He was the same man, the same monster he'd been four years ago. If she did nothing to prevent it, Lady Ellen would end up marrying him and be exposed to God only knew what kind of horrors. But if she did say something and the marriage didn't take place, Lord Durling would do everything he could to ruin Phoebe.

Which meant there really was no choice. Diana liked Lady Ellen, but she loved Phoebe, and, in this, her loyalty had to be to her family. Lady Ellen was sister to the Earl of Garthdale; a powerful man who could use his position to protect those he loved. Phoebe was the only daughter of a gentle scholar and his crippled wife.

Diana closed her eyes. What choice did she really have?

Diana didn't sleep well that night. She tossed and turned, plagued by dreams filled with people she didn't know, but who threatened her at every turn. She saw Phoebe stretch out her hands in supplication, but a chasm opened up between them and made it impossible for Diana to reach her.

In her dreams, it was Phoebe who married Lord Durling, not Lady Ellen. Phoebe, who turned to her with bruises on her face and tears in her eyes.

With that terrible image haunting her, Diana flung back the covers and got out of bed. As weary as she was, she had no desire to venture back into sleep. Not when dreams like that awaited her. She threw a warm shawl around her shoulders and headed for the drawing room.

She knew that the servants would be stirring below stairs, but had no wish to alert them to her presence. She tiptoed quietly into the drawing room, thankful she had no need to worry about Chaucer making a noise. He was no doubt snoring at the foot of her aunt's bed, just as he did every night.

She crossed to the long window and drew back one of the curtains. The sun had not yet risen, but the sky was already brightening in the east, and as she sat on the window seat and gazed out over the city, she pondered what she was going to do.

Last night, Edward had apologised for his mother's behaviour, but he hadn't asked her to explain her relationship with Lord Durling. Instead, he had told her that while he sympathised with her, and agreed it was unfair that Phoebe be unjustly cut off from her friend, he had to side with his mother in saying there could be no further association between them.

His attitude had shown Diana that he didn't understand her plight, which, in turn, had forced her to admit that he really didn't care—about it *or* her. If he had, he would have given her an opportunity to set matters straight by asking what really happened between her and Lord Durling. But he hadn't asked, and she hadn't told him. And, as a result of her untimely meeting with Lord Durling, she no longer could. She *wouldn't* say anything to Edward when she knew what the consequences would be. Before she had only speculated that Lord Durling might intercede to do harm. Now there was no question that he would, and since the only thing that mattered to Diana was seeing Phoebe happily married, she wasn't about to jeopardise that by speaking out against the one man who had the power to prevent it.

'Diana?'

Startled, Diana turned. 'Phoebe?' She had been so deep in thought she hadn't heard the door open, or notice the slender form slip through. 'What are you doing up so early?'

'The same as you, I expect.' Phoebe quietly closed the door. 'I thought I heard you moving around, and when I peeked into your bedroom and saw you gone, I thought you might have come down here.'

Diana sighed. 'You couldn't sleep either?'

'No. I did try, but it was no use.' Phoebe sank down on the window seat beside her. 'Are you all right?'

Diana smiled. 'Of course. Why would you ask?'

'Because I saw Lord Durling follow you on to the balcony last night,' Phoebe said quietly. 'And I saw how upset you were when you returned.'

'That needn't signify that anything unpleasant passed between us,' Diana said, not wanting her to worry.

'No, but given that you don't like Lord Durling, I suspect something did. I've also been wondering if the connection between you and Lord Durling has something to do with the abominable way Lady Garthdale treated you yesterday.'

'Lady Garthdale is not well, Phoebe. She is still suffering grief over her husband's death.'

'Perhaps, but it wasn't grief that made her lash out at you.'

Diana pulled her shawl more tightly around her shoulders. 'It is nothing you need concern yourself with.'

'I wish I could believe that, dearest. What happened between you and Lord Durling? It must have been something very bad.'

Diana looked up and met the girl's questioning gaze—and knew that the time had come.

She couldn't put it off any longer. 'I wish I didn't have to tell you this, Phoebe, but I suppose it isn't fair that you don't know.' She fiddled with the tasselled ends of her shawl. 'When I was in London four years ago, I received an offer of marriage.'

Phoebe's eyes widened in astonishment. 'You *did*?'

'Yes. From…Lord Durling.'

'Lord Durling! And you didn't tell me?'

'Until now, it wasn't important that you knew.'

'But…you refused an offer of marriage from the man who is now engaged to marry Lady Ellen—'

'I didn't refuse him, Phoebe. I accepted his proposal.'

The girl looked at her askance. 'Then why didn't you…?'

'Marry him?' Diana turned back to the window. 'Because I learned something about him that made it impossible for me to do so. And the day before the wedding was to have taken place I went to him and told him it was over.'

'Gracious!' Phoebe exclaimed. 'No wonder the two of you were so distant in the park the other day. But what happened? Did you fall out of love?'

'Yes, but not for the reasons he would have everyone believe,' Diana said. 'Perhaps had I taken longer to know him in the beginning, I might have seen indications of what his character was, but, like you, I was impulsive, and anxious to fall in love. I wanted nothing more than to be married and have a home of my own.'

Phoebe shook her head. 'I can't imagine you being impulsive, Diana. You're far too sensible for such things.'

'Thank you, Phoebe, though I'm not sure whether to be flattered or offended by the remark.'

'Oh, but I didn't mean it in an unkind way,' Phoebe said quickly. 'It's just that you always know to do the right thing. You consider your actions, and you always seem so calm and in control.'

Diana's mouth twisted. 'So boring, you mean.'

'No, that's not what I meant at all!' As if realising she was doing a poor job of getting her point across, Phoebe went back to her original question. 'You said you broke off your engagement for reasons other than those Lord Durling wanted people to believe. Why? What did he say your reasons were?'

Diana stared through the window and into the streets below. 'He said I broke it off so that I might look for a wealthier husband.'

'What!'

'He suggested that I was a…cruel and heartless woman who was lacking in morals, and who could not be trusted to tell the truth because I had no conscience and felt no compunction about lying.'

'But that isn't true!' Phoebe cried. 'You're the kindest, the most honourable, the most decent person I know! How could any man say such hateful things about the woman he loved?'

'You mean the woman he *claimed* to love,' Diana said softly, 'for that's all it really was. I was too young to understand it at the time, but I've learned a great deal in the last four years.' She stopped, took a deep breath, and went on. 'I didn't stay long in London after I broke off the engagement. Thanks to the stories Lord Durling told about me, I found I was no longer welcome. The invitations stopped coming, and even my friends began to look at me differently. In the end, I had no choice but to go back to Whitley.'

'Oh, Diana, how awful!' Phoebe whispered. 'Why didn't you tell me any of this before we came to London? I would never have badgered you to come if I'd known.'

Diana patted the girl's hand. 'That's all right, Phoebe, it hasn't been all that bad. I've enjoyed seeing Aunt Isabel and Amanda again, and there are many in society who no longer hold me in contempt. It would seem that time is, indeed, a great healer.'

'But that doesn't take away from the fact that you must have hated the idea of coming in the first place.' Phoebe looked at her with apprehension. 'Why did you do it, Diana? Why did you really break off your engagement?'

Chapter Eleven

So, here at last was the heart of the matter, Diana thought, glancing at her cousin. But was Phoebe strong enough to hear the truth? She was so young; barely older than Lady Ellen Thurlow. But Lady Ellen was of an age to be married, which meant that Phoebe was too, and surely if a woman was old enough to be married, she was old enough to deal with some of the harsher realities of life.

'Phoebe, what I'm about to tell you must not go beyond these walls,' Diana said in a low voice. 'Whatever emotion you feel, be it anger, or shock, or even revulsion, you must not speak of it to anyone other than Aunt Isabel or myself, do you understand?'

'Well, yes, of course, but...was what happened truly so bad?'

'It was to me.' Diana slowly stood up. 'One evening, when Lord Durling and I were alone, he did a most contemptible thing.'

Phoebe's voice was a mere whisper. 'He did?'

Diana nodded, and pulled the shawl more closely around her shoulders. 'He raised his hand and struck me. Hard, across the face.'

Phoebe gasped. 'He *struck* you? But how could he do such a thing? A gentleman would *never* behave such a way!'

Diana's voice was dry. 'So society would have us believe.'

'But why did he do it? Had you been having an argument?'

'We had been having…a discussion.' Diana walked towards the fireplace, finding it easier to talk when she was moving. 'I really don't remember what about. Nothing of consequence, I'm sure, for Lord Durling wouldn't engage in conversations of an intellectual nature with me. He refuses to believe that women are capable of handling the complexities of science or politics.'

'But you have an excellent grasp of such things!' Phoebe exclaimed. 'I heard you and Sir James having a most animated conversation about economic reform over dinner one night.'

Diana's mouth twisted. 'Yes, but unfortunately, Lord Durling doesn't share your opinion. When I expressed a sentiment contrary to his, he told me I was being foolish and became quite angry. Not realising how annoyed he was, I laughed. The next thing I knew, I was lying on the floor, looking up at him.'

'Oh, Diana!' Phoebe rose and went immediately to her side. 'I hardly know what to say. I can't imagine a gentleman doing such a terrible thing.'

'Nor could I,' Diana said, remembering the pain and humiliation of that unexpected slap. Remembering how the stars had danced in front of her eyes when his open palm had struck her jaw, and the way she had fallen against the sharp edge of the table before collapsing to the floor. Her tender flesh had borne the mark of it for weeks.

'That was exactly one week before the wedding,' Diana said quietly. 'The next time I saw Lord Durling was two days before the ceremony, and he acted as though nothing had happened. As though everything was fine between us.'

'You mean he didn't apologise for what he had done?'

'He didn't even acknowledge that he'd done anything,' Diana said. 'When he saw the bruise on my cheek, he chided me for my clumsiness, saying I must have walked into a door, or tripped and hit my face. At no time did he *ever* accept blame for striking me. That's when I realised what kind of man he was, and knew that I couldn't go through with the marriage.'

Phoebe stared at her with an expression of shock and incredulity. 'I cannot believe he would have been so horrid. Or that he would have denied doing such a wicked thing.'

'If he denied it, even to me, I couldn't claim agreement to it on his part,' Diana explained. 'If I had spoken out against him, it would have been my word against his, and in such a case, how much weight do you think my word would have carried?'

'But you did tell people what happened,' Phoebe said, nodding as though she expected Diana to do the same. 'You did tell people he'd struck you, even if he didn't have the decency to admit it. You had the bruises to prove it.'

'I had bruises, Phoebe, but none that could be attributed to Lord Durling. After all, why would he strike the woman he intended to marry? The woman he claimed to love.'

'But surely he didn't…after what he had done…he did not still claim—?'

'To love me?' Diana gave the younger girl a cheerless smile. 'Of course he did. In fact, he played the part of the wounded lover most convincingly.'

The girl's eyes softened. 'Oh, Diana, what a dreadful ordeal. I cannot imagine such a thing happening. What did Aunt Isabel say? She must have been furious!'

'She was. She came up to my room after Lord Durling left, and when she saw what he had done, threatened to have the law after him. I, of course, begged her to say nothing.'

'But why? Surely you wanted to see him punished?'

'Of course, but I was only just turned seventeen, Phoebe. Even younger than you are now. And I was afraid of him,' Diana said, hard as it was for her to admit it. 'Afraid of the power he wielded, and of what he might do with it. In hindsight, it was the wrong thing to do, but at the time, all I wanted to do was run away and pretend it had never happened.'

'So you went back to the country.'

Diana nodded. 'Yes. My much-anticipated first Season was over. I'd met Lord Durling in April, we were engaged in the May, and before the end of June I was back in Whitley, licking my wounds and vowing never to return to London again.'

'But you did return,' Phoebe said in a hushed voice. 'You agreed to come back and to go around with me, even though you knew what you might face.'

Diana smiled as she drew the girl close. 'Yes, but as I said, it's not been so bad. It was just unfortunate that we happened to run into Lord Durling and Lady Ellen in the park the other day.'

Phoebe hung her head. 'Now I understand why Lady Garthdale behaved the way she did. She must have heard the lies Lord Durling told about you, and was afraid you would say something to Lady Ellen.'

'I dare say that was the case.'

'But you *must* say something!' Phoebe cried. 'Lady Ellen can't possibly marry Lord Durling now. If he struck you and denied it, there is no reason to believe he won't treat her the same way.'

'No, there isn't, but listen to me, Phoebe. You are not to mention a word of this to Lady Ellen or her mother, do you understand?'

'But—'

'Not a word! There is too much at stake.'

'But what could be more important than sparing Lady Ellen the pain and humiliation of being married to such a monster?'

'Sparing someone, who is closer and dearer to me, a similar kind of pain and humiliation.'

Phoebe gasped. 'You mean Lord Durling would hurt someone else because of something you might say about Lady Ellen?'

'Not physically,' Diana said, putting her hands on Phoebe's shoulders, 'but he would do everything he could to ruin her reputation. And as heartless as it sounds, I can't help Lady Ellen, but I can help—'

'*Me!*' Phoebe whispered. 'That's who you're trying to protect, isn't it, Diana? You're afraid that if Lord Durling finds out you've warned Lady Ellen against him, he will do something to jeopardise *my* chances of making a good marriage. That's what this is all about, isn't it?'

When Diana didn't answer, Phoebe's face fell. 'Oh, I knew it. I knew I was right. And you weren't even going to tell me, were you?'

Diana's hands dropped away from the girl's shoulders. 'I don't know *what* I was going to do. I would have told you if I thought you'd needed to know, but I honestly don't know if I would have said anything otherwise. I don't want to see you hurt, Phoebe. And I certainly don't want to see your chances of making a good marriage destroyed because of something I did.'

'But *you* didn't do anything! You were…a victim of circumstances. And it's no wonder that you are not kindly disposed towards marriage. I don't know that I would ever be able to trust a man again, if something like that happened to me.'

Diana smiled. 'Of course you would trust again. There are many good men out there, Phoebe. Kind, decent men, who respect women, and who would never do anything so hurtful. Men like Lord Eastcliffe and Captain Wetherby, and—'

And *Edward Thurlow*. Diana closed her eyes, forcing back the anguish of her thoughts. Yes, Edward Thurlow. One of the most admirable men she had ever met. A man who believed her to be one person, but knew her as another, and to whom she had lied in order to protect herself.

A man with whom she had been foolish enough to fall in love, and who through no fault of his own, would bring her nothing but heartache and despair!

*   *   *

Edward was in the park well before seven the next morning. He hadn't been able to sleep, even though he had gone to bed late and risen early. He'd found no escape from his thoughts, haunted as they were by the memory of Diana Hepworth's face.

Would he ever forget the way she had looked in his mother's drawing room? Forget the expression of horror and embarrassment on her face as his mother had cruelly lashed out at her?

He was quite sure the memory of that wretched encounter would stay with him for the rest of his life. And yet, as shocked and dismayed as Diana had been, it was her cousin, Phoebe, for whom she had expressed the deepest concern. When he had spoken to her last night at the reception, it was her cousin's welfare she had pleaded for. She had not criticised his mother for her unconscionable behaviour. She had asked only that the friendship between Phoebe and Ellen be allowed to continue.

Admirable conduct, Edward reflected, for a woman who was supposed to be a jilt and a liar.

The sound of an approaching rider stirred him from his thoughts, and as Edward looked up and saw Jenny approaching, he put his thoughts of Diana Hepworth aside. Not because he was unsympathetic to her plight, but because he had was reluctant to let that part of his life infringe on this one. He had so little time with Jenny as it was.

She looked particularly fetching this morning in a dark green habit trimmed with black piping, and an elegant bonnet that trailed a long, flowing sash down her back, under which she wore her dark hair caught up in a snood. Edward wished there was some way of spending more time with her. Would she allow him to call upon her at home, he wondered, or meet with him at a society function? She must attend some, though he knew he hadn't seen her at any of the assemblies he'd attended since her arrival in London.

But then, would he have recognised her if she had?

Edward sighed. It was highly unlikely since he had no idea what she looked like under those blasted veils. Veils that seemed to be getting darker and heavier each time they met. Was it still so important that she conceal her features from him? Was her face so well known that he would recognise it the moment he saw her? And what if he did? Surely she must know that it didn't matter to him. Not any more.

'Good morning, Jenny,' he said quietly.

She inclined her head. 'Edward. I didn't expect to see you here so early.'

He smiled. 'Riding is far preferable to lying awake in one's bed, endlessly tossing in a futile attempt to find sleep.'

She sighed. 'Perhaps it is something in the air, for I, too, have been awake for hours.'

'Perhaps we are plagued by secrets that do not allow us to find comfort in sleep,' Edward said, forcing back images of her lying in his bed, her dark hair spread around her, her lips sweetly curved as she gazed up at him. 'Secrets that, if shared with another, would no longer have the power to unsettle us.'

Was it his imagination, or did he see a faint smile through the netting? 'A convenient answer, my lord, but I do not think the problem is so easily resolved.'

'We could try. Will you not allow me to share your secrets, Jenny? Whatever they are, they will not change my feelings for you.'

'But you must not have feelings for me. We meet for conversation and—'

'Damn the conversation. This has gone far beyond the level of that, or at least it has for me. I look forward to seeing you every morning,' he told her. 'And on the days when you do not come, I feel as though I've missed something of importance. As though the rest of my day won't proceed as smoothly. I know that doesn't make sense, but neither does anything else about this. You said you weren't looking for anything to come of this. Neither was I. But perhaps it is *because* of our lack of expectations that something *has* come of it. Either way, I would be lying if I said I haven't come to feel a great deal of affection for you. Indeed, more than I should.'

He knew he'd caught her off guard. Knew it by the way her head dropped forward and a sigh slipped through her lips. 'But there can be no point to it, Edward, don't you understand? There are so many things you don't know about me.'

'What? Like this mysterious secret you keep referring to, but will not share?'

'That and...others.'

'Very well, then, let us try to narrow down some of the possibilities. Are you an escaped criminal fleeing from the Bow Street Runners?'

She drew in a quick breath. 'Of course not!'

'Then are you a thrice-married woman, hiding from one or more of her husbands?'

'Gudgeon! You know it is nothing like that.'

'Do I? You say I wouldn't care for you if I knew what you had done, but if you haven't committed murder or mayhem, how bad can your transgressions be?'

'Some would say very bad.'

'Some?'

'Those in polite society.'

'Huh! I suspect there are many in polite society, who harbour secrets of which they are not proud, and who have done *many* things wrong. Including the person who decreed that the wearing of veils over the face was fashionable,' Edward muttered.

'You do not care for veils?'

He heard the amusement in her voice, and felt his own lips curve. 'Not any more. Have you any idea how desperately I long to see your face? I think I've been very good not to ask before now, but…will you not raise your veil just once so that I might see the lady who has come to mean so much to me?'

She shook her head again, but Edward sensed it was not without regret. 'It is better that I do not.'

He watched her in silence, his eyes narrowing. 'Then answer me this, Jenny. Do you care for me?'

Her gasp was audible. 'You know I cannot answer that. It would be most improper—'

'Damn propriety,' he interrupted blandly. 'I want to hear you say that you don't join me on these rides because it provides you with a few hours of distraction in an otherwise boring day.'

'Of course that isn't why I come! The time I spend with you is far more than a diversion. Surely you know that.'

'How can I know, if you do not say so? A gentleman may wish to hear many things, Jenny, but that is not to say he can expect to.'

'That is only because there are many things a lady knows she cannot say. But I would not have you think that I…treat these encounters lightly,' she said in a halting voice. 'That would not be fair. And I do want to be honest with you, inasmuch as I can be.'

'Then are you saying you do care for me?'

She lifted her head. 'Yes. And like you, a good deal more than I ought.'

Edward felt as though a weight had been lifted from his shoulders. She cared for him, and he'd finally managed to get her to admit it. 'Do you know, I sometimes wonder whether you're not a spirit, so thoroughly have you bewitched me.'

The remark was so unexpected that she actually laughed, a rich, sensual sound that had Edward fighting an urge to pull her into his arms and knock that wretched bonnet from her head! He wanted to feel her body warm against his, and to hold her so close that every inhalation of breath brought her sweetness to him.

He knew his feelings made no sense, but who was to say that matters of the heart ever did? She *had* bewitched him. Completely and utterly.

'Tell me one more thing, Jenny. Is the secret you're keeping one that would preclude us from being together?'

It was a bold question. As bold as Edward dared ask, and he wasn't surprised that it was some time before she answered. 'That depends what you mean by…being together.'

'I'm asking if you've done something so shocking that it would preclude you from being considered marriageable?'

He heard her quick inhalation of breath. 'Edward, I—'

'No, don't try to evade the question.' He nudged Titan closer. 'I want the truth, Jenny. Are the secrets you're keeping of a nature that would prevent you from accepting an offer of marriage?'

'Not…any offer, no.'

'An offer from me?' When she slowly inclined her head, he bit off one word. 'Why?'

'Because your wife must be beyond reproach,' she said simply. 'Not even a hint of scandal must be attached to her name; no stories that would cause people to doubt her worthiness to be your wife. I am not able to make that claim.'

'Were the stories told about you true?' he asked, needing to know, willing to trust whatever she said.

'No. They were lies told by someone of consequence in an attempt to conceal the truth. And because of his position, they were believed.'

'But if *you* know they are lies, why do you allow them to torment you? Why do you feel the need to hide your face, and to keep your name from me? Do you believe I've heard these fabrications and believe them to be true?'

'You may have.'

'Then tell me what they are so that I can set your mind at rest.'

She sighed. 'You make it sound so simple, Edward. As though with a few words, the whole situation could be resolved and the problems made to go away. But it isn't that straightforward. It's easy to offer opinions when you are not involved in the situation—'

'But that's just it, Jenny. I *want* to be involved. Intimately involved—with you!'

Edward knew he'd gone too far. Knew it the moment the words left his lips and Jenny uttered a muffled cry. She pulled the mare's head around and set her to a gallop, defying propriety and leaving her startled groom to follow as best he could; leaving Edward to watch her; silently cursing for having handled the situation so poorly.

He'd spoken too soon. Jenny hadn't expected his feelings to be what they were, and it was wrong of him to have admitted them. He should have bided his time; waited until the moment was right to tell her all the things he wanted to say. Instead, he had rushed his fences and, in doing so, had caused her to run from him.

The fact that he had touched on a few sore spots in her life, perhaps opened a few old wounds, hadn't helped the situation, but strangely enough, that didn't bother him as much. Sometimes old wounds needed to be bled. Sometimes, Edward told himself, it was the only way of letting the poison out.

And there was poison here; the kind of poison created when hateful words and insidious lies were used against a woman who had done nothing to deserve them. But since she had also told him there was no truth to the stories—and because he believed and trusted her—there was nothing stopping him from acting on the decision he had been coming to over the last few days.

A course that would no doubt meet with resistance on all fronts, but that he intended to pursue regardless.

Chapter Twelve

Diana had a hard time settling to normal routine after her tumultuous meeting with Edward in the park. Her heart still fluttered every time she thought of what he had said.

I want to be involved. Intimately involved—with you.

That had certainly sent the blood rushing to her cheeks! And his earlier words had only made it worse.

...are the secrets you're keeping of a kind that would preclude you from considering an offer of marriage?

What was she to make of that? Diana had believed that one statement was indicative of a desire to set her up as his mistress, while the other had clearly hinted at a longing for a more honourable relationship. Surely he wasn't saying that he wished to marry her? How could he when he knew nothing about her! Yes, she rode a fine horse and possessed the manners of a lady, but so did many of the courtesans plying their trade in the streets of London.

His mother certainly wouldn't approve the match. Diana could just imagine walking into Lady Garthdale's drawing room and being presented as the woman her son intended to marry.

It wouldn't come to that, of course, because once Edward found out who she was, he wouldn't *want* to marry her. When he discovered that Jenny was actually Diana Hepworth, there would be no more morning rides in the park. He would realise he had been the object of a clever deceit, and draw his own conclusions as to why she had lied to him. Conclusions that would surely persuade him to believe he had no wish to see her again.

Could she bear the heartache? Could she live with the thought of never seeing Edward again?

'You seem rather distracted this morning, Diana,' her aunt commented from her chair. 'Has something happened to upset you?'

Diana kept her eyes down, wondering how much she should reveal. Her feelings for Edward were of an extremely personal nature, but she had always been honest with her aunt, and, in truth, she valued her opinion. And given that the lady already knew that she was meeting with Edward in the park, surely it wouldn't come as a complete surprise.

Diana sighed. 'I find myself in something of a quandary with regard to Lord Garthdale.'

The older woman smiled. 'Indeed. And what is the nature of this quandary?'

'Amongst others, I no longer think that having Jenny tell him the truth about Lord Durling is a good idea.'

Her aunt's hands stilled over their work. 'I thought we agreed it was the only way of helping Lady Ellen?'

'We did, but I fear now that the cost may be too great.' And, in as few words as possible, Diana told her aunt about her encounter with Lord Durling at the reception, and then watched her aunt's face darken with outrage.

'Damn the man! Pardon me, Diana, but there are times when even a lady is moved to profanity. How dare he threaten you in such a manner! Truly he is the worst form of vermin.'

'Be that as it may, we cannot deny that it must have a bearing on what we do now. I cannot tell *any* member of Lady Ellen's family the truth, because I won't put Phoebe's happiness at risk.' Diana reached for a new length of silk and threaded it through the eye of her needle. 'By the way, Phoebe knows what happened four years ago.'

Mrs Mitchell sat back. 'She does?'

'Yes. We had a chat before dawn this morning.'

'Gracious, child, whatever were you doing up so early?'

'Trying not to fall back into unpleasant dreams,' Diana admitted. 'And, as it turned out, Phoebe couldn't sleep either, and followed me down here. When she asked what was wrong, after more or less telling me she suspected it had something to do with Lord Durling, I decided there wasn't much point in not telling her the truth.'

Mrs Mitchell sent her a questioning glance. 'Was she shocked?'

'Horrified. Appalled that a gentleman would behave in such a manner, *and* that I hadn't told anyone the truth at the time.'

'Well, at least we are in accord there,' Mrs Mitchell said drily. 'And I can't say I am sorry she knows, Diana, as difficult as it must have been for you to tell her. At least, now all the cards are on the table.'

Diana hesitated, biting her lip. 'Unfortunately, there's more. Before I told Phoebe about Lord Durling, I warned her that she wasn't to say anything to Lady Ellen or her family because others might suffer for that knowledge. Again, she more or less put two and two together, and figured out that *she* was the one I was trying to protect.'

'Oh, dear.' Mrs Mitchell put aside her tambour. 'What did she say to that?'

'That it is no wonder I have no wish to be married, and that while she understands *why* I'm trying to protect her, we must nevertheless do everything we can to prevent Lady Ellen from marrying Lord Durling.'

The older woman smiled. 'Dear Phoebe. She would say something like that. But to be honest, Diana, I can't help but agree with her. I cannot bear the thought of that poor girl becoming the property of such a beast.'

'Nor can I, but if Lady Garthdale won't listen to anything we say, and we cannot speak to Lord Garthdale, how is the wedding to be prevented? I doubt Lord Durling would be foolish enough to mistreat Lady Ellen *before* they are married.'

'No, for I am sure if word got back to Lord Garthdale that he had, Lord Durling would find himself facing pistols at dawn.'

'But who is to say that once they are married, he won't take her north to Chipping Park?' Diana said. 'That way he could be assured of having her to himself for months at a time.'

'Indeed.' Mrs Mitchell's fingers beat a staccato on the arm of the chair. 'This makes for an extremely awkward situation.'

'Yes, it does, Aunt. And I, for one, shall be very glad when I am back at Whitley and all of this is behind me.'

'Perhaps, but returning to Whitley will only trade one kind of unhappiness for another.'

Diana gazed at her. 'What do you mean?'

'Why, Lord Garthdale, of course. If you leave now, you will just be leaving behind the man you love, and that certainly isn't going to make you happy.'

A rush of pink stained Diana's cheeks. 'But I don't...that is, I haven't...'

'You needn't try to deny it, my dear, your face gives you away,' Mrs Mitchell said kindly. 'I've oft said it is easier to be an observer of life than a participant in it. I assume Lord

Garthdale still doesn't know that you and Jenny are one and the same?'

Guiltily aware that everything her aunt said was true, Diana shook her head. 'No.'

'But you are still seeing him.'

'Yes.'

'Has he said anything to you about his feelings for you as Jenny?'

'He's admitted he *has* feelings for me…her,' Diana said, still finding it strange to think of herself as someone else. 'And he has been asking some rather pointed questions.'

'Of a respectable nature, I hope.'

'Oh, yes, perfectly respectable,' Diana assured her with a smile, 'though I do wonder how to answer them.'

There was a knock at the door, and Jiggins came in, bearing a salver upon which rested a single card. Mrs Mitchell took it, and upon reading the name, smiled. 'Well, isn't this interesting,' she said, handing the card to her niece. 'It appears you may have an opportunity to ask, if you care to.' She nodded to the servant. 'Thank you, Jiggins. Kindly show Lord Garthdale up.'

Diana barely had time to compose herself before the man she loved appeared in the doorway. He was no longer dressed in casual riding attire, but wore light-coloured pantaloons and a beautifully tailored dark blue jacket. His Hessians gleamed, and the distinctly masculine aroma of soap, fine linen, and light cologne rose to tantalise Diana's nostrils. Glad she had changed into one of her flattering new gowns, she rose to greet him, painfully aware of the fluttering of her heart—and of a sudden desire to flee.

Chaucer also got up, legs stiff, ears forward at the sound of an approaching male. He growled low in his throat, but stopped when he saw Edward, as though sensing this was not a man who was easily intimidated. Nevertheless, he barked once, and then looked to his mistress for approval. Mrs Mitchell duly patted him on the head. 'Good boy. You can go back to bed now. Lord Garthdale,' she said, smiling at their guest. 'How good of you to call.'

'Mrs Mitchell.' Edward came forward and bowed. 'I hope my timing is not inconvenient.'

'Not in the least. Diana and I were just enjoying some quiet conversation. And Chaucer is always happy for company, as you see.'

Edward grinned, and offered his hand to the dog, allowing him to sniff it. When Chaucer wagged his tail, Edward fondled him gently behind the ears, bringing a look of such bliss to the creature's face that Mrs Mitchell was moved to remark, 'I am afraid you've made a friend for life, Lord Garthdale. For all his size, Chaucer is quite shameless when it comes to begging for affection.'

Edward smiled. 'I have several dogs of my own, none as large as this, but I know how ardently they crave affection. It is one of the things I find most endearing about them.' With the smile still on his lips, he turned and bowed to Diana. 'Good morning, Miss Hepworth.'

'Lord Garthdale,' Diana said, feeling the strangeness of greeting him for the second time that day.

Fondly ordering Chaucer back to his bed, Mrs Mitchell resumed her seat by the window, and invited Lord Garthdale to make himself comfortable on the sofa. Diana returned to her chair and picked up her embroidery, needing to do something with her hands.

'I hope you don't mind my speaking plainly, Mrs Mitchell,' Edward said, 'but I was not pleased with what took place at my mother's house. I had an opportunity to speak to Miss Hepworth last night, but not to you or Miss Lowden, and since my mother's anger was directed at all three of you, I thought it only right that I come and offer apologies on her behalf.'

'It is good of you to do so, Lord Garthdale, but surely your mother is capable of making her own apologies,' Mrs Mitchell said in a dry voice.

'Yes, but she is not like to do so,' Edward said ruefully, 'and you *are* owed an explanation. I now know it is the nature of the attachment that existed between Miss Hepworth and Lord Durling that caused her to react so poorly to your visit, but that does not excuse her behaviour.'

'Thank you, Lord Garthdale. While I tend to agree with you, I suppose your mother's reluctance to entertain us is understandable,' Mrs Mitchell said. 'No doubt she anticipated some lingering animosity between Diana and Lord Durling, and with Lady Ellen in the room, wished to hear nothing said against him. Not that my niece *would* have made such ill-mannered remarks.'

Edward inclined his head. 'Of course. Being aware of Miss Hepworth's situation, I can understand why she would wish to avoid the topic altogether. However, something you said as you were leaving aroused my curiosity, and is part of my reason for calling on you today.'

Diana looked up, but her aunt's attention remained fixed on their visitor. Her expression, one of mild curiosity, did not change. 'And that was…?'

'You said you had a reason for calling upon my mother. One you felt to be in her best interests to hear. You also suggested that if she didn't listen, she might have cause to regret it in the future.' Edward's gaze briefly touched on Diana before settling back on the older woman. 'That led me to believe it might have something to do with Ellen's forthcoming marriage.'

This time, it was Mrs Mitchell who sought Diana's eyes. A glance passed between them, before Mrs Mitchell turned back to her guest and cleared her throat. 'I'm sorry, my lord, but there is nothing I would say to you or your mother.'

His surprise was evident. 'Am I mistaken in believing there was?'

'No. I'm simply saying that upon reflection, I think it would be best if I kept my own counsel.'

'Forgive me, Mrs Mitchell, but it was my impression that what you wanted to say was of considerable importance.'

'It was, but circumstances have changed since then and I am no longer at liberty to say anything.'

'But I don't understand. If you felt the matter important enough to seek out my mother in the first place, and were turned away for your trouble, why would you not tell me now that I am here and willing to listen?'

'Because time lends wisdom to our thoughts, Lord Garthdale, and, in reviewing the matter, I realised it was not my place to say anything. Now,' Mrs Mitchell said, obviously feeling ready to move on, 'can I offer you tea, Lord Garthdale?'

Not surprisingly, Edward wasn't at all pleased. He looked at Mrs Mitchell, who met his gaze with imperturbable calm, and then at Diana, who endeavoured to do the same. Unfortunately, it wasn't long before she had to look away, returning her attention to her embroidery, painfully aware of the ticking of the clock, and of the beating of her own heart.

Fortunately, Chaucer chose that moment to roll over and make a low, whuffling sound in his throat. His legs began to twitch and his jowls to quiver as he blissfully chased rabbits in a performance so comical that Diana couldn't help but be amused. Regrettably, though it served to relieve some of the tension in the room, it failed to bring a smile to Edward's face.

'Thank you, Mrs Mitchell, but I won't take up any more of your time. I came to offer an apology and to give you an opportunity to say what you were prevented from saying.' He rose. 'However, as circumstances have altered, and you feel there is no longer anything to be said…'

He left the sentence unfinished, leaving Diana to wonder if he was purposely trying to make them feel guilty. She shifted a little in her chair.

'Was there something you wished to say to me, Miss Hepworth?'

Too late, Diana realised that he had been watching her for any indication that she might wish to say something. She forced herself to meet his eyes, and shook her head. 'No, Lord Garthdale. Only that it was good of you to call and to extend apologies on your mother's behalf.'

For a long moment, he looked at them. First at Mrs Mitchell, then at Diana, almost as though he was daring them to let him leave. But let him go they did, because they both knew that to say anything now would only negate their earlier claim, and cast them both in a very poor light.

When Diana finally heard the front door close, she slumped down in her chair, feeling as though she had come through the battle but without knowing which side had won. 'Gracious!'

'Indeed!' Mrs Mitchell said, rising to pull the chord. 'I am very glad *that* encounter is over. There was a moment there when I was not sure I would get through it without breaking down and telling him the truth.'

'You did a wonderful job, Aunt Isabel, though I still wonder if we were right to do it,' Diana said. 'Was it a mistake to let him walk out of here without telling him the truth about Lord Durling?'

'Of course it was,' Mrs Mitchell said, guilt sharpening her tone. 'By not telling him, we have kept a secret about a man we know to be a beast, and who should have been exposed years ago. However, if we had told Lord Garthdale the truth and he hadn't believed us, we might have found ourselves far worse off than before.'

Diana frowned. 'How so?'

'Because it is entirely possible that Lord Garthdale's loyalty already rests with his future brother-in-law, and if that is the case, he would have felt compelled to go to the man and tell him what we'd said. Then Phoebe's future would have been well and truly compromised.' Mrs Mitchell shook her head. 'No, under the circumstances, I really don't see that we had a choice.'

Diana wanted to believe that her aunt was right. Wanted to believe that they had done the right thing in not being honest with Edward, and that a desire for Phoebe's happiness justified the possible sacrifice of another's. But in her heart, she knew it did not. If anything should happen to Lady Ellen, Diana knew that she would never forgive herself. She would never live down having kept silent today, no matter how well intentioned their motives might have seemed.

Edward spent the evening at his club. He hadn't felt like staying home, but neither had he been inclined to go out and partake in any of an endless number of society events. Instead, he lingered over his newspaper, trying to distract his thoughts from the disappointing call he had paid on Mrs Mitchell and her niece that afternoon. Disappointing, in that he had known full well that they were keeping something from him. The question was *what*? What had they intended to tell his mother only a few days ago that now must go unsaid?

Whatever it was, Edward knew that both Mrs Mitchell and her niece were privy to it. He had seen the look Diana had exchanged with her aunt. And he was just as convinced now as he had been then that it had something to do with Ellen's future. So why wouldn't they tell him? What had happened to make them change their minds? What could have been so important one day—and of no consequence the next?

'Evening, Garthdale,' a familiar voice said.

Edward glanced up and saw Lord Durling approach his table. The gentleman had obviously been doing the rounds. He was dressed in evening attire and his appearance was, as always, immaculate. Not a speck of dirt marred the pristine perfection of his white silk stockings, nor was there a crease to be found in the skin-tight smoothness of his breeches. Even his cravat was crisp and unsoiled, the snowy white fabric arranged in the intricate folds of a perfect Orientale.

Edward sometimes wondered if everything about Durling wasn't just a little too perfect.

'Durling. Done for the night, or just stopping in for a rest between assemblies?'

'The latter, I'm afraid.' Durling's grimace was marginally convincing. 'I promised Lady Pharquar and Mrs Bentley I would attend their gatherings, and I've yet to visit either. Thought to stop here for a moment's peace. All this gadding about does tend to wear one out.'

'I wonder you still do it,' Edward said, smiling to mask his impatience. 'After all, you're soon to tie the nuptial knot. Surely it isn't necessary that you continue to attend all of society's functions.'

Durling laughed. 'True, and I do attend fewer than I used, but I like to keep abreast of what's happening in society.'

Yes, I'll bet you do, Edward reflected narrowly. Durling was a great follower of court gossip. He liked being seen at all the fashionable assemblies, and he enjoyed passing on what he had seen—which explained why he would never be a close friend of Edward's. Edward had no time for rumours, or for those who spread them. Still, it behoved him to make an effort, if for no other reason than that the man was to be his brother-in-law, and surely, in the scheme of things, fastidiousness was hardly a reason to dislike a man.

He invited Durling to join him. Durling did, saying as he settled into the armchair opposite, 'I see you've chosen to avoid the crowds this evening. Probably a wise thing to do.'

'Wisdom had nothing to do with it. I simply wasn't in a mood to be sociable. At least, not in the ballrooms of society.' Edward leaned back in his chair and watched the other man for a moment. 'Tell me, Durling, your engagement to Diana Hepworth. Why haven't you mentioned it to me?'

Durling slowly looked up. 'I assumed you already knew.'

'I didn't. Why did she break it off?'

'Does it matter?'

'Yes, as it happens.'

Durling shrugged, and signalled to the waiter. 'She had her reasons.'

'Care to tell me what they were?'

'Not really.' Durling smiled, but Edward thought it looked forced. 'Why so curious?'

'Because the lady is back in town and our paths have crossed several times.'

'Romantically so?'

'Not at all. Miss Hepworth is here to act as companion to her cousin. And as *that* young woman has formed a close alliance with Ellen, we frequently find ourselves in the same vicinity.'

When the waiter arrived, Durling ordered a bottle of brandy. 'Has Ellen said anything to you about my relationship with Diana?'

'No. I'm not even sure she knows you had one.'

'Then I fail to understand why you feel the need to bring it up.'

And I fail to understand why you're so anxious to avoid talking about it, Edward reflected. But all he said was, 'Curiosity, I suppose. After all, the lady was engaged to you, and now you're engaged to my sister. I don't think it's too much to ask what happened.' He fixed Durling with a deceptively mild gaze. 'Do you?'

In a timely interruption, the servant appeared at the table with the brandy and two glasses.

'Care to join me?' Durling enquired. 'I think you will find this very much to your liking.'

Edward nodded his agreement. 'Thank you. I never say no to a fine brandy.'

Durling filled up Edward's glass, and then his own. Setting the decanter back down, he took up his glass and cradled it in the palm of his hand. 'Miss Hepworth told me she didn't want to go through with the wedding because she no longer wished to be my wife.' His voice was matter of fact. 'She said she was desirous of seeking a more prosperous alliance with a man of greater rank and fortune.'

Edward frowned. 'She *told* you that?'

'Actually, she informed me of it in a letter, which I received the day before the marriage was to have taken place.'

'Good Lord. What did she say when you went to see her about it?'

Durling swirled the brandy in his glass. 'I didn't go to see her. She'd already told me how she felt. Why would I go and listen to anything else she had to say?'

'Perhaps to make sure you hadn't misunder-stood her intentions.'

'Oh, I understood them well enough.'

Edward slowly rubbed his finger along the side of his glass. 'Miss Hepworth paid a call upon my mother and Ellen the other day, in the company of her aunt and cousin. I believe it was her aunt's idea. Unfortunately, when my mother learned of Miss Hepworth's identity, she asked all of them to leave.'

'Probably a wise thing to do,' Durling remarked. 'I doubt Miss Hepworth would have had anything kind to say about me.'

'What makes you think she would have said anything about you at all?'

'Because I know the lady.' Durling downed a mouthful of brandy. 'Diana, for all her appearance of gentle amiability, can be a spiteful creature. When she found out that I had told people what happened between us, she accused *me* of being vengeful, and of ruining her reputation. She believes that to this day. As such, I have no reason to believe she will wish Ellen happy in her marriage to me, or even encourage her to proceed with it.' He slowly set the glass down on the table, avoiding Edward's eyes. 'So, what *did* Diana say about me?'

'Nothing. Mrs Mitchell had barely finished exchanging pleasantries with my mother, when I arrived and made my greetings to the party. When I addressed Miss Hepworth by name—which must have been the first time my mother heard it—she told them in no uncertain terms to leave. Given the brusqueness with which they were treated, I went to visit Mrs Mitchell today to offer my apologies, and to ask her a few questions.'

It seemed to Edward that Durling's face paled. 'And what did she say?'

'Again, nothing. She refused to answer my questions.'

'Which was, of course, her prerogative,' Durling said.

'Agreed,' Edward said, wondering why he heard relief in Durling's voice. 'But it didn't make sense to me that she had changed her mind so quickly.'

'Perhaps not, but that too is to be expected of women. What they are adamantly convinced of one day, they are obdurately opposed to the next. But let me be very clear about one thing, Garthdale. Matters might not have worked out between Diana and myself, but that has nothing to do with my relationship with your sister. I love Ellen, and I intend to make her the happiest woman in England. I give you my word on that,' Durling said, holding out his hand.

Seeing no reason not to take it, Edward did. 'See that you do. I'd hate to have to call my own brother-in-law out over some personal family grievance. Shockingly bad *ton*.'

He said it with a smile and Durling laughed, but it was forced—and they both knew it.

Durling left soon after that to continue with the night's round of merrymaking. Edward stayed where he was, reviewing the man's comments with regard to Diana Hepworth. Strange that his opinion of the lady should be so different from his own. Diana didn't strike him as the kind of woman who would behave in such a manner, and he had certainly seen nothing vindictive or bitter in her nature. Had she been a different person four years ago? Was it possible she had been so selfish that securing a wealthy viscount hadn't been enough for her?

Granted, Durling might not be as rich as some, but his family's holdings were not inconsiderable, and he was an extremely handsome man. And yet, a young woman of seventeen, possessed of neither wealth nor title, had refused to marry him, and had not offered any excuses why.

Did that signify guilt? Did it mean that the reasons Durling had given him were, in fact, valid?

Edward stared into his brandy. Why would a young lady of good family break off an engagement to a handsome peer, and not volunteer her reasons for doing so? Especially when the reasons her jilted fiancé were putting about were so damning to her reputation.

Something wasn't making sense, and Edward had a feeling that the part of the story he didn't know was of far more importance than the part he did. The question was, where could he go to learn the truth? Who knew Diana Hepworth well enough to know what she had been like four years ago when all of this had happened?

Chapter Thirteen

'Lord Garthdale,' the butler announced into the sunny room where two elegantly dressed ladies sat at their respective desks, perusing their respective lists.

'Thank you, Cumberland. Lord Garthdale, what a pleasant surprise,' Mrs Townley said, rising to greet him.

Edward smiled. 'I happened to be passing and thought I would call in to see how the wedding plans were progressing.'

'As well as can be expected,' Mrs Townley said, though her voice hinted at amusement. 'Amanda is quite sure I shall forget something.'

'Now, Mama, I did not say you would forget anything,' Amanda replied, also rising. 'I merely said there are so many details to attend to, it would be possible to overlook one and not even be aware of it.'

'I assure you, my dear, I do not intend to overlook anything.'

'If it is of any consolation, Ellen is going through the same contortions,' Edward told them as they all resumed their seats. 'I'm sure there would be no more work involved if she was marrying into the royal family.'

'Now there is a dreadful thought,' Mrs Townley commented. 'Imagine having the Prince Regent as a son-in-law.'

'Some would be delighted,' Amanda pointed out.

'Not those with any sense,' her mother remarked. 'But at least you have no worries in that regard, Lord Garthdale. Lord Durling hardly moves in that set.'

Edward said nothing. He had been looking at Amanda when the comment was made, and had noticed the slight frown that appeared between her brows.

'Yes, I imagine it would be enough to have any mother wringing her hands,' he said, tucking it away. 'Speaking of which, I wonder, Miss Townley, if we might take a turn about the garden. There is a matter Ellen wished me to discuss with you.'

Amanda rose, a graceful column in pale yellow muslin. 'I should be delighted, Lord Garthdale.'

The gardens behind the town house were exceptionally lovely, but on this occasion, Edward paid them little mind. 'Miss Townley, I wasn't being quite truthful when I said that Ellen wished me to speak to you.'

'Oh?'

'The fact is, *I* wished to speak to you in private about your friend, Miss Hepworth.'

Amanda stopped dead. 'Diana?'

'Yes. More specifically, about her relationship with Lord Durling.' As Amanda's blue eyes widened, Edward said, 'You do not like speaking of it?'

'It is not a question of liking or disliking it. I am merely surprised that you would think to ask me.'

'I ask because I know that you and Miss Hepworth are friends, and because there is something I would very much like to know about her.'

Amanda cautiously inclined her head. 'What would you have me tell you?'

'Is she greatly changed from the person she was four years ago?'

Amanda's brows lifted. 'That is a rather peculiar question, my lord.'

'Perhaps, but I have good reason for asking. I met Lord Durling in my club last night,' Edward told her. 'And because I was curious, I asked him what happened between him and Miss Hepworth. Specifically, what her reasons were for breaking off their engagement.'

'And did he tell you?'

'He told me something.'

'But you did not believe him.'

Edward decided the situation warranted his being honest. 'No, though I have no compelling reason not to believe him.'

Amanda didn't look at him as she said, 'Have you asked Diana the same question?'

'I didn't think there would be any point.' Edward stooped to pick up a bright green caterpillar that was inching its way into the middle of the path. 'From what I gather, she told no one, other than Lord Durling, what her reasons for breaking off their engagement were. And by saying nothing, she has allowed society to believe whatever they want.' Edward let the caterpillar wriggle in his palm before setting it safely back in the garden. 'I simply thought that as her friend, you might have heard her side of the story.'

Amanda shook her head. 'Diana did not confide her reasons for not wishing to go through with the marriage, Lord Garthdale, and she returned to the country very soon after ending it. But I will tell you this. It wouldn't have been because she was desirous of making a better match.'

Edward slowed. 'Yet that is what Lord Durling would have people believe.'

'Perhaps, but it isn't the truth.' Amanda fixed her gaze on his face. 'Tell me, Lord Garthdale, why do you want to know if Diana is a different person today than she was four years ago?'

'Because the lady I've come to know doesn't sound like the lady who jilted Lord Durling.'

Amanda looked relieved. 'I am very glad to hear you say that.'

He lifted his shoulders in a shrug. 'I can say nothing else. A woman who would call off her wedding the day before it was to have taken place, and for the kind of reasons given by Lord Durling, speaks of someone self-centred and without feeling. The lady with whom I am acquainted is neither.'

'Exactly,' Amanda said quietly. 'Diana would never do anything to hurt someone she cared about. And I know for a fact that she cared deeply for Lord Durling.'

Edward's eyes were dark on hers. 'So you're saying there's more to this than Durling's letting on.'

'I am saying,' Amanda said carefully, 'that Diana would not have ended the engagement unless she'd had a very good reason for doing so.'

Edward weighed her answer, then carefully phrased his next question. 'Miss Townley, if Ellen were your sister, would you wish to see her marry Lord Durling?'

Two spots of colour appeared in Amanda's cheeks. 'My lord, I really could not say—'

'Amanda, please,' Edward said. 'I promise that whatever passes between us today will go no further, but if there is something about Lord Durling I need to know, I beg you to tell me now, before it is too late.'

He saw the turmoil in her eyes, sensed the inner battle she was waging, and knew he had his answer. 'I see. So there is something about him.'

'Go to Diana, my lord,' Amanda implored. 'Ask her what you've asked me. I feel sure that if you were to speak to her, she would tell you what really happened.'

Edward looked at her and saw the concern in her eyes. 'Yes, perhaps that's what I'll do.' He touched her cheek in a friendly, consoling gesture. 'Don't worry, Amanda, everything is going to be fine. I give you my word.'

He saw her back to the drawing room, and then took his leave. But as he climbed into the carriage and told the driver to take him to George Street, Edward was more convinced than ever that there was more to this than met the eye. And he was determined that this time when he left Diana Hepworth, he would have *all* the answers he needed.

Edward's arrival came as a shock to Diana. Not because she didn't wish to see him, but because she had no expectation of doing so. Why would he bother to call again? Her aunt had already told him she had nothing to say, and Diana certainly didn't believe it was because he had any personal interest in her. As far as she was concerned, he'd made his feelings—or lack thereof—quite clear.

But when he asked her to join him for a drive, and didn't include her aunt or Phoebe in the invitation, Diana began to wonder if something truly was amiss.

To her surprise, he did not head for Hyde Park, but set the horses in a different direction all together. 'I hope you don't mind, but I prefer to avoid the park at this time of day,' he said briefly.

Diana shook her head. 'I don't mind. At this time of day, one only goes there to see or be seen, and I have no wish to do either.'

He flicked a glance in her direction. 'Are you still so uncomfortable in society?'

'Somewhat. Though most people seem to have forgotten what happened, there are those who cling to it, and I do not like being made to feel of so little consequence.'

'I wonder at your not making more of it at the time,' Edward said, his attention back on the road. 'You could have said *something* in your own defence. By saying nothing, you let people believe what Lord Durling said about you.'

'Why would I not let them believe it?'

'Because I question how much of it is true.' Edward turned and met her eyes with a boldness that took her breath away. 'You confuse me,

Miss Hepworth. You are painted in one way by society, but in a very different way by your family and friends.'

'Perhaps I tailor my face to fit my audience.'

'That crossed my mind, but I don't believe you're the type. From what little I know, I would say you would behave exactly the same way with me as you would with anyone else.'

'It could be that your assessment of my character is at fault,' Diana pointed out, not sure why she felt the need to play the devil's advocate. 'Sometimes it is impossible to accurately judge a person's character on such brief acquaintance.'

'True, but some people are more transparent than others, and I have always believed myself to be an excellent judge of character.'

He was watching her with an expression that made it difficult for Diana to breathe, and just for a moment, he was the man she rode with in the mornings; a man who spoke to her with softness in his voice and amusement in his eyes. It struck such a deep chord within her that she had to look away.

'I've upset you,' he said.

'No. I was just…thinking about something.' But she didn't say anything more, and let the silence stretch between them, using it to collect her thoughts and to prepare herself for whatever was to come.

'Is your cousin enjoying London?' Edward asked, changing the subject.

Glad for it, Diana nodded. 'Yes, very much. But then, Phoebe is not terribly difficult to please. She is such a dear girl, and finds this all very exciting.'

'Has she professed herself in love yet?'

'She does seem to have developed a partiality for one young man.'

'And is he a suitable candidate for her hand?'

Diana smiled. 'My aunt believes him to be, though he is not as well situated as she would like. And she is, of course, concerned that Phoebe not display too much fondness for him. After all, it is still early in the Season, and she is sure to meet other gentlemen who will attempt to win her heart, and for whom she may feel a greater affection.'

'I take it the gentleman is not possessed of fortune or title?'

Diana glanced down at her hands, rubbing the thumb of one into the gloved palm of the other. 'He is the younger son of a good family, and is, at present, serving in the militia. When he resigns his commission, he is hopeful of securing a living within the church.'

'The church?' Edward frowned. 'Would your cousin enjoy life as a clergyman's wife?'

Diana smiled. 'Phoebe will be happy wherever she is, as long as she loves her husband and he loves her. And I think she would do well as a clergyman's wife. Her disposition is such that she would soon become a favourite with his parishioners, and it goes without saying that she would be a wonderful support to him.'

'Would *you* support such an alliance?'

A slight frown furrowed Diana's brow. 'If they loved each other, why would I not?'

'Because you have just said that your aunt would rather see her settled with someone in a position to offer her more in the way of material possessions. Would you not like to see your cousin as mistress of a fine house, with servants to attend her, and carriages to take her wherever she wished to go?'

Forcefully reminded that she had once thought such things important, Diana shook her head. 'Not if it comes at the expense of love. Phoebe would never be happy with a man for whom she could not feel the greatest love and admiration.'

'So you would not counsel her to seek one at the expense of the other?'

'Never!'

Edward returned his eyes to the road. 'Tell me, Miss Hepworth, were your parents happily married?'

Diana thought it a strange question, but having no reason not to answer it, said, 'My parents lived for one another, Lord Garthdale. They weren't happy unless they were together, which was of great consolation to me when they died.'

'It was?'

'Yes, because as heartbreaking as it was for me to lose both of them at once, it would have been even more tragic to see one of them forced to live on without the other. I suspect it would have been a half-life at best.'

Edward was silent for a long time. So long, that Diana turned to look at him. 'Have I said something wrong, my lord?'

'Not at all.' He turned his head and met her questioning glance. 'You have merely added to the confusion surrounding who you really are.'

Diana didn't attempt to answer. To do so would have only put her in the position of making excuses for herself, and she had no intention of doing that, even for him. So she changed the subject to one neither of them could take personally. 'Tell me, Lord Garthdale, what are your feelings with regard to the establishment of schools for the education of your tenants' children?'

The look on his face was clear indication of his surprise. 'I have always believed it to be an excellent idea, Miss Hepworth. Ignorance fosters ignorance, and I believe it is the nature of all people to wish to learn, especially children, who are generally more receptive to education than adults.'

'However, it is often the cost of such education that prevents these children from receiving such benefits, or the fact that their parents need them to help work the farms, isn't that right?'

'Yes.'

'So how would you go about putting forward a solution to help your own workers cope with the expense and the lost time?'

Not expecting such concerns to be of interest to her, Edward took pleasure in outlining the plans he had been discussing with his steward for the implementation of just such a system. He explained why he felt the need to educate children was of such importance, and how receptive, and indeed eager, a few of his tenants were at the idea.

And for every comment he made, Diana gave him an intelligent and well thought-out reply. Her passionate belief in helping those less fortunate than herself struck a chord within him, and Edward was impressed by the agility of her mind and her willingness to voice her opinions. She could—and would—entertain ideas she hadn't considered in the past, once the merits of them were made known to her, and she was happy to debate the popular opinions of the day when it came to social structure and class hierarchy. Her sense of humour was equal to his, and Edward found himself laughing with her over something he was sure most other young ladies would not have found in the least amusing.

In fact, the more time he spent with Diana, the more he was reminded of Jenny. They had the same dry wit, the same appreciation for life, and the same willingness to argue a point with zeal and conviction. Indeed, now having made the connection in his mind, Edward wondered if that wasn't the association he had been trying to establish the first time he'd seen Diana. He'd thought that she reminded him of someone, and now he knew who that someone was. Because, when he thought about it, the similarities were striking. Both Diana and Jenny were tall and slim, and they were remarkably alike in build. Both had dark hair, though Jenny favoured the wearing of hers in a snood, while Diana liked hers drawn up and fastened high on her head. She also wasn't compelled to wear a veil the way Jenny was, and Edward had to admit, he enjoyed looking at her.

Perhaps because they were so pleasurably occupied with talk of the future, Edward didn't spend time talking to her about her past. He didn't raise the subject of her relationship with Lord Durling as he'd planned, or ask her to explain her reasons for breaking if off, because he realised, with some surprise, that he was reluctant to be the one to bring the shadows back to her eyes. For that reason, he purposely kept the conversation to subjects of interest to both of them.

But as he was returning home after leaving Diana at George Street, Edward also had to admit that he was no further ahead than when he'd started out. He was certainly no wiser as to why Diana and her family had called on his mother, or what they had intended to say. He had asked her questions, but not the ones he'd planned on asking, and the answers he had received were not at all in keeping with what he'd expected to hear.

The only thing he was sure of was that someone wasn't telling the truth. Diana Hepworth was nothing like Lord Durling made her out to be. She wasn't egocentric or malicious, nor was she interested in bettering herself at the expense of others. She cared about people too much. And knowing all that, Edward could find no reason for Lord Durling to speak of her the way he had.

Unless it was Lord Durling himself who had something to hide.

Not long after Diana returned from her drive with Edward, Phoebe returned from hers with Captain Wetherby. She waltzed into the room with her pretty cheeks flushed and her eyes glowing like emeralds. 'Oh, good, I'm so glad you are both here, I was hoping to tell you all about my afternoon.'

'Did you enjoy your drive with Captain Wetherby?' Mrs Mitchell enquired.

'Very much! We went to Hyde Park, and I am quite sure half of society was there.'

Reminded that those were the very reasons for Edward's wishing to avoid it, Diana only smiled.

'But do you know what the best part was?' Phoebe asked, sitting down. 'Being able to talk to him quietly, just the two of us. There are always people around when we are at an assembly or ball, but today I had him all to myself!'

Mrs Mitchell frowned. 'I hope you did not let him see how pleased you were by the fact.'

'Of course not! You would have been very proud of me, Aunt Isabel. I was suitably reserved and didn't giggle or blush too much, even though we did have the most interesting conversations. He told me all about his family in Kent, and about growing up there. I think I should like to visit it one day, so prettily did he describe it.'

'Kent is very pretty,' Mrs Mitchell agreed, glancing with amusement at Diana. 'What else did Captain Wetherby say?'

'That he will be sorry when his time with his regiment is over, but that he is looking forward to taking up the living at…oh, now, where did he say it was to be? Dear me, I have completely forgotten. But I do think he will be good at it. He is such a kind, gentle man, for all his dashing appearance. I think he is the most wonderful gentleman in all London!'

Mrs Mitchell chuckled. 'How convenient, since Diana told me you were looking to fall in love with just such a man.'

Phoebe's face warmed. 'I don't know that I am in love with him. I like him very much, of course, but…' She stopped, bit her lip, then gazed at her aunt. 'Perhaps I do love him, if this shortness of breath and light-headed feeling I get whenever he's near is any indication.'

'Dear me. Shortness of breath and light-headed, is it?' Mrs Mitchell had trouble hiding her smile. 'I dare say those are fairly significant signs. Tell me, has the young man given you any indication of *his* feelings, since we are reasonably assured of yours?'

'He did say he thought I was the prettiest girl in London,' Phoebe said, a soft bloom of colour appearing in her cheeks. 'And that he's never felt…quite this way about anyone before—'

She broke off again, prompting Mrs Mitchell to say, 'Well, if that's the way of it, I dare say a proposal could be in the offing. The question is, will you accept him, Phoebe? He is, after all, a younger son, and, as a clergyman, he won't even have a house of his own. You will be expected to live in whatever establishment is provided for him.'

'I should be happy to live wherever he does,' Phoebe said softly, 'and I really don't care that he doesn't have a title. I should rather see him doing work he loves than work he is obligated to do as a result of his position.'

Mrs Mitchell nodded. 'I think you will do very well with your handsome captain, my dear. And if that is to be the way of it, I am happy for you. He will, of course, have to speak to your father, but it's likely in the interim that he will approach me. Best I know what to say when he does.'

Diana attended the Oglethorpes' reception that evening with mixed emotions. On the one hand, she was delighted that Phoebe had found a gentleman with whom she wished to make her future, and that he seemed to share her feelings, but on the other hand it meant that her time in London was drawing to a close and that she would soon be bidding farewell to Edward.

That left her feeling decidedly dejected, and she realised her aunt was right. It was going to be very difficult to leave him. It was hard to believe they had achieved such a closeness of spirit after such a short time together.

But, leave him she must, because she had led him down a merry path. There was little chance of his forgiving her for that.

'You look despondent, Diana. Not happy about being back in London?' said a familiar, unwelcome voice.

Diana tensed, and steeled herself to turn around. 'Lord Durling.'

'It's all right, you needn't look so worried,' he assured her. 'I am not about to cause a scene. But I thought it important that we talk.'

'I have nothing to say to you,' Diana said coldly. 'You made your feelings perfectly clear the last time.'

'Ah, but since then I've had a chat with my future brother-in-law, and it seems he is suspicious of your reasons for calling upon his mother.'

'Did he say I gave him cause to be suspicious?'

'Not you, per se, but he was curious about his mother's reaction to you. I suppose he wondered why she would take you in such dislike.'

'I should think the fact of our previous engagement would be reason enough.'

'Perhaps,' Durling allowed. 'He did say that neither you nor your aunt said a word about me.'

'Then what reason can you have for speaking to me now?'

His lip curled unpleasantly. 'It never hurts to ensure that we still have an understanding.'

She wanted to lash out at him. To say something that would wipe the smile from his face and rattle his confidence as badly as he had rattled hers. But Diana knew that he would always have the upper hand. His position in society was his assurance of that. 'Your threats are unnecessary, Lord Durling. I will not risk Phoebe's chances of making a successful marriage.'

'I didn't think so.' He smiled, but it was merely a movement of his lips. 'I understand there is talk of young Wetherby offering for her. You must be happy with the arrangement.'

Refusing to give anything away, Diana said only, 'It is too early to say. Nothing has been declared between them yet.'

'Perhaps not, but if it is what she wants, I am sure she will win him. She is a sweet child.'

Dislike flared into alarm. 'How do you know that? Have you spoken to her?'

'I had no need to,' Durling said, as his eyes drifted towards the dance floor. 'Ellen speaks of her very often.' He stepped back and bowed with mocking formality. 'Good evening, Diana.'

She didn't bid him farewell. Turning quickly, she left the room, knowing that anger and frustration had brought an unbecoming flush to her cheeks.

Why couldn't he leave her alone? Why did he have to keep plaguing her like this? Hadn't he caused enough havoc in her life? Hadn't she earned the right to live a peaceful, uneventful life?

'Miss Hepworth, are you all right?'

Edward!

Diana slowed, took a breath, and turned around. 'I am well, my lord, thank you.'

'You don't look it.' He took a step closer. 'In fact, you look quite flushed. No doubt as a result of your conversation with Lord Durling.'

Diana's eyes flew up to his, unaware that her brief interlude with the man had been observed. 'You are mistaken, Lord Garthdale. Lord Durling said nothing to upset me. He was merely asking after my cousin.'

'I wasn't aware that he knew Miss Lowden.'

'He knows of her, as he does all my family.'

'So you are able to talk civilly to one another?'

'For the most part,' Diana said. Edward didn't need to know that it took every ounce of willpower she possessed not to scream at the man.

A passing acquaintance hailed Edward, and then, at the sound of a country dance starting up, Edward sighed. 'Forgive me, Miss Hepworth, I fear my presence is required in the ballroom.'

Diana inclined her head. 'Of course. Pray do not allow me to detain you.' She gave him a cool smile and walked away, aware that her feelings of jealousy and disappointment were completely irrational. *He wouldn't have been in such a hurry to leave had you been Jenny*, the voice said. *He would have stayed and laughed, and most likely have asked you to dance.*

Diana pushed the unwelcome thoughts aside. It was utterly ridiculous, of course, because she *was* Jenny. But Edward didn't know that. And even though she sensed a softening in his attitude towards her, he still made no move to encourage her or to lead her to believe he held her in any particular regard. But her feelings for him were getting stronger all the time. Every day it grew harder to see him and to conceal the depth of her affection.

Which meant there was only one thing she could do. She would have to go away. Her time with Edward had been too precious to end with memories of dishonesty. If he thought about her in the future, she wanted it to be with kindness. But every time she appeared in the park as Jenny now, she was furthering a deceit that would ensure Edward's enmity if he should ever stumble upon the truth of it. He might even be inclined to believe the tales Lord Durling had told about her, and that would be unbearable. If he had to have bad feelings about one of them, Diana didn't want it to be Jenny—which only left her one choice.

It was time to bring it to an end. For the good of everyone involved, Jenny would have to disappear.

Chapter Fourteen

Though the sun shone bright the next morning, Diana felt as though a cloud followed her all the way to Hyde Park. Another night spent rolling in her bed hadn't changed her mind. Her resolve was as firm now as it had been yesterday.

Today would be the last time she rode with Edward. There was nothing to gain by prolonging their association now. Every time she saw him, she thought about Lady Ellen, and every time she thought about Lady Ellen, Diana thought about Phoebe, and what manner of retribution Lord Durling's anger would take.

If Diana had believed there was some way of sparing Phoebe his wrath, she might have been more hopeful, but nothing she came up with seemed guaranteed to work. She'd thought about going to Captain Wetherby and telling him what was going on, but who could say whether or not he would believe her? Were his feelings for Phoebe strong enough that he would ignore any stories he might hear? Would he discard them out of hand, seeing them as the lies they so obviously were?

He might, but that wasn't to say that it would stop there. Even if the marriage took place, who was to say that Lord Durling wouldn't make trouble for Phoebe in her new role? Gossip was a cruel and hurtful thing, and seldom did people stop to find out whether or not it was true. Phoebe's reputation as a clergyman's wife could be called into question, and that in turn could impact her marriage, and her husband's standing in the community.

Was she willing to carry the weight of that on her shoulders too?

The simple answer was no, and because of that, Diana also knew that her decision to bring this to an end as quickly as possible was the right one.

She wouldn't tell Edward that today was the last time he would see her, because he might try to persuade her to stay. Lord knew her willpower ran dangerously low when he was near and he might say something she was better off not hearing. If she left without saying goodbye, he wouldn't have the chance.

Then, once Phoebe received her proposal, Diana Hepworth would disappear too. She would go back to Whitley, and her time with Edward would become a wonderful memory that she would cherish until her dying day.

Diana was so immersed in her thoughts that it was a few minutes before she realised that she was still alone in the park. She pulled the mare to a halt, and gazed around, wondering if Edward had decided to take another path. But there were few riders about, and none of them resembled Edward. Had he decided not to come?

Had he found out about her?

A hundred possibilities flashed through Diana's mind—each one worse than the last—which accounted for the fact that when she did finally hear the big bay hunter approaching, she had to take extra care to control the tremor in her voice. 'Edward! I thought you weren't coming.'

He pulled up on the reins and brought Titan to a prancing halt. 'Forgive me, Jenny, but I received a most unusual letter before I left, and it served to delay my departure.'

She heard the concern in his voice. 'Nothing serious, I hope?'

'I don't know. The sender of the note is a young lady whom I do not know well, but whose integrity I have no reason to doubt. The question is, do I respond to it?'

'Does the letter demand a response?'

'It does, in that she has asked to meet with me regarding a matter of considerable importance.'

'Then why would you not, if you have no reason to doubt her?'

Edward pressed his lips together, as though trying to decide what to do. 'I haven't kept you informed of this situation, Jenny, because I didn't want it infringing upon our time together. But with the arrival of this note, I admit, I would welcome your opinion. Since you have no involvement in it, perhaps you can have a clearer mind about it than I.'

'Is it a personal matter?' Diana enquired cautiously.

'It involves my family, and though I don't know precisely how, I feel it could have repercussions for my sister.'

Diana felt the blood leave her face. ...*could have repercussions for my sister.* Had he learned something about Lord Durling?

'Forgive my curiosity,' Diana said slowly, 'but who is the letter from?'

'A young lady new to town. I doubt you would know her.'

'No, but it is possible my aunt might.' Suddenly, Diana very much wanted to know who the mysterious letter was from. 'She is quite well connected in society circles.'

Edward sighed. 'Then I suppose there is a chance. The lady who sent me the note is a Miss Phoebe Lowden.'

Diana couldn't speak. *Phoebe had sent him a letter?* What in heaven's name was the child thinking of? Why would she do something so foolish? And what kind of message did her letter contain?

Striving for a voice that didn't quaver, Diana said, 'Perhaps it would be best if you…told me what was going on.'

'There's really not much to tell,' Edward said, but he told her what he could of the situation, including a brief description of Diana Hepworth, her past relationship with Lord Durling, and the fact that the man was now engaged to marry his sister.

'I suspected there was something Mrs Mitchell wanted to tell me,' Edward said, 'but when

I called on her, she refused to say anything. I'm wondering if the younger girl knows what she wanted to say, and felt it was important enough to get in touch with me.'

Diana nervously licked her lips. 'Did Miss Lowden say when she wished to see you?'

'She asked that I call at three o'clock today. At her aunt's house.'

Three o'clock. The time her aunt had arranged to go out and meet a friend for tea, and that she had agreed to meet Amanda to go shopping, Diana realised. An outing Phoebe had declined to join, which meant she had fully intended to see Edward when the house was empty. And with sudden clarity, Diana knew why.

She was going to tell him the truth about Lord Durling!

It was the only explanation. Phoebe was going to tell Edward why Diana had ended her engagement to Lord Durling, because she knew that the *only* reason Diana wouldn't say anything was in an effort to protect her. So Phoebe was taking the decision out of her hands in the hopes of preventing Ellen's marriage. She was going to tell Edward what Lord Durling had done, and risk the consequences.

What a stubbornly disobedient—and incredibly valiant—child!

'Do you think I should meet with her?' Edward asked.

No! Diana wanted to shout, wanting to do anything that would prevent him from finding out the truth. But he had asked for her help. How could she not give it to him?

'Of course you should meet with her,' Diana said, knowing it was the only logical answer. 'It's obvious the young lady has something of importance to tell you.'

'But why would *she* come to me with this, rather than Miss Hepworth?'

'Perhaps Miss Hepworth is not in possession of the same information,' Diana said, still finding it strange to be spoken of as though she wasn't present.

Edward shook his head. 'It doesn't make sense that the younger girl would know something the older one did not, especially if this *is* in regard to Lord Durling and his engagement to Miss Hepworth.'

Diana squirmed a little in the saddle. What could she say that would not jeopardise her position? She had to remember that she was hearing this as a stranger, and respond to it as such.

'Is it possible Miss Hepworth doesn't know her cousin sent you a letter?'

Edward's eyes narrowed. 'You're suggesting the younger girl may wish to tell me something the older one wouldn't approve of my hearing?' He thought on that a moment. 'That would make sense. The two girls are very close. If Miss Hepworth isn't there when I arrive, I'll know Miss Lowden planned it that way.'

Diana took a slow, deep breath, aware that she was starting to feel quite ill. She was now openly playing a role. She was pretending not to know Diana Hepworth, blatantly denying any knowledge of what Edward was talking about, and thereby plunging herself deeper into the abyss of lies and deceit. There wasn't a hope of extricating herself with a shred of honour now.

'Whatever you do in regard to Miss Hepworth and her cousin, Edward, I know it will be the right thing,' Diana said, resting her hand lightly on his arm. She was so close to him, she could smell the fragrance of his soap, mingling with his own masculine scent, and she knew she would never forget him. 'I will only say that you must let your conscience be your guide. Things are not always as they seem, and sometimes it is good to hear what others have to say.'

'I shall do what I feel best, of course, but…why do I feel as though you're saying goodbye, Jenny?'

She could feel the intensity of his gaze on her face, and knew she couldn't lie. 'Because I am. We knew the time would come when I would have to go home.'

'But not after so short a time. Surely it needn't be so soon.'

'I am anxious to get back to my life,' Diana said, keeping her voice light. 'Anxious to get back to Wh…my home.' Dear heavens, she'd nearly given herself away! 'And while I have enjoyed my brief stay in London, it is not where I am truly comfortable.'

He didn't seem to know what to say—likely because he knew there was nothing he could say. And, sensing that, Diana knew it was best she leave now. It was too hard to see him like this; too heartbreaking to know that she was the one responsible for his sadness. Because she knew, as he did, that when she rode away today, it would be over for good.

'I asked you this once to no avail, Jenny, but I am going to ask you again,' Edward said quietly. 'Will you not raise your veil for me? Will you not let me see your face just once before you go?'

Diana felt tears sting her eyes. 'I think the mystery of the veil has bewitched you, Edward. My face is nothing out of the ordinary.'

'Perhaps, but it is not only the face of the lady that makes her special.' He nudged Titan closer, and reached for her hand. 'It is the lady herself, and everything about her.' To her surprise, he unfastened her glove and slipped it off. Then, raising her hand to his lips, he turned it over so that the palm was up, and pressed a tender kiss into it.

Diana could have wept. The gesture was so intimate that her entire body trembled. Her heart quickened as he raised his eyes to hers, and she saw in them the emotions he wasn't even trying to hide. But nothing could have prepared her for his next words.

'Marry me, Jenny.'

She gasped, disbelieving. 'Marry you!'

'Yes. I can procure a licence within a matter of days. All I need is your name—your real name—and a few other particulars.'

'But your family…your mother—'

'We needn't tell them until it's done. Once you are my wife, no one will dare try to come between us.'

His *wife*!

It was so tempting that Diana had to press her lips together to keep from shouting, 'Yes!' Edward wanted to marry her! He had *asked* her to marry him; without any knowledge of who she was, and fully aware that she was keeping something from him, and for one long, foolish moment, Diana was tempted to do it. Tempted to throw caution to the wind, and to be irresponsible for once in her life.

But she couldn't. She couldn't deceive him like that. Not when there was so much that needed to be said. So much that had to be explained. 'I can't, Edward.'

'Yes, Jenny, you can. I don't care what you've done, or what people say about you. I want you to be my wife. Tell me you feel the same,' he whispered fervently. 'Tell me something within you isn't begging you to say yes, and to say to hell with the consequences!'

He was so close to the truth that Diana felt as though he had reached inside her soul and dragged it out. 'I *do* want to, Edward, but you must know I can't.'

'No, not that you can't, Jenny, that you *won't*. There's a world of difference between the two. However, I also know there's no point in my trying to force you to marry me because this ultimately has to be your decision. And so, I'm willing to give you the time you need. I shall wait for your answer for as long as it takes.'

'Edward—'

'I shall wait,' he continued softly, 'until you tell me you no longer wish me to wait. Until then, there will be no other woman in my life.'

Diana closed her eyes, fighting back tears. She was overwhelmed, both by the depth of his love, and by what he was prepared to do for her. But it was asking too much. 'You mustn't wait, Edward. It is not fair—'

'What's not fair is not having had the chance to court you,' he said softly. 'What's not fair was never being given the chance to get to know you the way I wanted to.'

'But you owe it to your family to choose a wife.'

'I have chosen a wife. She just hasn't chosen me.' He slid the glove back on to her hand, and fastened the buttons with all the care of a lady's maid. 'I shall continue to ride here every morning, as I do now. If you decide you want to be with me, you have only to join me. If you decide you do not, send me your veil.'

Diana blinked. 'My veil?'

'Yes. That will be the sign that you no longer wish to see me, and that it is over between us. Until I receive that, there won't be anyone else in my life. Know that for the truth, Jenny,' he said. 'And now go, and may the days until we see each other again not be long.'

It was Edward who rode away first—but this time, Diana didn't even try to be brave. She didn't bother pretending that she wasn't fighting to hold on to every last sight of him. She watched him until he disappeared, hardly able to believe that he had asked her to marry him— and that she had actually let him go.

Immediately upon arriving home, Diana went in search of Phoebe. She found the girl in the breakfast parlour, staring morosely into her cup. 'Phoebe, you and I need to have a chat,' Diana said without preamble.

Phoebe looked up, startled by the brusqueness in her cousin's voice. 'Diana. Whatever is the matter?'

Diana gave the servant a curt nod, and waited for him to leave before saying, 'Why did you send Lord Garthdale a note saying that you wished to see him?'

Phoebe's face went white. 'How did you find out?'

'Never mind how I found out, what on earth possessed you to do such a foolish thing?'

'But how—?'

'Phoebe!'

'Oh, all right. I had to send it!' Phoebe said, her bottom lip quivering. 'I knew you would not say anything to him, and I couldn't let you put my welfare before Lady Ellen's.'

'But I explained what was at risk for you—'

'Yes, but what is that compared to what is at risk for Lady Ellen?' Phoebe cried. 'I had a choice to make too, Diana. A choice as to whether or not Lady Ellen learned the truth about Lord Durling while she still had time to do something about it. And I realised I couldn't live with the knowledge that she might be allowed to suffer, just so that I could make a good marriage. What enjoyment could I find in mine, knowing what she had to look forward to in hers?'

'Oh, Phoebe.' Diana pulled out a chair and sat down. 'I cannot fault you for your consideration of your friend, but if we say something to Lady Ellen or her family and the wedding does not take place, you *will* be made to suffer.

Lord Durling will destroy whatever chance you have of finding any kind of happiness with Captain Wetherby.'

Phoebe took a deep breath. 'If Captain Wetherby would believe such things of me, he is not worthy of my affection in the first place.'

'But he won't know he's hearing lies!'

'He will if he comes to me and asks me for the truth. And if he loves me, that is what he will do. Lady Ellen is my friend, Diana, and I won't see her hurt. Not when I have the power to prevent it.'

Diana dropped her head on Phoebe's shoulder. 'I don't wish to see her hurt either, dearest, but when I think what you stand to lose—'

'Let me do this, Diana. Please. Let me speak to Lord Garthdale this afternoon. We don't even know that he *will* believe me, but I have to try.'

Diana sighed. 'Oh, Phoebe. You are truly a good soul. And if this is really how you feel, I won't try to stop you. But your involvement ends here.' Diana sat up. 'If Lord Garthdale is to be told the truth, it will not be by you.'

'But you just said—'

'I said that I wouldn't speak to him in an effort to spare you. But if you are determined to jeopardise your future, it is only right that *I* be the one to deal with Lord Garthdale. I shall try to keep you out of it; if anyone asks, it was I who spoke out of turn.' She gave Phoebe a wan smile. 'With any luck, that may buy us a little time.'

The knowledge that she was to see Lord Garthdale that afternoon did not make Diana happy, partly because she knew it would be an emotionally draining experience, and partly because she was convinced that by telling him the truth, she was condemning Phoebe's relationship with Captain Wetherby to failure.

Diana was just as glad her aunt was out visiting a friend. While she would have welcomed her advice, she wasn't sure she was up to telling her what she was about to do. Somehow it seemed easier to face the fire alone.

Shortly after noon, Diana went to the dining room, but found she could not eat. Frustrated, she went back to the drawing room and began to pace as she went over everything she had to tell Edward. She was still pacing when Jiggins announced the arrival of Miss Townley twenty-five minutes later.

Diana gasped. Amanda! She had completely forgotten that the two of them were to have gone shopping. And Edward was due to arrive in less than fifteen minutes!

'Thank you, Jiggins, would you show Miss Townley up?'

As the butler withdrew, Diana pondered what she could offer her friend in the way of an excuse. Fortunately, she had no need to say anything. Amanda took one look at her face and said, 'What's wrong, Diana?'

'You mean in that I am not dressed to go out shopping with you?'

'No, I mean in that you look as though you've had the most dreadful news and can't think whether or not to tell me.'

Diana grimaced. 'You have become a great deal more astute than you were four years ago, Amanda. Either that, or I am not as skilled at hiding my emotions as I thought I was. But I do owe you an apology. I completely forgot that we were to have gone shopping this afternoon.'

'Never mind the shopping,' Amanda said, looking at her closely. 'What's happened? I can tell you're extremely upset about something.'

'I am, but I'm not sure I can talk about it right now. It is a rather complicated situation.'

'Does it concern you?'

'Yes. And others, by virtue of their relation-ship to me.'

'I see.' Amanda went quiet, frowning as she fumbled with her reticule. 'Perhaps it is just as well we do not go shopping. I, too, have some-thing I have been wanting to talk to you about, but wasn't sure whether or not I should.'

Diana glanced at her in concern. 'Oh, Amanda, I'm so sorry, I have been so wrapped up in my own affairs, I didn't realise.' She sat down beside her friend. 'It has nothing to do with Lord Eastcliffe, I hope?'

'Heavens, no,' Amanda assured her. 'Every-thing is proceeding wonderfully in that regard. But…there is something I've wanted to tell you ever since you arrived in London. And after Lord Garthdale's visit yesterday—'

'Lord Garthdale came to see you?'

Amanda nodded. 'He said he wanted to hear how the wedding plans were progressing, but that wasn't really his intent. He had something particular to ask me.'

'What about?'

Amanda raised soft blue eyes to Diana's face. 'About you and your relationship with Lord Durling.'

Diana felt her mouth go dry. 'What did he want to know?'

'Before I tell you that—' Amanda stopped, and bit her lip. 'Remember the night of my party, when I was going to tell you why I stopped writing?'

'Yes, of course.'

'Well, it wasn't because Mama asked me to stop. After I came back from spending the winter with Aunt Hester, I found myself in the extraordinary position of being courted by several gentlemen, none of whom had so much as looked at me in the past.' She stopped, and took a deep breath. 'One of them was...Lord Durling.'

Chapter Fifteen

'Lord Durling?' A chill crept up Diana's spine. 'Well, this certainly comes as a surprise. How did you feel about him?'

'I am sorry to say that I encouraged him,' Amanda admitted. 'Partly because I found him so utterly charming, and partly because he had never so much as looked at me before.'

Diana nodded, well able to understand the girl's feelings. She too, had been surprised and flattered by Lord Durling's attentions. And, like Amanda, she'd had no reason to revile him. 'But you obviously did not continue to see him,' she said cautiously.

'No, because I found out—' Amanda broke off, and stared at Diana. 'This is very hard to say.'

With a growing sense of alarm, Diana reached for her friend's hand. 'Just say it, Amanda. Whatever it is, I'm willing to listen.'

Amanda nodded, then swallowed hard. 'Well, Lord Durling had arranged a shooting party at Chipping Park,' she began hesitantly. 'I went with my parents, and as most of the guests were known to me, I thought it would be great fun. Lord Durling had been very attentive to me the week before, and I think Mama was expecting him to offer for me that very weekend. The frightening part is, I might have accepted, had it not been for—'

She stopped again and this time, Diana knew that something was very wrong. 'What happened, Amanda?'

Amanda's lips quivered, and suddenly, she reminded Diana of the girl she had been four years ago. 'It was…our first night there. I had left the dining room, intending to go back to my room before joining the other ladies in the drawing room, but became quite disoriented. Chipping Park is a huge place.'

'So I've heard.'

'Well, I obviously went the wrong way and found myself in a long corridor. Realising I had made a mistake, I turned around, but stopped when I heard…voices.'

'Whose voices?'

'Lord Durling's and…a young girl's. I think she must have been brought in from the village to help for the weekend. But she didn't deserve…'

When Amanda closed her eyes, Diana felt her heart begin to race. 'What happened, Amanda? What did you hear?'

'I can hardly say it. Even now, after all this time.' There was a long pause before Amanda opened her eyes and said, 'He *beat* her, Diana. I heard him. And I heard her pleading with him to stop, but he wouldn't. He just slapped her again and said that…if she told anybody what happened, he would find her and—' Amanda broke off, struggling for composure. 'It was the most awful thing I've ever experienced.'

Diana was aware of the room spinning, aware of heat enveloping her, and a thin veil of perspiration misting her skin. 'What happened then?'

'I'm not sure. I was so frightened I didn't know what to do. I was terrified Lord Durling would come out and find me standing in the hallway. I don't think he would have done anything to me, but I didn't want him knowing that I had heard anything of what he'd done to that poor girl.'

'Was she all right?'

'I've no idea. I never saw her again. When I asked the housekeeper if anything had happened to one of the staff, she just looked at me as though I was talking nonsense. The problem was I couldn't identify the girl because I hadn't seen her face, and Lord Durling hadn't said her name. And given the number of staff that was at the house that weekend, I suppose it's possible the housekeeper didn't know who I was talking about. But I tend to think she did and preferred not to say anything. Maybe they all knew what he was like—'

She broke off, but Diana had heard enough. Legs shaking, she got up and walked toward the window.

So, Lord Durling's treatment of her had not been an isolated case. He was an abusive man; one who frequently took his anger out on defenceless women. A man no one would suspect of having such a dark side to him.

Diana pressed her hands to her stomach, aware of the nausea roiling within. Listening to Amanda had brought it all back: the pain, the shock, the horror of finding out that she had been deceived. That the man she had trusted—

the man with whom she had thought herself in love—was a monster.

And in that moment, she knew exactly what she had to do.

'Did you tell anyone else what happened?' Diana said, her back still to her friend.

'I couldn't. I was...too horrified. I'd never known a man beat a woman before. It didn't matter that she was a servant, she was still a woman.'

'What happened after that?'

'I eventually found my way back to the drawing room, but I couldn't stay,' Amanda said quietly. 'I told Mama I wasn't feeling well, and that I wanted to go to my room. I'm sure the way I looked was more than enough proof of my words. Mama sent me immediately to bed and when I said I felt no better in the morning, we returned to London. I didn't see Lord Durling before we left, and I only saw him once in town, and only then to tell him that I no longer wished to see him.'

'He must have been surprised by your sudden change of heart,' Diana said.

'He was, but he didn't call again so he must have known I was serious. Mama was confused, of course, but I couldn't bring myself to tell her what had happened. Thankfully, I met John not long after that.'

'Did you tell him what you'd heard?'

Amanda shook her head. 'I've told no one, Diana. No one…but you.'

Diana was silent for a long time. 'Is that why you stopped writing to me?'

The blush that appeared on Amanda's cheeks was extremely telling. 'I felt I was being disloyal in having seen the man you had once been engaged to marry,' she whispered. 'But after what happened in the country that night, I began to wonder…' She hesitated. 'I was afraid I might have discovered something about him that you either didn't know, or that you didn't want anyone else to know.'

'You mean the fact of his violent nature?'

Amanda looked up. '*Did* you know?'

'Yes. It was the reason I refused to marry him.'

'But you never said anything!'

'Neither did you.'

Amanda blushed. 'How did you find out?' Her voice was hushed, as though she was afraid someone would overhear. 'Did you see him strike one of his servants in London?'

'Not exactly.'

'Did you hear tell of it from one of them?'

Diana looked down at her hands, then raised her eyes to Amanda's. 'Remember the bruises?'

Amanda stared at her, uncomprehending. Then, as what Diana was trying to tell her sunk in, her face went ghostly pale. 'Oh, no! Oh, dear God, *no*! Never say that he did that...to *you*?'

'Yes. And apart from my aunt and my cousin, you are the only one who knows.'

It was too much for Amanda. Her composure shattered and she burst into tears. 'Oh, Diana, why didn't you say something? You never said a word. Not a...w-word.'

'No, because it wasn't something I could talk about at the time.'

'But...I had no idea,' Amanda sobbed, digging in her reticule for a handkerchief. 'When I h-heard the terrible things Lord Durling said about you, about your...reasons for breaking it off, I didn't know what to think. I knew you wouldn't jilt him on a whim. You're n-not like that. And it didn't make sense. He was rich, and handsome, and considered an excellent catch.'

'He still is.' Diana's mouth twisted. 'Lady Garthdale considers her daughter extremely fortunate to be marrying him. But there is something I want to ask you,' Diana said suddenly.

'Something you mentioned when you first came. You said Lord Garthdale came to you, asking questions about me.'

'Yes,' Amanda said, as the tears finally slowed. 'When I was…walking with him in the garden, he asked me what you were like four years ago.'

Diana's mouth went dry. 'What did you tell him?'

'That he should be asking you, rather than me.'

'What did he say to that?'

'I got the distinct impression he was going to.'

Was that why he had called on her and taken her driving the other afternoon? Diana wondered. Had that been the question he'd really wanted to ask? She thought about the meeting she was shortly to have with him, and wondered if he would bring it up.

'Amanda, does Lord Garthdale know that Lord Durling was interested in you?'

'I don't know. Probably not.' Amanda wiped away her tears. 'Lord Durling was not blatant in his attentions to me. I think he felt he should still act the part of the gentleman grieved in the wake of your departure.'

'Amanda, I have to ask you this, and I wouldn't ask unless it was extremely important, but…would you be willing to tell Lord Garthdale what happened that night at Lord Durling's house?'

Amanda paled. 'Oh, Diana! I don't know. I hadn't thought—'

'Your willingness to speak out against him may be the *only* way of preventing Lady Ellen's marriage to him,' Diana said urgently. 'I want to convince Lord Garthdale that Lord Durling is cruel, and I am happy to be the one to do it, but if it's just my word against Lord Durling's, Edw—Lord Garthdale may not believe me. But if you were to lend your support to what I was saying, it might convince him that I was telling the truth and help prevent Lady Ellen's marriage. And I have to do that, Amanda. I have to try!'

Amanda was silent for a long time. She gazed down at the twisted handkerchief in her fingers, pulling at it, then smoothing it out while Diana held her breath, knowing that whatever Amanda said would play a huge part in what she did next.

Finally, she nodded. 'Yes, I'll talk to him if you need me to. I'll do whatever I can to protect

Lady Ellen from that monster,' Amanda said quietly. 'And I don't care what Lord Durling threatens me with. In less than a week, I shall be the Countess of Eastcliffe, and I know that John would never stand for any of Lord Durling's lies!'

'Thank you, Amanda.' Diana smiled and hugged her close. 'I am counting on it!'

Diana vacillated between moments of dread and moments of anticipation as she waited for Edward to arrive. He was scheduled to arrive on the hour, and it was now five minutes to. She was sure she glanced at the clock a hundred times in between.

As painful as it had been to hear Amanda's confession, Diana knew how important it was. Because with the knowledge that Lord Durling had mistreated someone else had come the certainty that she finally had what she needed to challenge his word. If Amanda was willing to tell Edward what she knew about Lord Durling, on top of what Diana intended to tell him, it might be enough to start Edward asking questions, and to put a halt to his sister's marriage.

Finally, the clock struck three. As it was sounding the last chime, Jiggins appeared in the doorway. 'Lord Garthdale, miss.'

'Thank you, Jiggins. Would you be so good as to bring the decanter of sherry and two glasses?'

The butler bowed and withdrew. Diana turned and smiled at the man she loved. A man one part of her had bid goodbye to that very morning. 'Good afternoon, Lord Garthdale.'

'Miss Hepworth.' Edward glanced beyond her and around the room, one eye lifted in an expression of surprise. 'Forgive me, I understood I was to meet Miss Lowden here.'

'You were, but there has been a change in plans. Thank you, Jiggins, that will be all,' Diana said as the butler returned with the sherry. 'Please see that we are not disturbed.'

'Very good, miss.'

After he left, Diana turned to Edward. 'Would you be so good as to pour?'

'As you wish.'

Diana smiled. 'No doubt you find the idea of a lady drinking spirits in the afternoon somewhat unusual, but I think you will understand when I have told you what I must.'

Edward unstopped the decanter. 'You make it sound rather alarming.'

'It is. I venture to say that you will be shocked, surprised, and angry at the conclusion of it.'

He poured out two glasses of sherry and handed one to her. 'All in the space of one short visit?'

'Yes. Because it concerns the welfare of someone you love.'

Diana got his attention with that remark.

'You are without a chaperon, Miss Hepworth,' Edward said. 'Am I to conclude by your aunt's absence that she is unaware of our meeting? Or that she is aware and has given her permission for you to speak to me alone?'

'My aunt is not aware that I am seeing you, Lord Garthdale, though she would not have prevented the meeting taking place. She is not here because she made prior arrangements to visit a friend. Phoebe, of course, knows that I am seeing you, and what I am going to say, but I felt it would be better for everyone concerned if you and I discussed the matter in private.'

'I see.' Edward inclined his head. 'Then I think you'd best tell me what you feel I need to know as quickly as possible.'

Diana took a sip of her sherry, using the time to gather her thoughts. 'The day we called upon your mother, it *was* in the hopes of making certain facts known to her.'

'The ones Mrs Mitchell apparently changed her mind about telling me?'

Diana met his gaze without flinching. 'Yes.'

'Would I be correct in assuming that this has something to do with you and Lord Durling, and the reasons you did not marry him?'

Diana inclined her head. 'I thought it was time to tell you what really happened, since my reasons for breaking off the engagement are very different from what he would have you believe.'

'I fully expected they were, Miss Hepworth.' Edward walked across to the fireplace and rested one arm on the mantle. 'What surprises me is that you waited so long to tell me the truth.'

Diana was careful to hide her surprise. 'How do you know Lord Durling is not?'

'Because you're not the kind of woman to place a higher value on material possessions than you are on love,' he said gently. 'The conversation I had with you regarding your cousin's future was most enlightening. It confirmed my belief that the description I had of you was completely at odds with who you really are. The problem was, I couldn't figure out why you would have broken off the engagement.'

Diana looked away, aware of how critical the next few moments were going to be. 'I was very young when I accepted Lord Durling's proposal, Lord Garthdale. An excuse, perhaps, for not taking the time to know the man better, but given the haste with which most marriages are made, I wonder if anyone is truly aware of the character of the person before they marry them.'

'It is a question I have oft asked myself,' Edward said with a smile. 'Please go on.'

'I believed myself in love with Lord Durling,' Diana said, encouraged by Edward's willingness to listen. 'I was impressed by his charm and good looks, and, I regret to say, pleased by the fact that he was titled, and came from a good family.'

'So far you've said nothing to condemn yourself. Most ladies base their decisions on a similar set of criteria. At least you believed yourself in love with the man.'

Diana's smile was wistful. 'Yes, though given what happened, it is hard for me to recall any feelings of affection I might have had for him.'

'What happened to make you change your mind?'

Diana had never found this easy to say. She didn't now. 'Lord Durling and I had...a difference of opinion over a matter we were discussing. I made the mistake of laughing. He took exception to it, and made his displeasure known in a…physical way.'

Edward's smile faded. 'He molested you?'

'No.' There was no reason to blush, but Diana did. 'He struck me. With sufficient force to… knock me down.'

Edward didn't move. 'Did he say anything to you?'

'Nothing. He just watched me, as though expecting *me* to say something. I didn't, of course, because I was too shocked—' Diana broke off, swallowed hard, and forced herself to go on. 'The next time I saw him was two days before the wedding. I hadn't been able to bring myself to see him before that. I'd tried to rationalise what he had done, but I couldn't. I haven't to this day.'

Edward put his glass on the mantle. 'Did he apologise for his actions? Offer to make amends in some way?'

'No. He acted as though nothing had happened. He accepted no blame for it whatsoever.'

Edward stared at her in disbelief. 'He *denied* having struck you?'

'Yes, and he was shocked when I accused him of such vile behaviour.'

'What did you say to that?'

'I didn't know what to say. I never expected such behaviour from a man I considered a gentleman. A man I believed admirable in every way.' Diana looked down at her glass. 'It was his refusal to address the issue, as much as his striking me, that convinced me I could not go through with the marriage. I no longer trusted him, and I was deathly afraid that if I did marry him, I would have no choice but to stay and take his abuse, or be forced to leave his house in disgrace.'

It was clearly beyond anything Edward had been expecting to hear. 'I don't know what to say. I find it difficult to believe that a man like Durling would behave in such a manner.'

Diana glanced at him. Did that mean he didn't believe her?

'Did you tell anyone what happened?' he went on.

'Only my aunt. I was seventeen, Lord Garthdale. Not long out of the schoolroom and terribly naïve when it came to the realities of life. I never thought a gentleman would do such a thing—'

'No gentleman *would* do such a thing.' Edward's face hardened. 'I do not claim to know Durling well, but I've heard nothing to support his having a violent disposition. A temper, perhaps, but I myself have one of those. But to consider the man capable of striking an innocent woman, and to feel no regret—' He broke off, a muscle clenching in his jaw. He paced the length of the room twice. 'Did he mark you?'

Surprised, she frowned. 'Does it matter?'

'Surely if there were bruises, it would have indicated abuse of some kind, and lent credence to your story?'

'There were bruises,' Diana said quietly. 'But when I remarked on them to Lord Durling, he suggested I had inflicted them myself. Accidentally, of course. He didn't stoop to say that I had purposely disfigured myself, but he did suggest I may have walked into a door.'

'So even when faced with the evidence of his actions, he denied them?'

'Yes. And in doing so, made me aware of another truth. That being, that if I were to tell anyone what happened, he would most certainly deny it.'

'And that is why you didn't say anything.'

'Partly. And partly because…I was afraid of him.'

Edward was silent for a long time, and knowing he was reviewing everything she'd told him, Diana waited. He was weighing up what he knew of the man against what he knew of her, and deciding whose side he would take.

That was the crux of the matter, Diana realised. Her credibility against that of a peer of the realm's.

'Lord Garthdale,' she said quietly. 'I know I am speaking about a man who may be your friend, and who may soon be a member of your family, but I would not do so unless I believe he presented a genuine risk to your sister's well being. A man capable of hitting a woman once is capable of doing it again, and I know for a *fact* that he has. I am not the only woman Lord Durling has mistreated.'

Edward's eyes narrowed. 'Have you proof of his abuse towards others?'

'Yes, by way of the testimony of a young woman whose word I know and trust.'

'Would you be willing to tell me who she is and what she said?'

Diana turned around and walked back to her chair. 'She was invited to Lord Durling's country house for a shooting party. One evening, having left the dining room and unfortunately becoming disoriented, she chanced to come close to a room where Lord Durling was chastising one of the young maids. Lord Durling wasn't aware that anyone was listening and he beat her most wickedly. If called upon to do so, Amanda Townley will attest to his flagrant brutality.'

Edward's face darkened. 'Amanda!'

'Yes. I am also convinced that certain of Lord Durling's former servants could be persuaded to come forward and tell what they know of him.'

Edward again subsided into silence. Finally, he looked at her, and his eyes were as black as midnight. 'Is this what Miss Lowden intended to tell me?'

'Yes. Phoebe only learned the truth about Lord Durling last night. She was extremely disturbed and felt you had a right to know. She is greatly concerned for your sister's welfare.'

'And you are not?'

Diana understood why there was a chill in his voice. 'I am naturally concerned for Lady Ellen's welfare, my lord. That was why my aunt and I went to see your mother in the first place. We had hoped to make her aware of Lord

Durling's…unsuitability without going into specifics. Unfortunately, Lord Durling learned of
our visit and made me aware that he would not
hesitate to interfere in Phoebe's future if anything was said.' Diana raised her chin. 'I care
about your sister, Lord Garthdale, but I love
Phoebe. She is *my* family. I have to think about
her reputation, because I have no doubt whatsoever that Lord Durling will do everything he
can to ruin her.'

'As he did you?' Edward said softly.

Diana nodded. 'Yes. As he did me.'

His eyes darkened with fury. 'I can scarce
believe it. A man to whom I offered my hand
in friendship. A man who was to have been my
brother-in-law, nothing more than a coward who
would beat and threaten innocent young
women.' He returned to the fireplace, picked up
his glass, and drained the contents. 'The marriage will not take place, of course.'

Diana was so relieved she was forced to grab
the nearest table for support. 'Lady Garthdale
will not be pleased.'

'No, and Ellen will be devastated, but that is
not your problem. I will deal with Lord Durling
myself. You need have no worry that you or
Miss Lowden will ever suffer his threats again.'

Edward set his glass down. 'Thank you, Miss Hepworth. I am forever in your debt for having told me the truth. I know the disclosure was not an easy one, but if it is of any comfort, I dare say your courage has spared a young woman a life of considerable grief.'

Diana smiled, dismayed to find herself blinking back tears. 'That was all I ever wanted, Lord Garthdale.'

'I do believe it is.' He looked at her, and Diana saw something in his eyes that made her catch her breath. 'It would seem, Miss Hepworth, that you are even more admirable than I thought.' He walked towards her, and taking her hand, slowly raised it to his lips. 'You allowed society to castigate you, rather than let the truth of what happened be known, and have maintained that silence for the sake of your cousin.'

'Wherever possible, one endeavours to spare those they love,' she said softly. 'Are you not doing exactly the same for your own family?'

He smiled. 'I suppose I am. But one last question, Miss Hepworth. Did you inform Lord Durling of your wish to end your betrothal in a letter?'

'Absolutely not. I went to see him the day before the wedding was to have taken place and told him I wouldn't marry him. As much as I disliked the man, I would never have resorted to such a cowardly device.'

'I didn't think so,' Edward said. 'And now, if you will excuse me, there are urgent matters to which I must attend.'

'Of course. I hope you will keep me informed as to what happens.'

'If that is what you wish.'

'It is.'

He offered her a bow, and then left, making the room seem suddenly quiet, and a great deal emptier. But it was only as the door closed behind him that Diana sank into the nearest chair and wondered if she truly had saved the day—or just opened the lid to Pandora's box!

Chapter Sixteen

Edward knew that his meeting with Lord Durling would not be pleasant. He had dealt with cowards before and knew how they operated. Knew how, when faced with evidence of their crimes, they offered excuses and tried to twist the truth to suit their own needs. He had no reason to suspect that the man engaged to his sister would act any differently.

For that reason, Edward did not go into the meeting unprepared. Using sources at his disposal, he made careful enquiries into Durling's background, and found out that Diana Hepworth was correct in her suspicions about him. And by the time he sent Durling a note three days later asking him to call, Edward was sure that he had all of his facts in place.

Durling was punctual. He was shown into the library where Edward was sitting at his desk, enjoying a glass of port.

Durling greeted him with his usual affability. 'Evening, Garthdale.'

Edward did not rise. 'Durling.' Now that he knew the nature of the man, he found it hard to be civil. He had only to think of him lifting his hand to Diana to reinforce his feelings of intense dislike. 'I will not waste time with pleasantries. News of a most disturbing nature has reached me, and because it centres on you, I thought a private meeting between the two of us would be the most expedient way of dealing with it.'

Durling's smile faltered. 'What is this about?'

'Your relationship with Diana Hepworth. And the fact that I am no longer willing to allow you to marry my sister as a result of it.'

'What the—?' Dark colour suffused the viscount's face. 'What lies has she told you?'

'I am not inclined to believe they are lies. Miss Hepworth informed me of what really happened between the two of you four years ago.'

'The devil you say! What nonsense did she tell you?'

'That you struck her, and then denied it.'

He looked suitably shocked. 'And you believed her?'

'She put forward a most convincing case.'

Durling snorted. 'Of course she would be convincing, I told you she was vindictive. She wishes me to suffer when the fault for the break-up was entirely hers!'

'Was it?'

'Of course,' he snapped. 'I'm surprised you would believe otherwise!'

Edward had to admit the man was a superb liar. At one time, he might have believed him. But not now. 'I said I'll not waste time, and I won't. Miss Hepworth did not cite only her own history with you, Lord Durling, but advised me of another case of abuse within your household. And to be fair to you, I did take the liberty of checking into the histories of several young women who've left, or were terminated from, your employ. In particular Miss Mary Withers and Miss Flora Delphin.'

Durling flushed. 'You would take the word of two women who were fired for attempting to rob me?'

Edward raised an eyebrow. 'Is that what you accused them of?'

'Indeed, because that's what they were guilty of! They thought that because I was wealthy, I wouldn't miss a trinket or two, but I soon let them know otherwise. I'll not have dishonest servants in my employ! I would have expected a man in your position to understand that.'

'I do. If I find a dishonest servant amongst my staff, I send them on their way. But whether the two young ladies in your employ were guilty of theft or not, it did not give you the right to physically mistreat them.'

Lord Durling's eyes narrowed. 'You would side with them on this?'

Edward shrugged. 'When combined with what Miss Hepworth told me, and the result of my own investigations, yes. Because you may as well know, Miss Hepworth was very reluctant to tell me what you'd done. She is well aware that you could bring considerable influence to bear against her cousin, and that you could ruin her reputation as surely as you ruined Miss Hepworth's. But I would advise you against it,' Edward said softly. 'In fact, if I were you, I would make arrangements to leave London as soon as possible.'

'Leave London?' Durling's eyes widened. 'You jest, surely.'

'Not at all. Because as well as comments from former employees and Miss Hepworth, I have the word of one other person, whom I have known for some time and trust implicitly, that you are guilty of a grievous act of abuse in beating a young girl to within an inch of her life. You are a coward, Lord Durling, and I would have to be mad to allow Ellen to marry you.'

A thin layer of sweat broke out on Durling's face. 'Have you told Ellen of this?'

'No, but I intend to first thing in the morning. I think it only fair that she and the rest of my family know what kind of coward you are, and why I have forbidden the marriage. And, in an effort to clear Miss Hepworth's name, I intend to see that justice is done.'

Durling blanched. 'What do you mean? That you would publicly acknowledge what she says? That you would let it be known...in society?'

'A young woman has suffered for your lies, sir. I see no reason for her to go on doing so.'

'But you would *ruin* me!'

'Suitable recompense, I think, for having destroyed the reputation of an innocent young woman four years ago, and quite possibly, the lives of several other young women since.'

There was nothing Durling could say, and he knew it. His handsome face, once flushed with anger, had taken on a sickly appearance, and he was sweating profusely. Without a word, he turned on his heel and left. The moment he did, a young footman slipped into the room.

'You know what to do,' Edward said quietly. 'Be discreet, but don't let him out of your sight. I want to know where he goes and who he speaks to. I expect he'll be leaving London late tonight or very early in the morning. See that he does. And take whatever help you need.'

The footman nodded, and quietly left the room. Edward poured himself another glass of port, sure in the knowledge that his orders would be carried out, equally sure that Durling would slip out of the city under the cover of darkness.

Because he *was* guilty. Nothing in his interview with Durling had led Edward to believe that anything Diana had said was a lie. Durling had not apologised. He hadn't tried to make excuses for his behaviour. He had simply tried to cast Diana in the role of the instigator, and in that, he had failed, for the lady had more integrity than Durling ever would.

Edward thought about that as he slowly walked toward the window. Diana Hepworth had turned out to be a most admirable lady. An honest woman, faithful to those she loved and willing to fight for their well being. The kind of woman he might have loved, had it not been for Jenny.

He sipped his port, mulling over something else that had been bothering him. He was sure he'd seen something in her face. Hope, perhaps, or longing. Maybe even affection. And that troubled him, for he had no wish to hurt her. But as much as he admired and respected her, he couldn't return her feelings when his heart was given to another.

At the thought of the lady who had captured his heart, Edward sighed. God only knew if he would cver see her again. She believed she was not worthy of him; that she couldn't be the countess he needed. *Ah, but you could, dear Jenny*, Edward thought sadly. *You could.*

But what if Jenny didn't come? It was still his duty to marry and sire an heir; that had not changed. And his desire to find someone with whom he could talk as an equal hadn't lessened. Could Diana Hepworth be that woman? She was a lady to whom family meant everything; a woman who had earned his respect and admiration in so many ways. Surely he could do a great deal worse than to choose her to be his wife.

Perhaps, Edward decided, but it was still Jenny he loved, and until he received clear indication from her that she no longer wished him to wait, he would do nothing. He had given her his heart, and his word. And to a man of honour—and a man in love—nothing else really mattered.

News of Lord Durling's unexplained departure from London quickly made the rounds of society drawing rooms, as did a more subtle filtering of the real reasons for his rift with Diana Hepworth four years ago. Not surprisingly, many hours were spent in discussion of the matter, and though no specifics were given, it was clear that Diana Hepworth had not been guilty in any way, and that the parting had been as a direct result of what Lord Durling had done.

Naturally, with Edward's endorsement of her, Diana was welcomed back into society with open arms, and it seemed that everyone she met was anxious to be made known to her. Mrs Mitchell was understandably amused and gratified by the turn of events.

'Well, you will have no need to rush back to Whitley now,' she said happily. 'You can stay here and see to your own future, now that

Phoebe's is settled.' Mrs Mitchell beamed at the young girl sitting in the corner, with Chaucer's head resting in her lap. 'You look a happy puss, my dear.'

Phoebe laughed. 'Why should I not be happy? The most handsome gentleman in London has asked me to marry him, Diana's good name has finally been cleared, and Lady Ellen is no longer engaged to marry the dreadful Lord Durling. What more could we ask?'

'What, indeed?' Mrs Mitchell said, though her eyes were unusually perceptive as they settled on Diana's face. 'And what of you and Lord Garthdale, Diana? Do you think he will make his feelings for you known?'

'Lord Garthdale has a *tendre* for Diana?' Phoebe exclaimed. 'Why did no one tell me?'

'Because there is nothing to tell,' Diana assured her. 'I do care for Lord Garthdale, and I know he likes and respects me, but I have good reason to believe that his heart is already given to another.'

Phoebe's eyes looked ready to pop. 'Lord Garthdale is in *love*? But why hasn't Lady Ellen said anything to me about this?'

'It's quite possible Lady Ellen doesn't know,' Diana said, 'so you must say nothing either,

Phoebe. It is a relationship Lord Garthdale does not wish to be made public.'

Phoebe pouted. 'It really is *too* vexing to be in possession of such delightful information and not be able to share it. I shan't, of course, but I am sorry to hear that he loves someone else, Diana. He really would be better off with you, and I've half a mind to tell him so.'

'Oh, I don't know, Phoebe,' Diana said, sharing an amused glance with her aunt. 'You might be surprised at how well you like the lady, if you were given the chance to meet her.'

Amanda Townley's wedding to the Earl of Eastcliffe provided a welcome diversion for all of them. As expected, it was a lavish affair, and Diana thoroughly enjoyed seeing her dear friend married to the man she loved. Amanda looked breathtaking in an elegant gown of white lace over satin, with flowers in her hair and the smile on her lips of a woman about to embark on the most exciting part of her life. She would indeed make a wonderful Countess of Eastcliffe.

For her own part, Diana enjoyed the day far more than she expected to. Now that she was welcome in society again, there was no need to play the part of the retiring chaperon. She was sought after as an eligible lady, and there were always gentlemen asking her to dance, or paying her compliments. It truly was remarkable how quickly the tides of fortune could turn.

'You look very pleased with yourself, Diana,' Edward said, coming up to her at the wedding breakfast with two glasses of champagne. 'And, may I say, exceptionally lovely.'

Diana accepted a glass of champagne and hoped he would put her heightened colour down to the excitement of the day. 'Why, thank you, my lord, it is good of you to say so.'

It was still hard to believe how much this part of her life had changed. Since the day she'd told Edward the truth about Lord Durling, their relationship had taken a wondrous turn in that he now treated her as a friend. He had asked for permission to use her first name when they were alone, and naturally, Diana had given it to him, happy to recapture some of the intimacy she had shared with him as Jenny. And now, scarcely a day went by that he didn't call at George Street to see her. Sometimes he took her and Phoebe driving, other times he just sat in the drawing room with her and her aunt and talked. But whatever the occasion, Diana always felt the same breathless excitement when he was near, though she was careful not to show it, or to overstep the bounds of their friendship.

The relationship remained something of a mystery to society, who had been quick to note the growing friendship between Lord Garthdale and the lovely Miss Hepworth. Certainly everyone knew he was paying calls on her, and that the two were frequently to be seen together at society functions. And yet, he did not offer for her, or lead anyone to believe that he intended to. And since he seemed disinclined to take her as his mistress, their relationship was viewed as something of a curiosity. Rumours naturally circulated that there was someone else in his life, but since nothing could be confirmed, and no one could put forward the identity of the other woman, the rumours remained unsubstantiated.

'Are you enjoying the day?' Edward said, breaking into Diana's thoughts.

She opened her fan in a graceful movement. 'Very much. Amanda looks so happy, I'm so glad I was here to see this. But I have enjoyed all my forays into society of late, Edward, and I am well aware that it is you to whom I owe my thanks.'

'Me?'

'Of course. You are the one who set straight the misconceptions about my past. I've lost count of the number of people who've come up to me to express their regrets at what happened four years ago. And Aunt Isabel is positively thrilled. Every day a new round of invitations come in.' She leaned closer to him and said, 'I knew you were well connected, Edward, but I did not think even you could make things happen so quickly.'

He chuckled at her words, but his smile reflected his satisfaction. 'The secret is in knowing who to tell. When one knows who to speak to, it is remarkable how quickly word gets around.' Edward looked out across the room, and then cleared his throat. 'Diana, would you walk with me a moment? There is something I would like to say to you.'

Diana closed her fan, wondering at his sudden seriousness. 'Of course.'

He accompanied her into the garden, a riot of reds, pink, yellows, and bright fuchsia, the colours of an English country garden at the height of summer, and though they talked of several things, Diana knew that none of them were what had prompted him to bring her outside. She knew him too well.

Finally, as she bent to inhale the fragrance of a rose, he came to a halt, and said, 'Diana, you and I have become friends these last few weeks, have we not?'

She straightened slowly, aware of a feeling of warmth at his words. 'Yes, Edward, I like to think we have.'

'I thought so too. Which is why I don't want you to misunderstand what I'm about to say.'

'I'm sure I shan't.'

'Yes, well, I'm not so sure, because there is…a personal matter with which you are not fully acquainted, though of which I'm sure you've heard, but it is one that prevents me from offering you the kind of thanks you are truly owed.'

Diana looked at him in surprise. 'I expect nothing of you, Edward. Why would you think—?'

'No, please, Diana, let me say what I must,' he interrupted gently. 'I would not wish you to think less of me over this, because you truly are a remarkable woman. You have endured a great deal of unpleasantness over the events of the last four years, yet you have not been hardened by the experience. You refuse to shun those who rejected you, and have said nothing derogatory about Lord Durling, even though you had every right to do so.' He gave her a rueful smile. 'Indeed, your aunt has been far more vociferous in her feelings than you. But, that aside, you are everything that is admirable in a woman, and I know that *any* man would be proud to call you his own.' His dark eyes captured hers. 'I would be myself if the circumstances were different. But I won't mislead you, Diana, because there is someone else, and she is the reason I am unable to offer you what I, and quite likely society, think I should.'

Hardly knowing what to say, Diana simply said, 'You owe me no explanations, Edward, and I care little about what society thinks. We know what is between us, and what anyone else thinks of our relationship is of no concern to me.'

'Ah, but it is to me, because you are not insensitive to the whispers. You are an extremely beautiful woman who, by virtue of her courage, has also become a highly sought-after one. And you needn't look so surprised,' he said, when she obviously did. 'You must know that you have become quite the toast of the Season. And yet you do not encourage any of the gentlemen who dance attendance on you, but seem content to spend your time with me, in spite of the fact that I continue to treat you as nothing more than a friend.'

Diana lifted her shoulders. 'Perhaps I am not looking to become involved with anyone. Perhaps I enjoy being escorted about town by a handsome gentleman with whom I can feel completely at ease.'

He laughed, and Diana was delighted to see him do so. But then, because she needed to know what he wasn't saying, she asked, 'This other young lady of whom you speak, Edward. I take it she *is* at the heart of the secret romance everyone is talking about?'

A faint smile edged his mouth. 'It is as much a secret as anyone is able to keep, I suppose. Indeed, you would probably think me foolish if I told you the why's and wherefore's of it. However, we cannot choose where our hearts find happiness, and, I admit, she has totally captivated mine.' He looked at her, and his smile widened. 'You would like her, I think. She has many of your qualities, and her sense of humour is equal to your own.'

Diana glanced away, irrationally tempted to laugh. How was she supposed to answer that? He was pointing out the similarities between her and another woman, without realising they were the same person! More importantly, however, Edward was telling her, as kindly as he could, that he was in love with someone else—and that someone was Jenny.

In essence, he was telling her, without knowing it, that he was in love with *her*!

'I will be returning to Whitley soon,' she said, needing time to think that through.

He looked at her in surprise. 'You are not staying for your cousin's wedding?'

'I will return at the appropriate time but, for now, I wish to go home.'

'To Whitley, in Hertfordshire.'

'Yes.' She found herself curiously touched. 'I didn't think you would remember.'

'I have a good memory for some things and a dreadful one for others, but I like to think I remember the important things in life. And you, my dear, shall always be one of them.' He went quiet for a moment. 'I shall miss you, Diana. I've grown very fond of your company, and I'm sorry I didn't come to know the truth sooner. I think perhaps my conduct was troubling to you at times, and I wouldn't want to think I'd caused you pain. I also want you to know that I meant

what I said about the circumstances being different—'

'I know,' Diana said, gently pressing a finger
to his lips. 'But since they are not, let us say no
more about it. I told you I am content with the
way things are.'

He clasped her hand in his, and lightly kissed
her fingers. 'I hope so. And I hope I will have
an opportunity to visit you one day in Whitley.
I imagine it is a very peaceful place.'

'Yes, it is.' *And lonely.* 'How is Lady Ellen?'
Diana asked, needing to change the subject. 'I
only saw her briefly tonight before she and your
mother left.'

Edward sighed. 'She is unhappy, as is only to
be expected. But I think she is starting to get
over it.'

'I know what a terrible shock it must have
been for her,' Diana said softly. 'I know how
devastated I was.'

'I'm sure you do. Especially when I found out
the true nature of the man, and think of the terrible way *you* had to find out. But with luck,
Ellen will meet someone else who will make her
happy. In fact, I've a mind to introduce her to
a young man I know who might suit her very
well.'

'I'm glad. Speaking of that, you never told me how your interview with Lord Durling went,' Diana said.

Edward shrugged. 'There isn't much to tell. He denied everything, accepted blame for nothing, and made no comment except to belittle the integrity of everyone I mentioned.'

Diana shuddered. 'I pity the young woman who ends up his wife.'

'As do I. Fortunately, it won't be anyone in London, now that the truth has been made public.'

Knowing she had to ask, Diana said, 'Is your mother coming round? I can't imagine that she was happy with the turn of events.'

'Actually, she's taken it very well. For all her narrow-mindedness, Mama does care about her children. Once she discovered the truth about Lord Durling, she was as adamant as I that the marriage should not take place, and she is doing all she can to help Ellen through this difficult time. In fact, I think her desire to see Ellen recover may be just what she needs to finally pull herself out of the morass of her own grief.'

'Oh, Edward, I am pleased to hear it,' Diana said. 'As you must be.'

'I admit I am. She still has a long way to go,' he added with a smile, 'but every now and then I see flashes of the woman she used to be. And while I think of it, please tell your aunt that my mother would be most happy to receive her, if she is inclined to pay another call. And she is hopeful of seeing you, Diana, if you can find it in your heart to forgive her.'

Diana looked at him, knowing that, because of him, she could never hold a grudge against any member of his family. 'I believe that everyone deserves to be forgiven, Edward, especially when the circumstances are of such a personal nature. Your mother feared I would say something to abuse the man who was to marry her daughter. She was, in fact, protecting Ellen by asking us to leave. I cannot fault her for that.'

He sighed, and shook his head. 'Would that I had your sense of compassion. I have often been guilty of forming opinions and then been unwilling to change them, even when given reason to do so.'

'Ah, but it is never too late to change,' Diana said softly. 'And if the reasons for changing are important enough, it becomes even easier. But pride often stands in the way of doing what is right.'

As he so often did now, Edward reached for her hand and raised it to his lips, smiling as he bestowed a tender kiss upon it. 'I shall endeavour to remember that. And perhaps, in time, we shall enjoy…a different relationship than we do now. But I felt I owed you the truth, Diana, for only with truth can a man earn forgiveness. I have given my promise to a lady for whom I care deeply, and whom I may never see again, but until she tells me otherwise, I cannot go back on it. Nor do I wish to.'

Diana blinked back tears. Oh, what an admirable man he was. He was honouring the commitment he had made to an unknown lady. A lady he knew only by her first name and with whom he had fallen in love. Surely she couldn't let that go for nought? Did she not owe it to herself—and to him—to find out if they had any chance at happiness? And if they did, to do all she could to ensure that it was given the chance to grow.

Surely that justified the baring of her soul—and whatever consequences might result.

The sun was just rising through the trees as Edward trotted Titan into the park. It was a beautiful day, the air still crisp, but hinting at warmth to come. Robins sang with enthusiasm in the nearby trees, and he could already hear the faint buzz and chirp of insects around him.

It had been two weeks since Amanda's wedding, and almost four since he had last seen Jenny—and Edward still found it hard to believe how terribly he missed her. He didn't want to acknowledge how empty his life had become. Every morning he came to the park, hoping to see her again, and every day he returned home, more disappointed than the last, knowing it was another day he risked receiving a package.

Would she send her veil back to him? That was the agreed-upon sign. If Jenny wished to have nothing more to do with him, she need only send him back her veil and he would know that it was over.

Ironic that the one thing that had kept them apart might be the last thing he ever had from her.

Unfortunately, as the days slipped away, and there was still no word from her, Edward had to face the fact that it was likely he would receive it. If Jenny's feelings for him had changed, she would have come to him by now.

He was close to the place where they had first met when something suddenly darted across the path.

A cat, thin and scrawny, nervous, as such creatures were, dashed out from the brush and scampered across the path.

Edward reined in, and stared after it in disbelief. The *same* cat? No, it wasn't possible. It couldn't have been the same one that had jumped out in front of Jenny's mare nearly two months ago and started it all. Could it?

'Good morning, Edward.'

He looked up—and saw her. There, in front of him, no more than twenty feet away. She was seated on a familiar dapple-grey mare, and wearing a dark green habit trimmed with black piping, and a dashing hat with a veil down over her face.

'*Jenny!*' He could hardly believe his eyes. He looked beyond her, expecting to see her groom, but there was no one there. She had come to him alone? What did that mean? That she had changed her mind and decided to stay? Or that she had come to offer him one last goodbye?

'I can hardly believe you're here,' Edward said, his voice huskier than usual. 'I had almost given up hope.'

'I am so glad you didn't. I couldn't leave, Edward,' she said, urging the mare forward. 'Not without telling you the truth.'

Her voice came as a shock, because it was entirely different. Higher, and without the huskiness he knew so well. So reminiscent of another's. But at the moment, he was so distracted by seeing her again that nothing else really mattered. He was also more concerned with *what* she'd said than the voice she'd said it in. 'You don't have to tell me anything,' he said. 'All that matters is that you're here. I don't need any confessions.'

'Ah, but you do, because forgiveness cannot be gained without complete honesty. You said that to a lady recently, and I have been giving it a great deal of thought ever since.'

Edward frowned. *He'd said that to a young lady?* What did Jenny mean? Who could he have said it to, and if he had, how had she come to know about it?

'Forgive me, but I don't remember—'

He broke off, aware that she was slowly raising her hands to her face, her gloved fingers closing on the edge of the net. Ever so slowly, she began to lift her veil.

She was about to reveal her face to him.

Hardly daring to breathe, Edward watched as a small, pointed chin came into view, the skin the colour of peach-tinted cream. Above that, a mouth, as tempting as he had imagined, full-lipped and sensual. Then a nose, small, dainty, utterly delightful.

The veil continued to rise, revealing high-boned cheeks dusted a delicate pink, then dark lashes rimming eyes as clear and as blue as the sky that stretched overhead. But in that same instant, Edward realised that something was wrong.

As impossible as it seemed, he *knew* the face that was being revealed to him.

'Diana!' He stared at her in confusion. 'But how…why—?'

'Can you not guess?' she said quietly. 'Surely my reasons for doing what I did are obvious to you now.'

It only took a few moments for Edward to go over everything he knew of her. Everything he had learned, and everything she'd told him. And when he did, he realised she was right. Of course it wasn't difficult to figure out why she'd done it. Diana Hepworth had come to London in disgrace. At least, that's how she would have seen it. She'd come back, intending to avoid society, and so had ridden with a veil over her face, and spoken in a different voice in order to avoid recognition. Perhaps she had feared meeting Durling himself in the park, and had taken steps to ensure that he wouldn't recognise her. And, given Durling's character, how could he blame her?

But it was still nearly too much to grasp. His own dear Jenny, none other than Diana Hepworth. A woman who in her own way had earned a prominent place in his heart.

There were a hundred questions he wanted to ask, but one came immediately to mind. 'Why ''Jenny''?'

A beautiful smile curved her mouth. 'Because it was my mother's name. And my middle one.'

'And your voice?'

That one made her blush. 'The first few times I rode with you, I was suffering with a terrible sore throat, and the huskiness you heard was not feigned. But as my voice started to heal, and the risk of exposure increased, I purposely kept it disguised. I didn't want you finding out that Jenny and Diana Hepworth were one and the same.'

Edward looked at her. Looked at the face he had wanted to know for so long, hardly aware that he already did, and that he had almost from the beginning. 'To say that I'm surprised would hardly be doing justice to what I feel,' he admitted. 'I'm not even sure that I *know* what I feel.'

'Shock, I imagine,' Diana said. 'And anger. Perhaps betrayal. I lied to you, Edward. I pretended to be two people. In the simplest of terms, I deceived you most cruelly.'

He thought about that. Thought about the fact that she had lied to him, and that she had done so on more than one occasion. And yet, remembering everything she had said to him, both as Jenny and Diana, how could he revile her? Knowing what she had been through, how could he feel anything but admiration and respect, for she had not lied to him in the area of greatest importance?

She had not lied to him about her feelings. Perhaps she *had* pretended to be two women, but she had not tried to encourage his affections in either of those roles. It was Jenny who had refused to ride with him on a regular basis and Jenny who had turned down his offer of marriage. And as Diana Hepworth, she had tried only to set matters right for his sister, and to do all she could to make sure of her cousin's happiness.

She might have lied about who she was, but she had never been dishonest about her feelings.

'Why didn't you say something the night you told me the truth about Lord Durling?' Edward asked.

Her smile was heart-wrenchingly lovely. 'Because I thought you had heard enough for one night. You'd just found out that your sister was betrothed to an abusive man. That was more important than learning that I was Jenny and Diana Hepworth both. And I freely admit, the thought of telling you I was seemed an extremely daunting prospect. I had no idea how you would react.'

'And now that you've told me, how do you feel?'

'Relieved,' she admitted, 'and a little afraid. I didn't know what you would do when you found out who I really was. But it was our conversation at Amanda's wedding that gave me the courage to tell you the truth. I couldn't bear to listen to you tell me that you were in love with Jenny, and then just walk away. I felt I had to come and see if we had a chance. And whatever happens now, at least I know I have no secrets from you.'

'And where *do* we go from here, Diana?'

'I don't know. That is for you to say,' Diana said. 'You led me to believe that you had strong feelings for Jenny. Only you can say if you have those same feelings for Diana, now that you've learned the truth about her.'

It seemed to Edward that they might have been the only two people in the park. He heard the sounds of other horses and other voices, yet his entire focus was on the woman before him.

The woman he thought he'd never see again.

Edward slowly dismounted, knowing Titan would stay where he was, and walked over to Diana. He looked up into her face, saw the uncertainty in her beautiful blue eyes, and then silently held out his hands.

With a soft cry, she freed her leg from the pommel and slipped down into his arms, choking back a sob as they closed around her and drew her close.

'Oh, Edward, I was so afraid,' she murmured against his jacket. 'So afraid you would turn me away.'

He could hardly speak for the joy of finally holding her in his arms and the relief at knowing he hadn't lost her. 'And you have no idea how terrified I was that you wouldn't come back, dearest. I couldn't bear the thought of living without you. Nothing's been the same since you left.'

'I'm so sorry, Edward,' Diana whispered. 'I didn't mean to—'

He kissed her into silence, muffling her words with the hunger of his lips. She tasted of honey and champagne, and like a man who'd gone too long without food he feasted on her sweetness.

'You don't owe me any apologies,' Edward said when he finally raised his head. 'I understand why you did what you did, and, knowing the truth about you, all I want now is for our lives to start over again. If that's what you want too.'

'It *is* what I want. More than anything!' She touched his face with her hand, and her eyes glowed with happiness. 'I love you, Edward. I have for some time.'

'Then will you marry me?' he whispered. 'Will you be my wife as soon as I can arrange it, for I have no wish to spend another day without you.'

'I can't imagine anything I would like more. Yes, I will marry you, Edward. Just as soon as you can arrange it.'

He turned his face and pressed a kiss into her palm. 'I shall call on your aunt this very afternoon.'

'She will be happy to receive you.'

'But will she be surprised?' he asked, pulling her close and sprinkling gentle kisses on her eyes, her cheeks, her nose. 'Did you keep the secret from her as well as you kept it from me?'

'Actually, it's very difficult to keep secrets from my aunt,' Diana admitted, sounding a little breathless. 'Especially since she already guessed how I felt about you.'

'I'm not surprised. I have always held Isabel Mitchell to be a very astute lady.'

Diana watched his lips draw near, and smiled. 'It's a good thing I did have the veil to protect me, Edward. Otherwise you would have guessed the nature of my feelings long before now.'

'Would that have been so bad?'

She laughed, and leaned into him. 'No, perhaps not.'

'Good. Then will you make me a promise?'

'Anything.'

'I never want to see you with a veil over your face again,' he said, his breath warm against her skin. 'With the exception of your bridal veil, I don't want there to be a single moment when I can't look into your eyes and see exactly what you're thinking.'

Diana clasped her fingers behind his head and smiled. 'Never, my lord. Because the only thing you will ever see on my face—is love!'

* * * * *

HISTORICAL ROMANCE™

LARGE PRINT

A CONVENIENT GENTLEMAN
Victoria Aldridge

The bank won't lend Caroline Morgan the money she so desperately needs until she gets herself a husband.

Caro finds Leander Gray, the younger son of an aristocrat and the only eligible man in town, collapsed in a local bar. He grudgingly agrees to a paper marriage and Caro is left wondering what she's got herself into. But when the gambler turns gentleman her feelings begin to change…

New Zealand
Love rush – Gold rush

A VERY UNUSUAL GOVERNESS
Sylvia Andrew

Edward Barraclough's happy bachelor existence is thrown into a spin when he is forced to look after his two orphaned nieces. Employing the right governess is vital and as unassuming and a little dowdy as Miss Petrie may appear, he suspects she's neither so humble nor respectful underneath!

Independently wealthy Lady Octavia Petrie is on the verge of confessing that Edward's mistaken her for someone else. Then, in a moment of sheer madness, prompted by his cynical attitude, she finds herself accepting the temporary position.

MILLS & BOON®

Live the emotion

HIST0904 LP

HISTORICAL ROMANCE™

LARGE PRINT

THE WIDOW'S BARGAIN
Juliet Landon

When her Scottish home is invaded by a dangerous band of reivers, Lady Ebony Moffat's first thought is to keep her young son safe. For his sake she is prepared to make a bargain with the men's leader—her body for her child's life.

Sir Alex Somers is intrigued. In a reiver's guise he has raided Castle Kells, seeking out traitors at the behest of the King of Scotland. Alex means no harm to the boy. But with his desire for Ebony so intense, he can't help but be drawn by her offer…

Robert the Bruce
…Scottish borders, raiding parties, endangered lovers…

THE RUNAWAY HEIRESS
Anne O'Brien

Miss Frances Hanwell effects a daring night-time escape—in the Marquis of Aldeborough's carriage! Mistaking her for a kitchen servant, Hugh only realises his grave error the next day. With scandal imminent, a reluctant marriage seems the only course of action.

Reluctance turns to respect when Hugh uncovers the brutal marks of the unhappy life she's been leading. Suddenly, he will do all in his power to protect her…especially now, as an unexpected inheritance threatens to take Frances from him…

MILLS & BOON®

Live the emotion

HIST0204 LP

THE MYSTERIOUS MISS M

Diane Gaston

The Mysterious Miss M is a living male fantasy – alluring, sensual, masked. But when Lord Devlin Steele finds himself responsible for her – and her child – he comes to know the real Maddy: the loving, passionate woman who drives away the nightmares of the Waterloo battlefield.

But the aristocratic soldier can't support his new family. He will only inherit his fortune on marriage to a suitable lady – and Maddy is far from suitable. With the dangers of London's underworld closing in, how can he protect the woman he has come to love?

THE SOCIETY CATCH

Louise Allen

Miss Joanna Fulgrave is regarded as the perfect society catch, although the only bridegroom she'll consider marrying is gorgeous Colonel Giles Gregory. But her marriage hopes are dashed when it seems Giles is about to propose to someone else – and Joanna's family have already found her another match!

Fearing her family may force her into a loveless marriage, Joanna flees. Giles is hot on her trail, determined to catch her and bring her home safely – but will he be as determined to make her his bride. . . ?

MILLS & BOON®

Live the emotion

HIST1104 LP